Advance Praise for *A Cowboy's Dilemma*

"For fans of the Western Romance genre, this book is right up your alley- plenty of action along with a large dose of Romance. Follow the continuing adventures of Charlie Kelly and his beautiful and intelligent wife, Susan, as they carve a swath through the oil business, taking on gangsters and building a fortune. A wild ride!"

Jim Jones, Award-winning author and western musician

"Filled with interesting historical insights and a parade of bigger-than-life characters, A Cowboy's Dilemma brings the changing Old West of 1919-20 to life. This is the third in the Kelly Can series, but new readers can enjoy this story without missing a beat."

Anne Hillerman, Author of the award-winning Chee/ Leaphorn/Manuelito mysteries.

"In Joe Brown's book, riches are to be won and empires established during Oklahoma's cattle and oil boom of the early Twentieth Century. Charlie Kelly and his wife Susan, two flesh-and-blood characters, leap from the pages, driven by a passionate devotion for each other and their relentless will to triumph in this bustling, brutal, and high stakes environment."

R.G. (Bob) Yoho, Writer, Author, and Speaker

Other Books by E. Joe Brown

The Kelly Can Saga

A Cowboy's Destiny
A Cowboy's Fortune
A Cowboy's Dilemma

The Kelly Can Saga Book 3

A COWBOY'S *Dilemma*

By

E. Joe Brown

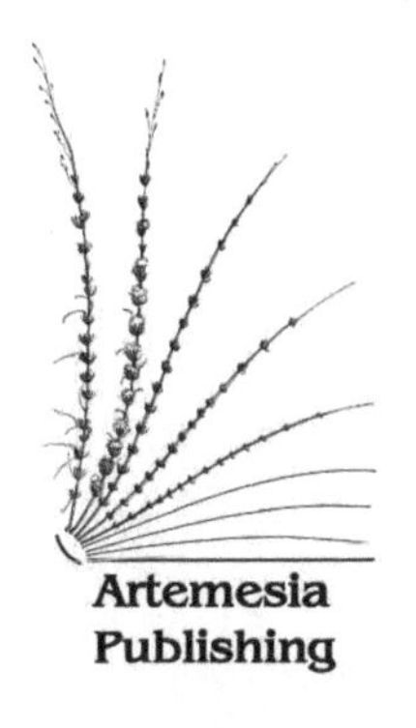

ISBN: 978-1-963832-18-1 (paperback)
ISBN: 978-1-963832-31-0 (ebook)
LCCN: 2025941023

Printed in the United States of America.

Artemesia Publishing
9 Mockingbird Hill Rd
Tijeras, New Mexico 87059
www.apbooks.net
info@artemesiapublishing.com

First Edition

Chapter One

The Day After the Day After

October 1919

CHARLIE KELLY STOOD AT the foot of the bed, his six-foot five-inch frame towered over the person that lay there. He loved the black-haired beauty who lay asleep, her naked body entwined in the sheets. She was his wife Susan, who, thirty-six hours before, had been held captive by two hoodlums wanting revenge for their business losses to the powerful Kramer Group owned by the Kellys.

Charlie walked around to the bedside, bent down, and kissed her. "Sweetheart, we need to git on the road. Our home at The Double Bar K ranch ain't gittin' any closer."

She rolled over and moaned. "Do we have to?"

"I'm afraid so."

She climbed out of bed, yawned, and saw that Charlie hadn't dressed. "Well, aren't you the handsome devil I call husband?"

"I better be. I waited for you to wake up to shower and git ready. Want ta join me?"

"You bet."

After their shower, and as they packed for their trip home, Susan said, "Last night, as we sat at our table and shared the bottle of Cabernet, you said something about trouble with the Chicago Outfit. I think it was something like that. What did you mean?"

"Night before last, as the group was plannin' how we were goin' to rescue you from Willard and his goon, I got a phone call from Hank Thomas, our Landman. He was up at Burbank and had been out at our oil well site. Someone had shot our oilfield storage tanks full of holes. It couldn't have been Willard because he was here in Cushing holdin' ya captive. I think it's the Chicago mob tryin' to scare us or settle a score. Do you remember Zane, our cement quarry manager, sayin' he learned the other bidder on the quarry auction in Sapulpa was someone from the Chicago mob? I think we may be lookin' at a new enemy whether we want it or not."

"Charlie, I'm scared. What if they come after us the way Willard did with me two nights ago?"

He patted her shoulder. "That's why we're creatin' a new security company with Bailey Muldoon as our lead."

"It can't happen fast enough to suit me, big guy."

"I agree. Let's git outta here."

***

As they stood under a massive chandelier at the Cushing Hotel's impressive mahogany registration desk to settle their bill, Susan yawned. She laid her head against Charlie's shoulder as she squeezed his arm. "I'm hungry. Can we eat here at the hotel before we head out?"

Charlie looked down at her sleepy eyes. "Sure, why don't you go into the restaurant and git us a table. I'll finish here and load our suitcases in the car. I'll be there in a few minutes."

"Okay, Sweetheart." She stopped at the restaurant entrance and looked back across the lobby at her cowboy as he talked to the clerk. Her pulse raced as she marveled at his rugged, handsome looks and confident demeanor. Then she reluctantly headed into the restaurant.

"Hey, Charlie."

Charlie turned and saw Bailey Muldoon, the new Kramer Group Head of Security, and Richard Murphy from the Oklahoma Bureau of Investigation coming out of the elevator.

He walked toward them. "Mornin' fellas. Hope you were able to get some rest." He looked at Bailey. "Are ya headin' out? I guess you're goin' back to Ponca City?"

Although tall himself, Bailey looked up and nodded. "Yes, I need to go back and finish up some things. And Hank called me. I need to see the damage he was talking about at the well site. Then, as your new President of Kramer Security, I'll start putting together some ideas regarding what the Kramer Group, and of course you and Susan, need to consider as we develop the new company. Give Susan my best."

Charlie nodded. "I will and let me know what ya find up in Burbank," He turned and put his hand on Richard's shoulder. "Thanks again for all your help the other night."

Richard ran his hand through his graying hair, smiled, and shrugged. "Just happy I could be of service to you and Susan. How is she this morning? Is she still upstairs?"

Charlie chuckled, "No. She's in the restaurant. She said she was starvin'. I guess her appetite is still healthy. She'll be fine, but it'll take some time. Thanks for askin'."

Richard patted his chest. "I'm glad to hear it. And know this; you can always call me if you need anything."

Charlie said, "You bet, Richard. You two travel safe."

***

When Charlie entered the restaurant, he saw Susan sitting at their favorite table, which allowed them to look out onto Broadway, Cushing's main street. He watched the steam rising from his coffee cup as he took his seat.

He gave Susan a big smile. "Thanks, Honey. I'm ready for coffee. After we finish breakfast, the car is loaded, so all we need to do is fill the Cadillac's gas tank, and we're on the road."

She reached over and took his hand. "Good. I've already ordered our food."

He could see tension still written on her face as she fiddled with her spoon. "Are ya doin' okay, Darlin'?"

She continued to look down at her coffee cup. "Oh, I'm fine. I still find it hard to believe Roland Willard victimized us again. You would have thought he learned his lesson at the oil drilling site in Yale last year." Her gaze rose to Charlie's smiling face. "It may take me a little time to get past what he put me through the other night. You know, being bound, gagged, and tied to a chair was terrifying. Sweetheart, I knew you'd come for me. But I had no idea what Willard would do to you when you did." She slumped back in her chair. "Well, at least I'm not physically hurt."

Charlie took a sip of coffee and carefully chose his words. "You were kidnapped. It would take anyone some time to get back to normal. And Willard is dead. Our new pal Richard took care of it and I'm sure Tompkins, Willard's goon, will go to jail for life."

Susan sat up, her nostrils flared as her hands became fists. "Willard would have killed you, if Richard hadn't shot him." She relaxed a little. "And Bailey Muldoon, what a wonderful friend he has become. I'm so glad we hired him away from Pinkerton." She leaned forward enough to allow Charlie his favorite view of her cleavage as she gave him a sweet and determined look. "Enough said. I'm not going to let some asshole win. So, I'm looking forward to some private fun with my honey in our car as we return to the ranch."

Charlie leaned back. "I agree we both need to git over that night." He grinned. "It sounds like you're ready to start it now." He looked out the window at their blue Cadillac sedan. "Yep, it'll be a fun ride to the ranch."

Her eyes brightened, and her jaw relaxed as the tension disappeared from her face. She checked around the room, winked, popped several snaps, and pulled her shirt open enough to show there was nothing under it but her. "It sure can be. Do you see what you'll enjoy for the next few hours?"

Charlie's eyes got as big as the saucer his coffee cup sat on. "I sure do." He shook his head. "You're amazin'. In spite of everythin', you're thinkin' about us enjoyin' ourselves as we head home."

She straightened in her chair and stuck out her chin as she sat erect. "You're right, Charlie, my dear. It's another way to put that night behind me."

Charlie cleared his throat and tipped his head in the direction of the kitchen. "Waiter's comin' with our food."

She used a snap to close her shirt some. As the waiter placed Susan's plate on the table, Charlie saw him enjoy Susan's assets. The server didn't hide the smile showing his admiration for her amazing curves, long raven black hair, and beautiful face. The couple grinned at each other as the waiter walked away.

Susan began cutting her chicken fried steak. "By the look on your face, I think you liked watching the waiter's reaction as much as when I opened my shirt just for you."

"Ya got me. I don't mind it when men admire your beauty. In a way, it's a compliment to you and even me. They can look all they want to, but they can't have ya."

"No, they can't. Letting the waiter see my cleavage was me being a little rebellious, giving you and him a small thrill. And I guess it was me proving to myself how my feminine charms can be powerful. My father told me several years ago he saw how many of his business associates couldn't take their eyes off me when I was in the room with them. He said, 'Susan, use your good looks as a powerful tool when you can. You're going to have opportunities when you're running Kramer when some man is thinking about the curves of your body when he should be thinking about the business negotiation, he's in with you.' Charlie, I know some folks would think bad of me, and maybe you, for letting me do something like what I did, or what we do in the car going down the road. But, if it's for us, or our leverage in business and it gives us pleasure, I'm happy."

Charlie stopped cutting his steak and looked up. "You're amazin'. We're in our twenties and young compared to many of those men your father talked about. We both are a little rebellious in some ways. We're gonna bother some folks with decisions we make as we build the Kramer Group. But we must always be true to each other and to what gives us satisfaction and pleasure that only we can give each other."

Susan's face showed her agreement. She took a sip of coffee, then tilted her head. "Sweetheart, I agree and it's how I see we must live our lives. We've discussed this before and now I know we're completely clear and together on how we're going to approach our future."

They looked into each other's eyes and smiled.

After his last bite of steak, Charlie stood and drained the last of his coffee. "The food was great, and your company was too. We better git goin'." He pulled her chair back. "Before we leave, I need to call J. Paul Getty and Hank Thomas to confirm they'll be at the ranch tomorrow. We need to discuss some issues regardin' our newest company, Kelly Oil."

"Yes, of course. We're so fortunate you got to know Hank while working in the oil business at the Miller's 101 Ranch. Tell him hello for me."

"I will. I'm thinkin' J. Paul Getty may be someone we'll do some big oil deals with down the road, and it's great he and Hank get along."

Charlie used one of the lobby telephones to make two short calls. After replacing the receiver, he walked across to where Susan waited for him. He enjoyed watching how she towered over the bellhop she was talking to and how the man's eyes never made it up to her face.

As they walked out to their car, Charlie said, "I sometimes forget you're six feet tall. You made the bellhop look small."

She laughed. "Well, Darling, you make me look small when we stand together."

As they climbed into their car, Susan asked, "Did you talk to Hank and Paul? Will we see them tomorrow?"

"Yep, and now for two to three hours of pure pleasure as we head to our new home at the Double Bar K."

Susan was true to her word. She unsnapped their shirts as they drove out of town. She purred, "I enjoy the muscles on your hairy chest as much as you do the breasts on mine. You know, it's only fair, Sweetheart."

Charlie glanced at her and laughed. "I can see your point.

Anythin' you want. Honey, I'm all yours."

***

As they entered Pottawatomie County, Susan enjoyed seeing the rolling hills, blackjack oaks, and sunflowers along the roadside. She turned to face Charlie. "I'm so glad we bought the Double Bar K Ranch."

"I'm happy to hear ya say it, although I knew how ya felt. We'll have a lot of fun raisin' Angus beeves with the help of my old friend Boss Bellamy."

"If we're being truthful, it'll be you and Boss, but thanks for including me in your thoughts."

It didn't seem like any time had passed to Charlie when he drove off the main road, through the ranch gate, and pulled around to the back of the main house to park. He climbed out of the car, stretched out the kinks, opened the trunk, and reached for the suitcases.

Susan stood next to Charlie as she looked toward the barns. "The place looks wonderful. I forget how beautiful everything is here. Can I help?"

"I've got this. I enjoyed livin' and workin' at the most famous ranch in the state, the 101, but it sure is nice to have our own place. This ranch is smaller, but we sure produce some fine Angus cattle. Yep, this is a mighty fine place. Can ya find Cleta and Attie? All our things need washin', and I'm hungry for lunch."

"Sure, Darling." She turned to head to the house and saw the girls come out the back door.

With her dark hair framing a radiant smile their housekeeper Attie, a twenty-year-old whose height almost reached Susan's shoulders, came running to greet them. "Welcome home, Miss Susan."

Susan hugged her. "It's good to be home."

Cleta, the cook, joined them in the hug. "I've some food ready for you and Mr. Charlie."

A few minutes later, in the kitchen, Cleta and Attie both looked a little apprehensive. Cleta hesitated, then said, "Miss Susan, are you, alright? Mr. Charlie told us what happened when he called and said you were coming home today."

Susan looked down, then raised her gaze to Cleta and Attie. Forcing a wavering smile, "I'm going to be fine. The bad guys are either dead or in police custody, and Charlie arrived with help before I was physically hurt. Let's agree we'll get things back to normal."

The three ladies hugged again, and no more would be said.

***

Charlie and Susan sat at the table in the breakfast room off the kitchen. There they enjoyed a scenic view down the hill of the forest behind the barns and corrals as they ate.

Until he saw what Cleta had prepared—fried chicken, mashed potatoes, and corn on the cob—Charlie hadn't realized how hungry he was. Susan also dove into her meal. She had picked at her breakfast food, and now she was ready to satisfy her hunger.

After finishing his plate, Charlie said, "Cleta, can ya bring me some more sweet tea? And this chicken is some of the best ya ever made. Maybe another couple of legs would be just right."

Susan turned to Cleta. "Dear, please leave the pitcher; I want more, too."

After his second helping, Charlie pushed himself away from the table. "My goodness, what a meal. It looks like we have leftovers for a snack tonight."

Susan wiped her mouth with her napkin. "She can't feed us like this all the time," she pointed out the window. "We'll end up as big as a barn out there."

Charlie stood, bent down, and kissed her forehead. "I think they were glad to see us and needed to hear it from you. They planned the big meal to have something special. And you're right. We can't eat meals like this every day."

Susan took Charlie's hand. "Are you leaving us?"

"Yes, I need to find Boss so he can git me caught up on things around here. With Hank and Getty coming here tomorrow, I thought I would chat with our foreman today. He told me a while back he wants to acquire some additional land near here."

Susan stood and laid her napkin on her plate. "Well, I'm feeling sleepy. I'm going to take a nap. Go ahead. I'm looking forward to seeing Hank and Paul tomorrow morning, and some rest now will help me feel my best when they get here."

"Our meal would make anyone sleepy. I'm expectin' a good update on Kelly Oil from Hank in the mornin' and what Getty's up to I have no idea. I'll be back before too long. This warm fall weather makes me look forward to time this evenin' in the pool and on the patio."

"Me too; I can't wait. Say hello to Boss for me."

***

Charlie went straight to the barn and found his horse. As he arrived at his stall, Tony moved close so Charlie could stroke his muzzle. "Hey buddy, I sure missed you. My, you look great. I hope Boss and the ranch hands have been takin' you out for a ride some." Tony whinnied his approval and nibbled at Charlie's ear. The big sorrel with its gleaming golden mane stood still as Charlie tossed a saddle blanket across his back. It was as if both knew they would be enjoying some time together. Charlie sensed Tony was every bit as happy to see him, and he was to have an afternoon on the back of his beloved stallion.

Charlie heard a door open at the back of the barn. He looked up to see a large shadowy figure of a man back lit by the sun walking toward him. It was the gray-haired, grizzled old ranch foreman, Boss, who had become like family.

Boss paused and put his hand to his chin, then pointed it at Charlie. "Let's see. I believe your name is Charles, Charles Kelly, right?"

Charlie laughed at his humor. "Boss, how the hell are ya They hugged and slapped each other on the shoulder. "Boss, I need to remember what it's like to be on the back of a horse."

Boss chuckled. "I bet ya do. I'm doin' mighty good. He looked serious. "And how is Miss Susan doin'?"

"She's good; it'll take her some time. Well, ya know it was scary for her and me. How about goin' for a ride with me? Like I said, I need to remember what it's like on the back of a horse. And I'm sure Tony could use the exercise. How's your horse, Blackie, doin'?"

"Blackie's doin' fine. Let's go. I can tell ya all about what I've in mind for expandin' the place."

They saddled their horses and rode out. In the first part of the afternoon, Boss showed Charlie all the improvements they had made over the last several weeks, and there were new calves in the herd to see as well.

Around mid-afternoon, Charlie asked, "Why do ya think we need to add some acreage to the place? We're just gettin' settled in. Seems too soon to me to be addin' more land to manage."

Boss nodded and pointed, "Let's ride over and sit under the tree there and chat awhile."

They climbed off their horses and picketed them where they could graze.

They sat on a log overlooking green pastures with cattle grazing.

Charlie rubbed his chin. "Your horse sure is a beauty. Blackie must be close to sixteen hands and those hind quarters. My goodness, I forgot how powerful they are."

Boss grinned. "I'm mighty lucky to have him. Charlie, to answer your question I need to discuss something with ya. A beef buyer stopped by the day after ya left wantin' to talk to ya. He's been doin' business with Clay Stephens here for several years. I agreed to sell him all we could. But I kept our prime bulls, some heifers, and yearlings to continue growin' our herd. He said demand has continued to rise every year since the war. People are eatin' more beef, and Angus is the most popular. He would have bought twice as much as we had. It's why I say we need to expand. I have found some land up the road is available. I want to show it to you."

"Well, now that's different. It's wonderful to need to expand because of demand. Tomorrow, I have some meetings. Let's have a look at the land on Monday."

"Sounds fine. On another subject, our old buddies up at the 101 are already sendin' people our way. Your brother Dan, next door at the Bar B Ranch, is gettin' a bunch o' calls from ranchers and others wantin' horses and trainin'. He got a call from someone livin' up around Stillwater yesterday. We could add some acreage to our cuttin' horse operation, too. If we could find property up north, it would be even better."

Charlie nodded. "If we relocate to another part of the state, we'll need to hire more workers and a foreman. But I'll consider it. I need to get back to the house. I told Susan I'd be there for supper. And we want and need some time together this evenin' to relax."

They rode back to the barn and gave their horses to the stable boy. Tony and Blackie would be rubbed down and fed before returning to their stalls.

As they walked past the last two horse stalls, Boss pointed and said, "We finished converting these two stalls to the wine cellar you and Susan asked for. It's not fully stocked yet with the wine you requested. I hope ya can get some more brought in."

"I'll talk to Susan about it. We prefer Cabernet Sauvignon from Napa Valley California, Boss. Berringer Vineyards is our favorite. With all the talk about Prohibition, we wanted to load up as much as possible. We have our folks in Kansas City doing the same."

Boss nodded, smiled, and headed to his house, and Charlie went to find Susan.

***

Susan was in the kitchen, laughing and talking with Cleta and Attie when Charlie walked into the room. "Someone is having a good time. What's so funny?"

Susan wrinkled her nose. "Men."

Charlie wrinkled his nose at her, "Well, pardon me." He smiled. "I'm ready for some more fried chicken and fixins. How about you?"

Susan laughed, stood, and walked to Charlie's side. "I could eat another piece or two. Can we relax on the patio?"

"That's my plan."

Cleta prepared and brought the leftovers to the patio so Charlie and Susan could enjoy them on their loungers. Susan carried a bottle of Cabernet and two glasses and followed Cleta. As she set the bottle down, she said, "Thanks, Cleta. Please go and enjoy your evening. We'll take care of ourselves until bedtime. Tell Attie goodnight."

Charlie was already seated. "I'm glad we got here before the sun went down. This sunset is beautiful. Look at those colors. If you painted that mixture of white clouds, blues, reds, oranges, and yellows, no one would believe this. Susan, isn't this the best? It's great to be back at the Double Bar K. I enjoy our place on Westover Road in Kansas City, and our new home on Madison Avenue in Tulsa will be wonderful, too." Some awkwardness showed up in his voice as he continued. "But I'm happiest on a ranch, especially when it's ours."

Susan reached over and stroked Charlie's chest. "Darling, as we expand our empire and go for our dreams, we'll need those homes located in cities. But nothing fills my heart and soul with more joy than seeing you and Tony together. We'll always have this ranch to come to. I married a cowboy. A very special cowboy. I love my cowboy and this ranch we both call home."

Charlie squeezed her hand. "I love you more every day and would live anywhere to be with you." He sat up, poured the wine, and divided the food as Susan undressed. "Susan, I noticed earlier we're gettin' low on our supply of Cabernet. Oklahoma's a dry state, so we can't buy it here. We better get some more brought to us from Kansas City."

Susan said, "I guess we better. I don't understand why Oklahoma prohibited alcohol sales when it became a state, but I want my wine. I'll have Uncle Curt get us more sent down here somehow."

Charlie watched her taking off her clothes and nodded his agreement. "It is a warm evening, so I guess you're preparin' to have your evenin' dip in the pool?"

"Not yet; I'm just getting comfortable. You can, too, you know."

"I guess I will." He stood, took off his clothes, and returned to his lounger.

They enjoyed the food and swam a few laps in the pool. When they returned, Susan joined Charlie, sitting on his lounger.

She cuddled in his arms. "I've wanted this all day. In the car, it was hard for me not to ask you to pull over so I could attack you. You're handsome and loving, and the other night, you were so brave."

Charlie kissed her as passion boiled inside him. "Susan, I can't imagine happiness without you. You made the drive here today go by so fast. As I've said before, what ya did in the restaurant this morning and on the drive was you makin' love to me. You make me feel special when you do those things." He hugged her again. They enjoyed a long, tender kiss.

Susan poured them each another glass of wine as Charlie said, "I'm thinkin' our bed looks better to me right now than the pool. How about you?"

She gave a wicked giggle, picked up her glass, and headed toward the house.

Chapter Two

A Conversation About California

October 1919

CHARLIE STOOD ON THE patio in his loose-fitting calf-length underwear enjoying a crisp pleasant morning. A rooster crowed his welcome to a new day as Charlie gazed at some of his cattle grazing in the pastures. His mind raced through the dozen or so projects he and Susan managed for The Kramer Group. He laughed and shook his head. "Not bad for a small-town cowboy."

From behind him, "Say it again. Something about a cowboy?"

Charlie turned and had a big smile, seeing Susan almost naked in a sheer white nightgown. She carried two cups of coffee as she walked toward him.

"I was sayin' not bad for a small-town cowboy. Is the coffee for me?"

She giggled. "No, I'm taking it down to the horse barn for my boyfriend." She gave him a look. "Yes, of course, it's for you, silly. I thought you might want some." She tilted her head and smiled as she scanned the pastures and the woods lining a creek to the west. "It's so beautiful here. Quiet compared to Kansas City and Tulsa."

Charlie joined her gaze. "Like I said last night, I'll never want to give this up. I can now be comfortable in the city doin' business and enjoyin' the restaurants and such. But I'll always need to come back to this."

Susan pointed to the loungers. "Sweetheart, let's sit and talk for a moment."

Charlie walked over and sat. "Sure, is there a problem?"

Susan sat, took a sip of coffee, then laid the cup on the side table. "I don't think so. But I do have a question or two for you."

Charlie put his coffee down. "Please, ask me anything."

"My sweet Charlie, are you happy? I believe things are wonderful between us when it's only us. But..." She paused to pick the right words. "How are you liking all the "stuff" you inherited because of who I am? Big business decisions, thugs like Willard wanting what you have, and not having as much time to be the cowboy on a big, beautiful ranch you always dreamed of?"

Charlie looked down and shook his head. Then leaned back and looked off in the distance. "Wow! What an unexpected question."

She leaned toward him. "Maybe so. But it is a necessary one this morning. I understand what you mean when you say you need to come back here. I enjoyed my years of quiet along Rock Creek at Elmore City. But I needed to go to the city, too. We'll always want to have our sanctuaries. I can tell we both love working hard to build our businesses. But this beautiful ranch, our home on Kansas City's Westover Road, and the new place on Madison Avenue in Tulsa will give us places we can go to and get away from the rest of the world and relax when needed."

Charlie moved over to Susan's lounge and hugged her. "I agree we gotta have our sanctuaries. Darlin', you must believe me when I say our life together in the business world excites me. When I still worked for George Miller, supportin' the 101 Ranch's venture into the oil business, my eyes were opened wide. I loved the challenges of learnin' new things and dealin' with the cutthroat competition in the oil business. We're findin' a balance to all this, and I want us to add to what your father left us and make the Kramer Group as large and powerful as we can. But, I'll always be a cowboy and ranching, horses and cattle will be part of my life. And I think it's great we're bringin' business to the ranch. Hank and J. Paul Getty should be here in a couple of hours. I'm lookin' forward to hearin' what's on their minds. I hope it's good news. We're already goin' to be busy for the next several months with our acquisitions in Cushing, with what Boss has planned here at the ranch, and movin' into our new house in Tulsa. I've been thinkin' about how much we've started in the last few months. We've spent some serious money, and there is more to spend in the near future."

Susan snuggled under Charlie's arm and returned his hug. "Have you thought about how many jobs we'll be creating and all the mouths we'll help feed?"

He looked down into her eyes. "No, I hadn't. But it's how I want to think of it from now on. Thanks, Sweetheart, you've put me in a great mood. What a wonderful way to spend our resources. Between what you're not wearin' and what you offered as a perspective on what we do, you've got this day off to a great start."

Susan smiled, "We better shower and get ready."

Charlie kissed her forehead. "Ya bet."

***

Susan was sitting at the breakfast table when Charlie arrived. "My, you look pretty as always."

Susan had a puzzled look on her face. "Did you forget something?"

"What? I don't think so. What's wrong; you sound very upset."

"Don't you shave before showering? It looks like you missed a step, Darling," she said in a disapproving tone.

"Are you mad?"

"Not if you just forgot."

"No, I thought I would let my beard grow like so many of my cowboy friends."

"Charlie, if you want to kiss me. If you want to hug and touch my naked body, you go back into the bathroom and get rid of the stubble."

"But Susan..."

"No buts, my Sweetheart. I've told you I love your smooth and handsome face. It turns me on and turns a lot of ladies' heads. So, just like you say you enjoy looking at the curves of my body, my face, and of course my breasts, I enjoy your broad shoulders, narrow hips, your muscular chest, and that handsome face. We both enjoy sharing them with the public to some extent. But Sweetheart, I like you best with only your mustache. Go back and shave before our guests get here."

Charlie rose, shaking his head as he headed toward the bedroom. "Okay, my Dear. And I love you."

"I love you too, my sweet man."

***

Charlie returned to the table clean-shaven, and Susan stood and greeted him with a kiss.

After finishing her first cup of coffee Susan placed her cup on its saucer. "Sweetheart, we seem to have a lot of meetings with people at breakfast or over a meal, why do you think that is?"

He leaned back and took a sip of coffee before answering.

"Your father and I shared an early morning coffee on the Westover patio on our wedding day, and he said he used meals often as meetings. Especially breakfast, because he could be sure to git somethin' important completed before he was busy at the office. He said his time was so valuable and he couldn't afford to waste it. He grinned and said people need to eat and certainly can talk and eat at the same time, so he would combine the two. I guess I thought that was good advice."

"Well, that explains it. He had people over to the Westover house for a meal often. Now I understand why. I guess I was a little jealous that I was giving up some private time with you. But we do need to be careful how we use our time. But, I still want to keep as many meals only for us as we can."

***

Hank arrived first and joined Charlie and Susan. The three enjoyed the views out of the room's massive windows as they chatted. It wasn't long before Getty knocked on the front door. Attie led him to the breakfast area. Cleta brought in a carafe and poured him a cup of coffee.

The men shook hands and Susan shared a hug. She said, "My, Paul, I've never seen you in boots and a cowboy hat."

He removed his expensive felt Stetson and held it across his chest. "I couldn't come to your fine ranch in a business suit and wingtips."

They all laughed at his response and Charlie almost choked on his last bite of bacon. "Paul .... glad ya made it. Have ya eaten yet?"

"Yes, I ate at the Norwood in Shawnee. They cook a great breakfast, but let me tell you, I had the best steak there last night."

Susan grinned at Charlie and turned to Paul. "We're glad you enjoyed it. We provide all their beef."

Paul's jaw dropped, "Are you kidding me?"

Charlie said, "No, they were buyin' their beef from Clay Stephens, this ranch's previous owner. And we've continued the contract with them. We've added a few more restaurants since we took over."

Hank pointed out the windows. "Paul, isn't this pretty country around here?"

Paul patted Hank's shoulder. "I now understand why Charlie and Susan wanted to buy it."

Charlie turned to their cook standing nearby in the kitchen.

"Cleta, I guess we won't need any more food for now. Please make another pot of coffee. We'll be ready for lunch around noon." He took another sip of coffee and looked across the table. "Ready to talk some business, fellas?"

Hank leaned in and placed his elbows on the table. "Yep. We're back pumpin' at Burbank number two. It looks like we're gettin' about twelve hundred barrels a day, but I think I'll slow it down for a while. We're usin' a truckin' company out of Ponca City to take the oil to the refinery, and they are strugglin' to keep up with our output. The problem's temporary because we're in the process of buyin' our own fleet of tanker trucks."

Charlie smiled. "Good, Hank. But before we go any further, Paul, here's a cashier's check for the $20,000 to close our deal on the Osage County properties we discussed back at the Hotel Tulsa." He reached over and picked up some papers. "These are the contracts and deeds we need to sign."

Paul took the paperwork and pulled a pen from the inner pocket of his tweed jacket. He was quick to read everything and signed it. "Thanks. This money will set me up in Los Angeles." He pushed the paperwork back to Charlie.

As they continued with the papers they heard the phone ring. In a few minutes, Attie rushed into the room. "Charlie, Susan you have a long-distance phone call from a Marjorie Post?"

They both rose and Charlie said to Hank and Getty, "Sorry. We haven't heard from Marjorie since we met her on our honeymoon at Jekyll Island. This will take but a moment."

Charlie got to the phone first. "Marjorie, this is Charlie. Is everything alright?"

Marjorie said, "That's what I was going to ask you. Is Susan, okay? I've been trying to reach you for the last few days. I finally called the 101 Ranch, and they gave me this number."

Charlie held the receiver so Susan could respond. "Marjorie, Sweetheart, this is Susan. I'm doing better every day. It's so wonderful of you to call. Where are you?"

"I'm back down here at Jekyll Island. It's why I didn't hear about your ordeal until yesterday. Do you want me to come to Oklahoma?"

"I'd love to see you, and we would enjoy showing you our ranch, but it's not necessary for you to come now. It would be wonderful to have some private time to discuss what you're thinking about the chances we'll see the bill ratified by enough states to allow women the right to vote alongside their men." Her face was distorted with indignation. "We can run huge businesses, but we can't vote. I'm getting all excited. Maybe we can meet somewhere later this year or sometime soon."

"Well, if you say you're alright, and it sounds like you're doing fine, I'll wait to come see you. I'm in a messy situation myself. Edward and I are divorcing. As you both know, we've been having trouble for a while. Well, I'll let you go. Let's get together soon. Maybe in the new year."

Charlie said, "We're sorry to hear things worked out this way."

Susan said, "Marjorie, our home is always available as a sanctuary for you as it is for us. And yes, we must get together soon."

Marjorie said, "Goodbye, sweet girl, and I love you."

Susan said, "I love you, too."

As she hung up the receiver, Susan looked at Charlie. "What a pleasant surprise. But I wouldn't say I liked hearing her marriage has failed. We must stay in touch better than we have these past months."

He gently cradled her chin in his hand. "Agreed, now let's see what our fellas have been up to."

They returned to the breakfast table. Getty and Hank were looking out the window at the ranch and turned back as the couple walked in. As he took his seat, Charlie set the paperwork aside, "Now, back to our discussion. When are ya leavin' for California, Paul?"

Getty picked up his coffee cup, hesitated, and said, "I'm catching a train tomorrow out of Tulsa."

Susan said, "So soon? What's driving you to get out there now?"

Paul took a sip of coffee. "Last month, a driller hit a big one in the Huntington Beach area outside of Los Angeles. I own a property near the well site. Now, I want to get out there as soon as possible and explore it. I may have told you I used to live in Los Angeles, so it will be like going home but getting paid to do it. I've already called my leadman, and I'll have a crew ready to start soon."

Hank said, "I'd like to join ya, but I have several things I need to get done here in Oklahoma and maybe down in Texas first."

Charlie added, "I know you knew Hank back when he worked for Marland. Now, as our partner in Kelly Oil, he stays busy because we've purchased four refineries and a pipeline company in a recent deal we pulled off in Cushing."

Paul grinned. "You now own a big chunk of Osage County, too. I wish I'd been the one to steal Hank from Marland, but maybe we can still find a way to work together in California."

Hank said, "There's a lot of folks makin' big money up in the Osage Nation area, and we will as well."

Paul nodded. "Be careful as you work up there. Between the killings of Osage people and some of the roughnecks working in the oil fields, it's getting dangerous. But you're right; there's a lot of money to be made."

Hank nodded. "I hear ya. It may take me a while to get everythin' here goin' in the right direction. But I'll be out to California as soon as I can. What do you know about experienced drillin' crews out there?"

"There are more than enough workers. I recommend you move one or two guys you trust out there to be your leads."

Charlie asked, "Is the Los Angeles area where the big ones are hittin'?"

Paul nodded. "Right now, yes. But there's been a lot of oil found up in the San Joaquin Valley north of Los Angeles. Some are saying it's bigger there than it is here in Oklahoma." He stood and looked Charlie in the eye. "Are you interested in a joint venture with me?"

Charlie looked at Susan, then Hank, and back to Paul. He shrugged. "Maybe. What did ya have in mind?"

Paul left his chair and paced around the room head down. "I've the money to acquire land where I'll have the mineral rights. And I'll lease where there is no other way. I've an old friend who said things are selling out fast, and auctions pop up, and, of course, drive up the price. If you help me acquire rights, we can split the profits."

Charlie thought about it. "I ain't makin' any decision today. Hank'll be out there before too long, and we can decide then. Or if something unusual comes up, call me. It's not a matter of trust. People don't always agree on where to drill. I've already seen enough of it. Hank has shared with us some scary stories from his past."

Hank said, "When I get there, I'll first want to drive the area and see what it looks like."

They continued sitting around the table, talking about California, Texas, and some Oklahoma locations. Lunchtime arrived before they knew it.

Cleta had prepared steak sandwiches with baked beans and potato salad for them. After they finished their meal, Paul asked, "Cleta, have you ever been to California?"

She was startled by the question. "No sir, why are ya askin'?"

"I want your cooking every day. It was amazing. Cleta, I've eaten at restaurants around the world, and that's the best steak sandwich I've ever eaten."

Susan reared back and threw up her hands. "Oh great, now she'll want a raise."

They all laughed, and Cleta smiled, "Mr. Getty, thanks for those kind words, but the Kellys are hard to beat as employers, and I'm happy you liked my cookin'. And you just enjoyed more of Double Bar K beef."

***

After lunch the group decided to walk down the hill to the barns and corrals to show Getty some of their ranch and allow their meal to settle.

As they stood at a corral, Charlie pointed and said, "Paul, see the big, beautiful Angus bull? He's one of the reasons our beef is in such demand. Do ya see all the cattle out in the near pasture over there grazin'? We're mighty proud of them, too."

Paul nodded, "Very impressive, Charlie. I don't know ranching or cattle, but I can hear the pride in your voice. You're every bit as excited to talk about this as you are about oil. Yep, very impressive."

Charlie didn't try to hide his smile. "I am, Paul. I'll always be a cowboy, and ranching will be a big part of my life. I'm happy you're impressed with this part of our lives."

They walked around some more so Charlie and Susan could show off parts of the ranch. After a while, they returned to the house to continue their discussion.

As they settled in Hank asked, "Paul, do ya have any other land or rights to drill here in Oklahoma you might be interested in sellin' before you head to California?"

Paul looked up at the ceiling, then back at Hank. "I hadn't thought about it, but I have several possibilities. Some might be interesting to you. They include land with minerals up at Cushing, over in Garvin County, nearby in Seminole County, and even over close to the Capitol in Oklahoma City."

Hank smiled, "What would ya take for the whole batch?"

Paul slumped in his chair with his arms across his chest. "Let me think a minute." After a long pause, he said, "I guess $75,000 would be alright."

Hank looked at Charlie, who nodded his approval. Charlie said, "Paul, I can draft ya a check right now you can cash at the Exchange Bank tomorrow for $60,000 if we have a deal. You can have the deeds sent to Curt for processin'."

"Your offer is less than I wanted." He grinned and reached

over to shake hands. "I'll take it, and the deeds are in a safety deposit box at the Exchange Bank. I know you bought the bank. Harry Sinclair continues to run it, right?"

Charlie shook Paul's hand. "He does, and I'm glad you are willin' to sell." He looked at Hank and winked. "We at Kelly Oil need to accumulate more properties; if you had them, I'm sure there must be value in them."

Susan nodded. "Harry continues to have a leadership role for us, but we had one of our bankers from Kansas City move here to run the bank. Harry wanted and needed to create more time for Sinclair Oil."

Charlie left the room to write the check. When he returned, he handed it to Paul.

Susan stood. "It's getting to be late. Paul needs to get back to Tulsa if he's heading to California tomorrow." She looked at Hank. "Didn't you say you were going to Shawnee for dinner with someone?"

Hank hesitated. "Uh... all I'm sayin' is her name is Polly'. I'll be back in the mornin' at about nine if that's okay?"

Charlie grinned. "Who he has dinner with is none of our business, and nine'll be great."

Paul nodded. "Susan, you're right. It's time I headed toward Tulsa. Today's trip was successful for me. I'm $80,000 richer than when I arrived. I hope we can do some business in California or at least be rooting for each other's success."

***

After their visitors left Charlie walked over to Susan and kissed her. "I believe things went about as well as we could have hoped. And I saw there were a couple of steaks left. And some leftover beans and taters, too. Ya git some wine, and let's find our loungers on the patio. I know it's cool out, but I can build a fire in our fire pit. How does that sound?"

"Perfect. I need to go to the bedroom for a minute or two, but I'll meet you there."

Another beautiful sunset glowed to the west as they arrived on the patio. Susan brought the wine, and Charlie had the food. They both dressed for comfort, wearing robes.

Charlie said, "Sometime before too long we need to talk to Cleta and Attie about movin' to Tulsa with us. We'll have the quarters for them and Paul's right, Cleta is a fabulous cook, and with her food, I'm spoiled. She and Attie are like family."

Susan poured their wine. "I agree with you. We had to put off the closing because of what happened in Cushing. We must talk to them before we return to Tulsa." She lay back on her lounger and allowed her robe to fall to her side. "The warmth from the fire feels nice."

"I like the way the light of the fire looks as it dances across your breasts. It looks like you dressed for me."

"I did have you, or I should say, us, in mind when I changed. It looks like you did too."

They enjoyed tasty leftovers and finished their bottle of Cabernet.

Chapter 3

Expansion Plans

November 1919

IT WAS A COOL Autumn morning as the young couple sat in their living room with the fireplace providing them warmth. Susan enjoyed her *Harper's Magazine* and Charlie laughed as he read the new *Western Story Magazine*. As always, she loved giving her man a visual tease across the room. She would catch him looking and open her shirt enough to get a smile.

Attie walked into the room, "Mr. Charlie, I just made my daily walk to the road to check the mailbox, and I found this letter addressed to you."

Charlie took the letter from her. "Thanks, Attie. I wonder who it's from?"

Attie had turned to leave the room. She stopped and smiled as she looked back. "It's postmarked Perkins, Oklahoma. You know anyone from up there?" She hummed a tune as she continued walking out of the room.

Charlie looked down and saw the name Meehan in the envelope's upper left corner. "I sure do. Why would the Meehans be writin' me? And how did they know where to find me?" He tore open the envelope and found a one-page letter. He gave Susan a puzzled look and then read it aloud:

Charlie,

I contacted George Miller a few weeks ago on a business matter. I had hoped he might be interested in acquiring the Meehan Ranch. He was not. I mentioned you and learned you are no longer there. He said you're married. I hope you and your new wife are doing well. He thought you might be interested in my place. You must have accomplished a lot since you left us two years or so ago. George sure bragged on you. With a thousand acres, we are just getting by, and to be honest, I'm not able to add any more land, even leasing. I would like to talk to you about any interest you might have in purchasing my ranch. We would love to talk with you anyway and catch up. Call me at Perkins - 4507.

Respectfully,
Bill Meehan
P.S. Your old foreman Hank Cottrell says hello.

Charlie shook his head, looked up at Susan, and sighed. "What a wonderful ranchin' family. Their foreman, Hank Cottrell, has one of the best ranchin' business minds I've ever been around. He's a younger version of Boss."

Susan leaned toward him and placed her hand on his. "Would you be interested in buying their place?"

"Maybe, I'll wait to see what Boss and the guys say. They might not want to add anythin' right now. Of course, buyin' it would involve spendin' money."

Susan giggled. "Sweetheart, I'm sure if you want to buy it, we can afford it."

He moved closer and gently squeezed her hand. "Oh, I guess you're right, but I don't always need to buy somethin' just because I want it. Now it's different if Boss, Tom, and Dan want it. And they think we can use it and make it profitable. Understand?"

"I guess. We come from very different backgrounds. You didn't have the luxuries Father gave me as you grew up. But I think our differences are good in its way."

"Susan, it's part of it. But I'm talkin' pure business as much as anythin' else. There should be a good bottom-line reason to buy somethin', includin' the Meehan's ranch. It's a small ranch, but very well run. In the right situation, it should be profitable."

"Aren't Boss and the others supposed to be here soon?"

"Yep, anytime now. Sweetheart, are you ready to talk ranchin'?"

"I'm ready, Charlie. But I doubt I'll be able to get a word into the conversation when you four start talking."

Charlie saw Attie in the doorway. She turned and pointed. "You have some visitors."

Boss, Dan, and Tom walked in. Boss nodded toward the front of the house. "I saw someone comin' up the road as we walked through the front door. It might be your oilman. You call him a Landman, I guess."

Charlie said, "Was it a truck?"

"Yep, it looked like a Model-T."

"It's Hank. And yes, he finds our oil and sets up gettin' it out of the ground."

Cleta came in from the kitchen. "Gentlemen, I've coffee and some food on the sideboard here. You'll find cinnamon toast, deviled eggs, and bacon. Help yourself to whatever you like."

Everyone filled a plate before taking a seat.

A few minutes later, Hank arrived, and the group was complete. After they each had some coffee and a snack, they settled into their chairs around the table.

Charlie looked across at his foreman. "Boss, I understand you and the boys have some ideas, so how about sharin' them with the rest of us? I'm sure Hank and Susan are curious, too."

Boss leaned in, elbows on the table, "Happy to, Charlie. What I'm about to say could be new to Hank, although he and I talked about some of this the last time he was here. Charlie, as I said before, we need to expand what we are doin' because the demand for our beef grows every month. We coulda sold fifty percent more than we did the last time the beef buyer was here. And I learned at the feed store over the weekend there's 4,000 acres of land for sale. It's located about half a mile north of here. There's an old house—if you can call it a house—on the land, but no barn or other structures. We have no immediate need for the house, if at all, but it comes as a package deal. You buy all or nothing."

Charlie's eyes sparkled. "Have you seen the entire property yet?"

"With the owner's permission, I have ridden it several times. It has plenty of grassland, and the same creek runnin' along the back of your ranch continues onto it as well. I wish we could also buy the thousand acre property between here and there. It has a nice large pond on it. Getting it would allow us to double the size of this ranch."

Susan looked at Boss. "Have you approached the property owner adjacent to us?"

"Yes, and he didn't say no to discussin' an offer. He knows the larger piece is for sale and will make us pay a premium for his pastures."

Charlie glanced around the table. "Any other comments about these properties?"

Hank had picked his coffee cup up to take a drink but hesitated. "Yes, I have a question." He replaced the cup. "If you buy both of these properties, will it give you everything up to Hardesty Road which is the main east and west road north of here?"

Boss nodded and gave Hank a curious look at the question. "Yep, it would. And we don't need it all for cattle right now, but as I said, we need to expand our operation. Why do you ask?"

Hank looked at Charlie and grinned. "You do whatever you gotta do to buy up these parcels. I would bet my life we'll hit oil on 'em. I sure liked what I saw up near the main road. I know it's an anticlinal trap up there, and I wish we could drill it today. We'll easily have three or four wells on it and you've gotta do whatever it takes so it becomes your property."

Susan squeezed Charlie's forearm. "I think Hank just made our decision for us. With the possibility of finding oil on the north end, let's give Boss what he needs to make this ranch more profitable."

Charlie leaned back with outstretched arms. "Does anyone have more to add to our discussion?"

Dan raised his hand. "Boss may have brought this up next, but I'll go ahead. We need to expand our horse trainin' and development ranch. And it may include adding a new location. We are gettin' a lot of business from the Miller's 101, the Drummond Ranch near Pawhuska, and other ranches up in the northern part of the state. We can't handle all the current activity down here and service them, too. I wish we could find a place up near those ranches. I know it could be tough for me to cover both, but we need to do somethin'."

Susan looked at Charlie and started to say something. He motioned for her to wait.

She gave Charlie a puzzled look and a pout that seemed to say, *"You mean I can't talk?"*

Charlie looked at her, tilted his head, and grinned. He stood, walked over, picked a piece of paper off the kitchen counter, turned to the group, and smiled. "What if I had the answer to that problem already?"

Dan rocked back into his chair. "Of course you do." He shook his head as he grinned. "What are ya talkin' about, brother?"

Charlie held the Meehan letter up chest high and said, "I received this letter this mornin'. It's from Bill Meehan. I worked for him before I got to the 101. He's interested in sellin' his ranch. It's only got 1000 acres, but it is a fine operation. I know there's an adjacent property we might acquire. Hank Cottrell, the Meehan foreman, told me they have leased it from time to time. The Meehan ranch is located outside Perkins, and it should be good to work from as you handle the northern business you're describin'. We might get Ole Hank Cottrell and the Meehans to stay and work for us. Whattaya think, Dan?"

"You're right. Their ranch and its location sounds perfect. Why are they sellin'? What are the owners like?"

Charlie sat, then looked around the table with his eyes sparkling with excitement. "They're our kind of people. I was happy there. If I hadn't had such a strong desire to go to the 101, I would be there today." He looked at Boss. "Their foreman is much like Boss. He's about ten years younger and even shares many of the same views on ranchin'. I think they may be strugglin' as a cattle operation, but we would have a different approach to usin' the ranch."

Boss edged toward Charlie and said, "Yeah, Hank Cottrell, he was always like a little brother to me. But I never could get him to use Red Man plugs like me." After the laughter died down Boss continued, "Charlie, Tom and I were at an Oklahoma Cattlemen's Association meeting at Oklahoma A&M in Stillwater before we left the 101. You were off doin' your oil business thing with George. We met Bill Meehan and my old buddy Hank Cottrell. Those are two fine individuals, and I imagine their little spread is a beauty. I might be interested in havin' it be a part of Dan's horse trainin' affair."

Tom had remained quiet. He now decided to add his two cents. "Charlie, I'm concerned with how we handle everythin' when it comes to havin' enough cowboys. Horse trainin' takes a few more people than runnin' cattle. I know this is Dan's area, but you need to be thinkin' about how we manage this with our current staff."

Dan said, "Tom's right. The Meehan place might be the right answer, but havin' enough crew is important and we can't forget to include hirin' as we decide what to do."

Charlie, a little restless, stood again and walked over to the food. He turned back to face everyone. "Tom, thanks for giving me somethin' to consider. You're right. We must make sure we have enough folks to git the job done right in any decision we make. And we will do that as we negotiate any deal. Now, here's what I'm thinkin' about all this. We want the 5,000 acres between here and Hardesty Road. Boss, you and Hank do whatever you need to do to get with the two owners and buy their property. I'm callin' Bill Meehan here in a little bit, and I hope Susan and I can drive to Perkins tomorrow and visit with the Meehans. We need to be in Tulsa in a few days anyway. I'll try to establish what Susan's daddy called an agreement in principle before we leave Perkins if it makes sense after the visit. I want the same for the land here. Get somethin' agreed to by this weekend."

The group responded with head nods and shouts of agreement. Cleta called from her kitchen, "My goodness, you folks sound mighty happy. It's lunchtime. Are you ready to eat?"

Hank said, "We are, and I'd say this meal will be one of our happiest in a long time."

Boss patted Hank's shoulder. "After lunch, let's go see what we can stir up on those nearby properties today. I have a way to get ahold of both owners."

Hank nodded. "You bet, Boss. Let's get this settled as soon as possible. We don't want someone else to beat us to 'em."

Charlie saw everyone heading for Cleta's kitchen. Charlie pulled Boss aside. "I'm gonna go call the Meehans now. I'll join you guys in a little while."

He headed to his office and picked up the phone. "Operator, I need the Meehan Ranch in Perkins, Oklahoma." He gave her the number from the letter.

After a short conversation between operators, a familiar voice said, "Hello, this is Bill Meehan."

"Bill, this is Charlie Kelly. I got your letter."

"Charlie, it's so good to hear from you. How is married life treatin' you?"

"It's wonderful. I couldn't be happier. I want to discuss your ranch. I assume it's still for sale, right?"

"It is. So, you're interested?"

"I am. I would like to bring my wife with me tomorrow and come see the ranch again."

Bill laughed. "Of course, and we want to meet her. Will you agree to spend the night with us?"

"We'll be happy to. I can't wait to have Susan meet you and your family. How's old Hank doin'?"

"He's great. I know he'll be happy to see you. Can you be here by lunchtime tomorrow?"

"We can, and we'll spend tomorrow night with ya. Thanks for the invite. We need to leave on Wednesday to get to Tulsa for a meetin' on Thursday."

"Okay. We'll plan on you for lunch and talk about the ranch."

"Bill, give my best to Claudia and Tess. We'll see ya tomorrow."

Charlie walked into the breakfast room and found everyone eating and celebrating.

Susan looked up. "Where'd you go, Sweetheart?"

"I called Bill Meehan. You and I are drivin' to Perkins tomorrow. We'll spend the afternoon and night with the Meehans. We'll go from there to Tulsa."

Susan clapped her hands. "Honey. I'm excited to meet them."

Charlie nodded. "I'll call Sinclair and arrange to meet with him. And then we can drive over to see our real estate agent Grant to close on our Madison house on Friday."

Boss squeezed Charlie's shoulder. "So, now the pressure is on Hank and me to get somethin' goin' here."

Charlie grinned. "You're right." He turned. "Boss you can sign checks on the Double Bar K bank account. So, tie up the property with earnest money and a handshake, and we'll get everythin' closed as soon as possible, okay?"

Hank said, "Do you have a limit on what you'll pay for these parcels?"

"We should be willin' to pay fair market value without quibblin'. Since you liked what you saw. And we should have more than one way to make money with the land, let's be willin' to pay a little over market value if needed. This is a business decision, guys, so don't ruin our chance of gettin' the land. We'll make it profitable."

After an hour or so everyone left to do whatever tasks they had to get done.

Chapter 4

The Meehan Ranch

November 1919

EARLY THE NEXT MORNING, Susan walked into the bathroom where Charlie was using their shower. "Darling, how long do you think we'll be gone on this trip?"

He turned the shower off. "Susan, I think I heard ya over the water, did ya ask me how long we'll be gone."

"Yes, how long?"

"We may not be back for weeks. It could be near the end of the month."

"Okay, I'll pack for three weeks. I want to eat breakfast here and talk to Cleta and Attie before we leave."

"Sounds good, Sweetheart." He turned the shower back on, and he rinsed off the last of the soap. He stepped out of the shower, grabbed a towel, and dried himself. "Susan, I'm packin' comfortable clothes. I'll take one suit, but I doubt I'll wear it. It'll be Levi denim pants and boots most of the time on this trip."

Susan had stood at the bathroom door and waited for him to step out of the shower. With a smile on her face, she said, "Now you're giving me my favorite view." She held her arms out to her side palms up. "You've always told me wearing nothing at all is yours. So, I haven't dressed yet; any request from you as I prepare for our drive to Perkins?"

He shrugged. "You're in my favorite outfit now."

"Charlie, I'm naked. I can't arrive at the Meehan's ranch like this."

He grinned as he dried the back of his neck. "Well, I guess you're right. I must admit, when we are in the car, regardless of what you wear you do a wonderful job of givin' me as much of this beautiful view as possible. So, I'm sure I'll be happy."

She kissed him and caressed his chest. "Then, it's shirts or blouses and no dresses." She started to walk away and stopped and looked back over her shoulder. "I guess I'll be giving you a view every time we travel by car from now on."

"Yep, you'll put a smile on my face every trip."

Charlie walked over and took her in his arms and kissed her. Passion was evident in his voice. "Susan, you're everythin' to me, Sweetheart." He cupped a breast in his hand and kissed her again. They walked to the bed without leaving their embrace. Everything else was going to have to wait.

***

After packing, Charlie loaded everything in the trunk of the car and then went to the kitchen where he found Susan chatting with the ladies.

As he entered the room, Cleta asked, "What'll ya want me to fix ya, Mr. Charlie?"

He thought for a second and said, "It's gonna be a while before I git to eat your cookin' again. So, let's make it my favorite, steak and eggs. The steak cooked medium rare, three eggs over easy, biscuits, and fried taters."

"Got it, and your coffee is on the table. I've already got Miss Susan's order."

Charlie said, "Cleta, wait a minute please; Susan and I need to talk to you and Attie before we leave today."

Susan said, "Yes, both of you sit here at the table with us."

Attie, standing nearby asked, "We ain't in trouble, are we?"

"For heaven's sake, no," Susan said.

Charlie looked from one to the other and smiled. "The last thing you two would ever be in is trouble with us."

Susan caught Charlie's attention by placing her hand on his. "Let me start this conversation, please."

Charlie nodded, "Of course, this is all you, Sweetheart."

She looked to Attie and then Cleta. "Ladies, we want to make you an offer, and we hope you say yes." She took a breath. "We want you to work for us in our Tulsa home; we'll be moving into it soon."

Attie gasped. "We would move to Tulsa?"

Cleta asked, "When would this happen?"

Charlie answered, "Susan and I signed the offer papers on what Susan would call 'an elegant estate' in Tulsa last month. It has wonderful separate quarters on the property which will be perfect as a residence for a housekeeper and a cook. I know you each have your bedroom here, but you would have more privacy there."

Cleta fell back into her chair. "I don't know. Who would take care of you here?"

Attie said, "I've never been to Tulsa. I hear it's a big place. I don't know about living there."

Susan reached over and took Attie's hand as she looked at Cleta. "We want you to support us in both places. Charlie and I are willing to buy you an automobile and teach you to drive or provide you with transportation between each location and around Tulsa."

Charlie added, "We'll pay you more for doin' this for us."

Attie replied, "How much more? I'm already makin' quite a bit for a housekeeper now. You're payin' me $250 a month now. I don't know any other housekeeper makin' even close to as much."

Cleta agreed. "You folks have been generous with us. I, too, am paid well above most household cooks."

Susan looked at Charlie and winked. She then turned to Cleta and Attie. "How about if we double your salaries? As I said, we'll pay to set you up in Tulsa with transportation and anything else needed. You both are like family, and we want you with us."

Cleta began to cry, "You would?" She sniffled. "I'm willin' to go with you, and what you're offering us is so generous."

In an instant, Attie said, "Me too. We both are single and can make this work."

Charlie said, "Good, then it's settled. We won't be movin' into our new house up there for a while, so we'll have time to plan. Now let's have some breakfast."

Cleta jumped up and said, "It'll be here before ya know it."

It was 8:30 when Charlie and Susan drove through the Double Bar K's front gate, heading to Perkins, Oklahoma.

***

The Kellys enjoyed their time together and dreamed of how they would use their new Tulsa house as their main residence. When they got to the turnoff to go west to Perkins or east to Cushing it was 11:00. They were about ten miles from the Meehan ranch. Susan had been her typical playful self, and Charlie had loved her show.

Susan reached over and stroked his bare chest. "How long will it be before we get to the Meehan's since you said Cushing was about twenty minutes in the other direction?"

"Maybe fifteen minutes at the most."

"Oh my, I better get myself together." She began to button this and straighten that as Charlie chuckled.

"Sweetheart, you have plenty of time. I could always pull to the side of the road if necessary. You look fabulous. They are goin' to love ya, I promise."

"I want to be perfect for you. These people are some of your friends from before you arrived at the 101, right?"

"Yep, and they are warm and wonderful people. Believe me, they're gonna love ya. Okay?"

She combed her hair one more time and said, "I'll settle down. It's just I want you to be proud of me."

"Holy Cow, Susan, you know how I feel about you. It's me should be thinkin' that way."

"But I'm not a cowgirl. I'm still learning about ranch life. I'm a city girl who might do or say the wrong thing. I don't want to embarrass you or me."

Charlie glanced over at her and asked, "Would ya do me a favor?"

"Sure, I will, Honey, anything."

"Promise to be yourself. Be the city girl ya are, with all your charms and wonderful personality. Let me say it again, please be yourself. It's who I fell in love with and know my friends will fall in love with."

"Now you're gonna make me cry."

"Don'tcha dare."

Charlie saw the Meehan Ranch sign and slowed down.

"Here we are, Susan, on the final road to the ranch. We'll be there in two minutes."

The Meehan home sat upon a hill and Charlie gunned the motor as they drove the quarter mile past blackjack oaks that lined the road.

Charlie parked in front of the house, and they climbed the steps to the porch and front door.

He knocked, and the door opened after a moment.

Bill Meehan smiled broadly and patted Charlie on the shoulder. "Charlie, it's so good to see you. I saw you driving up." They hugged, and then Bill said, "Who is this pretty lady?"

With obvious pride and love in his voice, Charlie said, "This is my wife, Susan."

Bill offered his two hands with warmth. "It's a pleasure to meet you. Charlie is special to the Meehan family. My wife, Claudia and I think of him as the son who moved away. So, we would like to treat you like family too."

Susan looked at Charlie and then back to Bill. "I— I would consider it an honor."

Claudia and Tess, their daughter, rushed in from the kitchen and immediately hugged Charlie.

Overwhelmed with emotion, Charlie tried to gather himself. "I better sit down before I get all fuzzy. I knew I had missed ya, but I didn't expect this reception. And Bill, what a wonderful greeting for my Susan."

Claudia fussed with her apron. "We love Charlie and hated to see him leave us. But we knew he needed to chase his dream. Susan, it would appear he found his dream by how he looks at you."

Susan nodded. "I know what you mean. I had to be apart from this wonderful man for a long time after I knew I loved him. It was my dream come true when we were able to get back together. I knew early on as you did, he was a man with a big dream."

Charlie said, "Claudia's right though. I knew soon after we parted back then my true dream was and is you, Susan."

Tess took Charlie by the arm. "I'm hungry, and I bet Charlie and Susan are too. Let's eat."

Chapter 5

We've Got to Make This Work

November 1919

AS THE GROUP ENTERED the kitchen Charlie was again hit with emotion as wonderful memories came flowing back. Seeing the table full of food and the old wooden chair he had used for those months made him grin.

As they gathered around the table, in walked Hank Cottrell. And the hugs started again, but they were brief, so the food wouldn't get cold.

After finishing the meal with apple pie for dessert, Hank said, "Can we all go out back and sit under the big shade tree and talk a while? It's a nice warm day out and it should be mighty pleasant."

Bill wiped his mouth with his napkin. "Good idea, and everyone bring your glass of sweet tea with ya. Momma, can ya bring the pitcher out there?"

"Yes, Bill. I'll be right out."

Outside, pitcher in hand, she checked everyone's tea glasses before she took a seat next to Tess.

They chatted about the weather, Shoeless Joe Jackson and what a shame it was the White Sox lost the World Series, and various other subjects when Hank said, "We need to git to the reason Charlie's here, Bill. You ready to start us off?"

"You're right again." He looked over at Susan. "We sure enjoyed conversations like this back when Charlie was here as a hand." He turned to Charlie, "We've been squeakin' by since you left. If Hank didn't have the skills he does, we'd not be doin' as well."

Charlie swallowed some tea. "What do ya think is the biggest problem you're facin'?"

"We're not big enough to handle the ups and downs in beef prices. It was great during the war. Now the troops are home, and the demand for beef is growin' but there was a time right after the war when it fell. We enjoyed it as we rode the prices as they crept higher. As the prices fell the larger cattle outfits could take less per pound, and with their volume, they still make it fine."

Hank added, "We enjoyed it as we were runnin' as many head o' cattle per acre as we could. We even supplemented grazin' with feed, but we can't afford it all the time."

Bill leaned in. "We need more acres, and we don't have the money to buy it. So, we need to be sellin' out."

Charlie moved to the edge of his chair. "I git the picture. Now I have an idea I'd like to run by ya."

Bill said, "We're all ears. Whatcha got for us?"

"We need to add to our ranchin' business. And this location is perfect for what we need. Our horse development ranch, the Bar B, needs to expand to meet our demand for raisin' and trainin' cuttin' and reinin' horses. A lot of the ranches drivin' the demand we're strugglin' to meet are places up around here, including the Miller's 101. I need your place and the 1500 acres next door too, if I can negotiate to buy it. I would love to have you folks stay on and be part of the horse operation."

Hank said, "I've never even considered that might be somethin' you would bring up. I thought you're runnin' cattle on your spread down in Pott County."

"I am at our Double Bar K, Hank. But I bought the horse outfit next door too. I'm hopin' to double the size of the acres I have for cattle, and this would almost double the size of the horse operation if we can agree on terms for this ranch and the property next door."

Bill said, "Well, of course, if we sell ya this place, ya can do with it whatever ya want to. I've got limited experience workin' horses. Hank, whattaya think about this?"

"I don't know yet. I'm still mullin'."

Charlie said, "This is a lot to throw at ya. I was hopin' but I wasn't expectin' an answer today, and we haven't even discussed the price of the place yet. Whattaya need to sell it?"

Bill said, "I need to get $30,000 to come out okay."

Charlie leaned back and scratched his chin. "About what I was expectin'. I think I can more than justify your price, if I can git you and Hank to stick around. Keep in mind; I run about 500 head of cattle on the Bar B to support the horse trainin'. Here we would need to run some cattle too, if we could get the 1500 acres next door. So, Bill, there would still be a cattle operation to run. My brother Dan is an expert at trainin' horses. He would be in charge of this location too, but his first task would be to teach you and Hank what he needs from ya on the horse trainin' side."

Hank said, "I'm sure the horse trainin' would come to me. I worked on a horse outfit back years ago. With Dan's help, I could be just fine. But I can't speak for Bill."

Bill took a sip of tea and looked at Charlie. "Are you saying we would be workin' for you?"

"Yes. Fellas, my horse outfit is profitable. And I have every reason to believe this will be too. I'll be able to pay someone well to run it for me."

Hank scratched the back of his neck as he looked at the ground. "Well, Charlie, I'm not sure ya could afford to pay us both, so I'll find somethin' else, I'm sure."

Charlie didn't hesitate. "Whoa now, both of ya guys. I'm not ..."

Susan had heard enough. She stood and with loving concern on her face she looked at everyone. "Can I step in here for a word or two, please?"

Charlie cleared his throat. "Uh, sure, Honey, this might be a good time for me to let someone else talk."

Susan said, "I'm not a ranch person. I can ride and saddle a horse but don't pretend to be a cowgirl. I have a business degree in economics from Vassar College. And my father taught me well regarding running profitable businesses. My instincts tell me the current cattle operation here covers the expenses and provides a living, even one where you're squeaking by. What Charlie is considering will do much more. I also want you to know it's not critical for us for the first few years to be profitable. Charlie and I are doing well financially. My maiden-name is Kramer. My late father built some successful businesses, and now Charlie and I own and operate them. We're expanding them and enjoying it, so if Charlie wants the folks he loves like family to stick around and continue to be part of his life, I'll be happy to agree to it and do all I can to make it happen." She smiled and sat down. "I guess I'm done."

Bill said, "Charlie, you done good. You've done real good. She sure is somethin' special." He turned to Susan. "By the way, was your daddy Walter Kramer?"

"Yes, he was."

"I met him once. I went to a ranching business event in Kansas City about ten years ago. He was the main speaker, and I was impressed by your daddy. They had a biography about him in the program. I don't mean to embarrass you, but you two are rich. I mean rich."

Susan tilted her head. "Yes, we are. But that's just money. What makes me *feel* rich is the life Charlie and I have together. Bill, I look at you, Claudia, and Tess, and with your dear friend, Hank, I see a wealthy man. Now nothing would make Charlie and me happier than if we could create a way for you all to be part of our lives from now on, and you also benefit financially."

Claudia raised both hands palms up at Susan. "My oh my, we already knew why and how you or any woman could fall in love with our Charlie, but now we see how he could fall in love with you. I know we can work all these business things out, right, Bill?"

"Right, you are, my Dear."

Hank said, "Susan, that was powerful. I look forward to seein' a lot of you and Charlie."

Charlie's smile seemed too big for his face. "Well then, let's agree in principle we will buy the ranch for the $30,000 ya need. I want ya to arrange a meetin' as soon as possible with the owner of the property next door. Susan and I have some business to see to over the next several days. Set somethin' up and I'll have Dan and my foreman Boss join us."

Startled, Hank looked at Charlie. "Are you talkin' about Boss Bellamy from the 101?"

"It sure is. Boss is in charge of the overall ranchin' operation for me."

Hank rubbed the back of his neck. "Now he woulda been your boss at the 101, right?"

"He was. But now he's happy workin' for me. We'll fill ya in on everythin' when Boss is here with us."

Hank shook his head. "Must be an interestin' story."

Charlie stood and stretched. "Folks, I'm about businessed out. Can I have some more sweet tea, and maybe we can check out the barn."

Bill said, "Let's go; come on, Hank."

Charlie forgot the tea and the three of them walked shoulder-to-shoulder toward the barn.

The women followed the men and Claudia nodded toward Bill. "My man is so happy right now; we ladies have got to make this work."

Susan looked at her. "Claudia, we will. I promise you; we will."

Chapter 6
New Threats
November 1919

CHARLIE AND SUSAN ATE breakfast with the Meehans and Hank Cottrell before driving to Tulsa. Claudia Meehan remembered when he lived with them, Charlie loved her thick buttermilk pancakes with maple syrup and bacon. She made a big batch and got a big hug from Charlie when he saw what she had done.

Soon after the meal, the Kellys were on the road. Along the way, Susan said, "After such a huge breakfast, we better take a long walk when we get to the hotel."

They drove straight to the Hotel Tulsa, went to their suite, and unpacked.

In their room, Charlie walked over and embraced Susan from behind. "Do ya want to go for the walk around town now or wait a while?"

"I've changed my mind. I think I want to take a nap, then freshen up and go down to the Topaz Room for dinner. Okay?"

"Fine with me. I need to make a call to the Bar B anyway. So, enjoy your nap."

Charlie took a seat on the brown leather couch, which was beginning to show some wear, putting him within reach of the candlestick telephone. He picked it up and placed the call to Dan. After the connection was made Charlie said, "Hey brother, how are things down your way?"

"Great, Charlie. The owners of both of those properties are willin' to talk to you. Boss and I told them it could be sometime in the first part of next month before you would be home. They were fine with waitin'. Boss didn't quibble on price. I think it made them want to talk with you."

"Well, good. I need ya both to meet Susan and me at the Meehan ranch as soon as Bill can get somethin' set up. I'm waitin' to hear from him."

"Sounds like you got what you wanted, Charlie. I'll let Boss know. Anything else?"

"No, that about covers everything. Again, great work on the properties down there. See ya soon."

Charlie opened the newspaper which had been delivered earlier and got caught up on the news. After her nap, Susan walked into the room. Charlie looked up. "Well, there's several articles here in the paper about all kinds of problems across the country because of the movement to ban alcohol sales has started."

"I guess it doesn't surprise me. I'm glad we anticipated the issues we'll see people having to deal with. We have a supply of our wine and a source for more."

"I know, and I'm sure the criminals will find ways to make money while makin' life miserable for everyone." Charlie yawned as he went to the shiny mahogany sideboard and poured himself a cup of coffee. Susan was standing in the bedroom doorway when the telephone rang. She answered it while Charlie took a sip of coffee.

"Hello, this is Susan Kelly. Oh, uh, hello Zane, you okay? Uh, yes, he's here, hold a moment." She turned to Charlie. "It's Zane. He sounds concerned."

Charlie sat on the arm of the sofa and took the receiver. "Zane, what's on your mind?" He listened as his eyes narrowed, and his face frowned. "Really? Where are you?"

He jumped to his feet. "You're downstairs? I'll meet ya in five minutes in the restaurant."

Charlie put the phone on the side table. "Damn."

Susan placed her hand on Charlie's chest. "What's wrong, Sweetheart?"

He stood and headed for the door. He looked back. "We may have more trouble with the folks from Chicago. I'll fill ya in later."

***

As Charlie arrived at the restaurant, he learned the VIP room was in use. He asked the maître d' to set him up with a telephone at a table as far away from the rest of the customers as possible. Zane met him and the two shook hands as the maître d' got the table set up. After a minute he escorted Charlie and Zane to the table.

Zane sat across from Charlie. Frustration was obvious on his face, and Charlie could see Zane's knuckles were white as he clenched his fist on the table in front of him.

Charlie took out a pen and opened his notebook. "I can tell you're upset. What did ya find at the quarry this mornin'? Give me as much detail as possible."

Zane took a breath and let out a sigh. "I arrived at the main office at 7:30, and before 8:00, I received a call from our foreman at the new quarry. When the morning crew arrived, they saw a lot of damage at their offices. I drove over and found windows busted out and the main door kicked in. The place was a complete mess. The vandals had tried to get into our filing cabinets but failed. We keep them padlocked, and they are reinforced with concrete. There was a message painted on the wall. "Greetings from Chicago, Get out of Town."

Charlie shook his head. "Well, I guess we should have expected somethin' from those assholes. Rice Coburn, he runs our Strawberry Hill construction company up in Kansas City, has had some run-ins with them. He's told me they don't like losin'. I need to make this incident the last one we have to face from them. Did you call the police?"

Zane nodded. "Yes. I waited for them to get there before I came here. After the police questioned me, I asked to leave so I could give you a report in person. As I walked to my truck, I heard the police call the quarry a crime scene. In spite of my anger and frustration I had to chuckle to myself and thought *Well, what else would you call it.*"

"Absolutely. Okay, Zane, I need to make a few telephone calls. Have you had anythin' to eat since early this mornin'?"

"No, and I'm hungry."

Charlie waved to the waiter, and he came to the table. He pointed to Zane, "Please get him whatever he wants to eat and drink and bring me a piece of apple pie and refill my coffee."

Zane ordered as Charlie started his calls. His first was to Kansas City. "Curt, I wish ya were here."

"What's wrong? I hear anger in your voice."

"We had our mafia friends from Chicago visit our Sapulpa cement quarry last night. They did a lot of damage to the offices. They also left a message to make sure we knew it was them. I need to talk to our new President of Security Bailey Muldoon. Do you know where I can reach him?"

Curt interrupted, "He's here doing some personnel paperwork, hold on. I'll go get him."

"Good."

In less than a minute, Bailey got to the phone. "Charlie, this is Bailey, what do you need?"

"First, I assume ya resigned from Pinkerton and are in Kansas City doin' paperwork to get on our payroll, right?"

"Right. What's happening there? Curt seemed troubled."

"We've been threatened by the Chicago Outfit, at the new Sapulpa quarry. The Kramer Group has a history with these guys bothering Coburn's construction company in Missouri. Curt can fill ya in on those details. I need ya to come here and work with the local folks and maybe call Richard at the Oklahoma Bureau of Investigation and get his point of view on this."

"I'll finish my paperwork, talk with Curt, and arrange to be there as soon as possible. Where are you?"

"I'm at the Hotel Tulsa. There will be a room waiting for you. See ya soon."

***

Susan dressed and joined Charlie and Zane in the Topaz Room full of questions. "What's happened, Charlie?"

"It's a real mess. I have Bailey on his way here from Kansas City. He'll be here as soon as possible. The Chicago Outfit hit the new quarry last night. Zane has given me a report on what he saw. He's called the police, and after Bailey is here, we'll get our arms around this situation."

"The Chicago bunch again? I know they've been a thorn in Rice's side for a while. They were backing Pendleton Concrete and providing them with toughs to scare off other construction companies," she turned to Charlie. "Do you remember?"

"I remember they took shots at you and Rice before we were married."

Susan smiled and patted his arm reassuringly. "I thought we took care of them after we purchased Missouri Concrete and Uncle Curt had talked to the Missouri AG. Pendleton hasn't been a problem since then and Rice hasn't mentioned any more intimidation from the Chicago Outfit since then. But now you're telling me these Chicago gangsters may be here in Tulsa?"

"I'm afraid so. We'll handle it."

Susan ordered something to eat, and as they ate Zane asked for more information about Pendleton and the mobsters. Susan gave him the history about the Kansas City issues created by the mobster Tom Pendleton and the Pendleton Concrete Company.

"And you were shot at while on a construction site," Zane asked.

"Yes, but I wasn't in any real danger at the time."

"They're lucky I wasn't with you," Charlie said, an edge to his voice. "Maybe we'd not be having these problems now if I had been."

Susan smiled and said, "You are my cowboy protector." But Charlie noticed that Zane had gotten a bit pale.

Charlie looked Zane in the eyes. "You need to understand, it is not part of your job to ever put yourself or staff in any danger. You'll have security support around you and the quarry sites until we put the mob down. As I said, we have dealt with them before, and we'll deal with them again."

Zane nodded. "I know you will."

Susan reached over and patted Zane's arm. "We're working as fast as we can to create a safe place for all our employees to work. I'm so sorry this has happened. As my husband would say, we're gonna beat this bunch like drum and send them runnin' back to Chicago."

Chapter 7

Closing the Deal

November 1919

TWO DAYS HAD PASSED since Zane's news. Bailey Muldoon was still up in Kansas City but there hadn't been any new threats at the quarry. At breakfast today Susan had wondered when they might hear from the Meehans about their offer to buy the ranch. Charlie had replied that Bill Meehan was a deliberate man and was still mullin' over the offer.

Back in their suite Charlie sat on the sofa reading the sports page when the phone rang. "This is Charles Kelly. Oh, hello Bill, it's good to hear from you. Yes, we can be at your place then. I'll need to get ahold of Boss and Dan, but we'll be there." He put down the phone and called to Susan in the bedroom. "We're goin' to the Meehans tomorrow. I need to call Dan."

After two rings, Charlie heard, "Hello, this is the Bar B Ranch. Dan Kelly speakin'."

"Mornin' Dan. How's my little brother?"

"I'm good. What's on your mind?"

"You and Boss need to be at the Meehan Ranch tomorrow with Susan and me to finalize our agreement on their ranch. I've arranged to purchase the ranch, and I hope the property next door. I plan to close the deal then."

"Okay, Charlie. We'll see you tomorrow."

***

In their hotel room in Tulsa, Charlie opened his eyes. It was still dark outside, but Charlie could see the clock on the wall. It was almost 5:30.

He noticed Susan was still asleep. He caressed her right shoulder, then moved down her bare body as he kissed it. "We need to git goin', Sweetheart. We're supposed to be at the Meehans at 9:00."

Susan shrugged, not really awake. "Huh? What didja say?"

"Good mornin', my beautiful wife. I said we've gotta git goin'. We've about three and a half hours to be at the Meehan's ranch."

Susan flew out of bed, almost screaming, "Why did you let me sleep this long? I need more time..."

Charlie threw up his hands. "Hey, wait a minute. Honey, it will only take a little over two and a half hours to drive there. They're plannin' on feedin' us breakfast. All ya need to do is shower and spruce up a little. And I'd like ya to put the same white blouse back on. You looked great wearing it last night."

They were on the road to Perkins in thirty minutes.

***

They drove west, away from the rising sun, and toward Sapulpa, Drumright, Cushing, and on to Perkins. It was a cold morning but warm enough in the car as Susan unbuttoned her blouse. "You were right, we'll have plenty of time to get there. You like me in this white blouse and its pink sister, don't you?"

"I love anthin' ya wear, but ya had those tailored to fit ya perfect. They show every curve, and I do love those curves. I don't mind if others look. But it's all they're ever goin' to get to do! I enjoy showin' ya off to the world. And I think your beauty as well as your brains are assets to our businesses. Do ya git what I mean, Susan?"

"Yes, Darling, we've discussed this before, but I had it all figured out on the banks of Rock Creek back in Elmore City. You are physically appealing to me and to any woman. I love you best shirtless and in tight-fitting denims. Your broad shoulders and, oh my, your chest. I also love being on your arm around people and watching other women try to keep from staring. Charlie, I show you off to the world, too."

The drive was pure pleasure for the couple and seemed way too short. Charlie was turning right off the road, with the Meehan ranch gate in sight as Susan buttoned her blouse and checked her makeup.

Charlie knocked on the front door. "It looks like Boss and Dan are already here."

The door was opened by Tess. "Come in, your foreman and brother beat you here by thirty minutes."

Susan said, "Well then you met Dan, didn't you?"

Tess blushed and gazed at the floor, "I did. He sure seems nice."

"He's nice and he's a cowboy, like his brother. I thought you might find him handsome too."

"Miss Susan, you're making me blush. But he is tall, broad-shouldered, and very handsome, like your Charlie."

They went into the kitchen, where everyone was gathered around the table. Bill stood. "Good, you're here. Welcome back, and now Mother, we can eat. Charlie, do you and Susan want coffee?"

Charlie joked, "I must be at least a gallon low, so please."

Susan walked over and hugged Claudia. "I'll have some too. And how can I help?"

Claudia said, "Well, I think everything is ready." She looked a little embarrassed at Susan. "Maybe help me clean up later?"

"It'll be my pleasure. Just tell me what and when to do it, and we'll get it done."

Hank said, "Let's all eat, so I kin take Boss and Dan out and show 'em the place."

Bill laughed, "I think Hank's more excited than anyone. Charlie, we don't mean to be applying any arm twisting, but Hank loved the idea of working horses. And I have some good news about the land next door. It's yours for $25 an acre."

Charlie said, "That's good news, for sure. I'm with Hank, let's eat."

Charlie nodded at Susan and tilted his head to get her to see Dan and Tess couldn't stop staring at each other. Dan was not eating, and Charlie knew his brother would have four eggs, and at least a half pound of bacon with his toast and coffee on a regular morning as a kid back in New Mexico.

It wasn't long before Bill stood and said, "Hank, why don't we refill our coffee mugs and take Charlie, Boss, and Dan for a walk?"

Hank sprung from his chair. "I'm ready. Let me fill your mugs." He grabbed the coffee pot and began filling coffee mugs, and Claudia started to pick up plates. The men put on their coats and went outside, and the women stayed behind to clear the table, wash the dishes, and clean up.

Bill and Hank led a forty-five-minute tour of the barn and corral areas.

Hank looked at the visitors. "Would you like to saddle horses and ride the land? We can see a lot in an hour or so."

Charlie said, "I would love for Boss and Dan to see it. Gents, this is a mighty nice piece of Payne County. The rolling hills, the two-acre pond just over the first rise, and I guess there is still the forest of pecan trees."

Bill said, "You've got a good memory, Charlie. We had just harvested the pecans when Charlie got here back in '17, and we learned real quick how much he loves pecans. We restocked the pond with bass and crappie a few months ago. We let some local boys come fish, and they come back to help us at brandin' time."

They got horses saddled and soon enough Bill and Hank were showing off the best features of the Meehan Ranch to Dan and Boss. Despite the chill in the air they all had a pleasant time.

After the ride as they rubbed down the horses in the barn, Charlie said, "Bill, I'd like to take Boss and Dan and have some time to talk."

Bill nodded as he gathered up the coffee mugs off the hay bales. "Of course. Hank and I will go back to the house and wait in the kitchen. You take your time."

Charlie took Boss and Dan over to a set of chairs under the large elm tree. The leaves had fallen and made a blanket under the tree, but the day had warmed a bit so it was pleasant enough. He picked up and turned a chair to face the other two. After Boss and Dan took their seats, he glanced at Dan, smiled, then looked right at Boss. "Fellas, I need your opinions on this ranch."

Boss leaned forward with his elbows on his knees. "This here is a mighty fine spread for only bein' a thousand acres. The barn and other buildings are in good shape. The land has solid stands of buffalo grasses and lespedeza for grazin'. Bill and his family live in a fine house, too. The land next door is how many acres?"

"It's fifteen hundred acres with an old house and barn on it."

Boss stuck out his chin and said, "I'd buy this place if Bill is reasonable with his price."

Charlie said, "Dan, your thoughts, please."

"I agree with Boss. I would say the barn and other structures are in as good a shape as what we have down at the Bar B. I love the location of the pond. We could do a lot with twenty-five hundred acres up in this part of the state. Perkins is close by, and Cushing and Stillwater aren't far. I say buy it."

Charlie smiled and nodded approval. "I agree with ya. I'm prepared to pay as much for this place as I did the Bar B, because of its location. We need a place up here, and I know the ranch, and I know the people. They have kept everything in as good a shape as we would have. I'm sure we'll make a lot of money with this place."

Boss added, "Charlie, this place in this location and at this time, I believe is worth more than you paid for the Bar B. So, don't be too tight-fisted and miss out on buyin' it."

"I hear ya, Boss. I won't."

The trio walked to the house and into the kitchen. Charlie said, "I could use one more cup of coffee, and then can everyone settle in the front room?"

Claudia said, "I made a fresh pot, Charlie. You go on in there with the others, and I'll bring you a mug."

After everyone was seated and he had his coffee mug, Charlie took a sip and then began, "Bill, Claudia, Tess, and Hank, you all know I love this place. I'm sure ya thought you sold us when Susan and I left. I bet we weren't outta sight and everyone was sayin' he's buyin' our place. Well, here's the way it is. Boss and Dan have convinced me I'd be a fool if I..." He paused for several seconds. "If I didn't buy this place."

After the air came back in the room and the laughter stopped, Charlie said, "Now, Bill, we need to find an arrangement that'll work for everyone. I'll be happy to pay $25 an acre for the place next door. I'd like to officially make ya an offer of the $30,000 we discussed before for this place. Can the owner of the property next door be here today?"

Bill shook his head. "Charlie, he had a death in the family yesterday up in Enid, so he won't be here today. He hoped the $25 an acre was fair."

"It is, and like I said, I'll pay it. Now the final part of the deal is crucial to me. As I told ya last time we were here, I want ya'll to stay and run the place. Bill, you'll be overall lead here, and I will pay you a salary ten percent more than what you made in your best year here, plus five percent of the net profit as an annual bonus every Christmas. Hank, I will pay you ten percent more than you are making now to be the lead horseman here plus three percent of the net profits here as an annual bonus every Christmas. So, everyone gets a pay raise and less stress in their life. Dan will be your leadman, Hank, regarding all things to do with the horses."

Bill responded, "Your very generous, and the Meehans agree to these terms, Hank, how about you?"

"Oh, I'm with you. Charlie, I'll be happy to work with Dan. I'd like to come down to the Bar B and see what you have there."

Charlie said, "I've done all the talking, Boss, ya must have somethin' to share."

"I do." Boss looked at Charlie and grinned. He then looked at Bill and Hank. "Despite how Charlie did the hirin', I do run the ranches, and it will include this one. How we do it at the other location is Dan runs the Bar B and works for me. I must provide the resources he needs to get his job done. Which is training cuttin' and reinin' horses. I see this will be a smaller version of that. Bill, you'll work for me too, and I see you as my leadman. You'll enable Hank to focus on the horses and the trainers. You'll oversee the cattle and the total operation up here. I have a cattle operation at the Double Bar K with Tom Grimes as my leadman. Bill, you'll have access to cattle through Tom. I know this a lot to take in. But you and Hank need to come down and spend some time with us. I know it's hard for ya to get away, but I can send some hands up here to spend a few days with ya so you can acquaint them with this place, and then they can take care of it while you're down with us."

Charlie shook his head. "See what happens when ya let Boss talk?" Everyone gave a laugh. "But he's right about everything. I stole him from the 101 for that reason. He's in charge of our ranching operation. I need to call Curt Schlegell, our attorney, and give him the details of our agreement. He'll create all the necessary paperwork for the sale and the contracts for your employment. All employees have a nice benefits package which includes life insurance and some other things. Curt will fill ya in. I'll have him send the paperwork to the ranch at Earlsboro, and we can arrange a trip for y'all to come down and visit, and we'll git the paperwork all signed. It'll take a week or two."

Susan said, "Long-winded men. Charlie and I need to be back in Tulsa tonight. Thanks for a great breakfast, and we'll see you in Earlsboro soon."

Boss put his coffee mug down and stood. "Dan and I'll stick around a while longer and talk."

Bill stood up and shook Charlie's hand. "Sounds like a plan… Boss."

Chapter 8

Keys to Madison Avenue

November 1919

SUSAN HAD A RESTLESS night. She finally gave up, got up, showered, dressed, called downstairs, and had coffee brought to the room.

It was 6:00 when she heard Charlie yawn. She looked up and saw him stretch and pull the covers off him. He said, "The coffee sure smells good. How long have ya been up?"

She walked in from the living room and sat on the edge of the bed. "Over an hour. I couldn't sleep. I'm more excited about our new house than I've been about anything in a long time. I know we have the ranches and the Westover Road home, but this one I picked out and I love it."

"I'm happy about it too, Sweetheart. Our appointment is at 9:00 at Grant's office, right?"

She stood and pointed to the bathroom. "Yes, and I don't want to be late. Get in there and clean up."

"Don't worry; we'll be on time. I'll be fast so we can get goin'."

They were in the restaurant before 7:00. Susan fidgeted in her chair and played with her food.

Charlie pleaded, "Susan, you need to eat. You'll feel bad before we can get through the meetin' with Grant. At least eat some eggs and toast."

"Okay, I'll try. I can't remember feeling like this over a business matter. Maybe when I was waiting for you at the station in Kansas City. And sure, again the morning we got married. But never when signing papers for buying anything."

Charlie placed his hand on hers. "Today is special. We'll be the first people to live in this house. You said the house is just the way you would have wanted it if Rice and his team had built it for us. Since it will be our home here in Tulsa, it's special."

She lifted her head and looked at Charlie. "You're right."

***

They arrived at Grant Stebbins' office at 8:50. He was ready. It took about thirty minutes to get through all the paperwork, and he handed Susan the keys.

Susan took them and squeezed them to her chest. "It's mine. Oh, I mean ours. Charlie's and mine." She looked sheepish at Charlie. "We got it."

Stebbins chuckled as he too looked at Charlie. "Hey fella, the keys always go to the lady of the house. She'll share copies with whom she chooses."

Charlie laughed, stood, and offered his hand. "Grant, I believe you, my friend. Thanks for your help with gittin' this wrapped up for us. We want to be established here, and this was a big first step."

Stebbins walked around his desk. "It has been my pleasure, and you two will be tremendous assets to Tulsa. I look forward to seeing you around the city. Now go enjoy your new home."

Susan walked over to Grant and hugged him before leaving the office. They drove down the street to their house. Charlie pulled their car around to the back of the house and parked near the garage doors.

As he got out of the car, Charlie said, "This'll be nice with the attached garage. We can go straight into the house and stay out of the weather."

He unlocked the garage door and raised it. Then drove the car inside.

Susan said, "Let's go in and open the place up. I know it's a bit chilly today, but it was stuffy the last time we were here."

Charlie reminded her. "You also need to call the decorator so we can get this place furnished. I know you're gonna want a housewarming party soon."

"Yes, I am, and the sooner, the better. I was able to meet her here last week. All she needs to do now is order everything we agreed on. Grant was gracious and handled keeping the utilities on, but we will need to call all those places and get everything into our name. When we're done here, let's go back to the hotel and I'll use the list Grant gave us and make those calls. You can go down to the restaurant and have them set you up at a table and make the calls I know you need to make today."

"How did ya know I needed to make calls?"

She smiled, "Charlie, you always need to make calls to someone."

"That I do." Charlie chuckled. "How about I have the restaurant make us a picnic dinner? We can come back here later. Too bad the pool may not be heated or we could go for a swim."

"How about roast beef sandwiches with potato salad? We can bring a bottle of Cabernet, too."

"Sounds like we have a plan."

***

Later in the afternoon, after making their various calls, they were in their hotel room when the telephone rang. Susan disentangled herself from Charlie's embrace in the bed and answered. "Hello."

"Hello, Mrs. Kelly. This is Bailey. I just arrived here at the hotel. Is Charlie there?

"Yes, he is. Just a moment."

She handed the phone to Charlie. "It's Bailey."

"Bailey, are you here?"

"Yes, I'm in my room. When and where do you want to meet?"

"Get settled in, then come to the Presidential Suite on the twelfth floor. We'll be expecting you."

"I'll be there in ten minutes."

Charlie handed the phone back and Susan set it back on the cradle. "Bailey will be here in ten minutes. You might want to put on some clothes."

She laughed as she headed to the bedroom. "Well, you too, Charlie."

***

Bailey arrived, and the three of them found comfortable places to sit in the suite's living room.

Susan said, "Bailey, can we offer you something to drink?"

Bailey shook his head. "No, I'm good. If you don't mind my saying it, you look very happy today."

"That's because we just took possession of our new house."

Bailey turned to Charlie. "I apologize for not being here sooner. It took me a few days to get everything signed with Curt. I also made some exploratory calls to some men I know. So, what happened at the new quarry? I know you told me there was some damage. I believe you said the windows were broken, paint-splattered, and more. Do you have more details?"

Charlie couldn't sit still, so he rose to his feet and walked around the room. "It's all of the above, buddy. Did Curt fill you in on our dealings with the mob up in Kansas City?"

Bailey nodded. "He did."

Charlie said, "Well, they went to the quarry office during the night, kicked in the door, destroyed the furnishings, and broke out windows. They tried to steal files, but the file cabinets were locked and made with steel-encased concrete."

Bailey nodded, "I know what Curt told me, and so I can understand your concern. But Tom Pendleton is dead. Do we have any idea who the new local guy in Kansas City is?"

"No, but the message written on the office wall said, 'Greetings from Chicago. Get out of town.'"

Susan had been quiet as Charlie did the talking. Charlie looked at the anxiety on Susan's face. "Sweetheart, do ya need to say somethin'?"

"I'm scared, or at the very least mighty concerned, we may continue to have violent people threatening us. We've got to bring this to a halt as soon as possible. I won't live in fear of what may happen next to the Kramer Group or us."

"She's right. What do you say, Bailey?"

"Charlie, over the next twenty-four hours, I'll call Richard Murray at the Oklahoma Bureau of Investigation for his input. And I'll also call Curt, who will get me a copy of the report from the incidents in Kansas City involving the Chicago mob. I should have had him do that before I left. Richard can give me information on what is going on around Oklahoma, and I'll compare it to what was learned in Kansas City. I'll study all of it and come back to you in two days with a plan of action. Agreed?"

Charlie returned to the sofa. "Yes. On another subject, I know you were at least startin' to consider what you wanted in the security company. How far are you?"

"I haven't finished the outline yet. I do have some ideas regarding initial staff. What we will learn from this threat will teach us a lot about what security around high-value assets needs to look like."

Charlie said, "I understand. I'll let ya go and get started on your contacts and research. Is your room alright?"

"It's more than alright, but I may do little more than sleep there."

After Bailey left, Susan said, "We have many expensive assets, don't we?"

"We sure do. I'm thinkin' we made a good decision when we agreed to create a security company. We may do many things with it over time, but the first task will be to protect those assets because we depend on them."

Susan could see Charlie's concern on his face. "Honey, we don't have to go over to the Madison house tonight."

Charlie didn't hesitate. "Oh yes, we need to. I want to take dinner and a bottle of wine and get away for a few hours. I have come to know solving problems is somethin' I enjoy, and I think I'm good at it. But right now, I need to clear my head and start fresh in the mornin'. So, let's go."

They arrived at the Madison Avenue house with the picnic the hotel made, plus a bottle of wine. It was twilight, their favorite time of day. Susan headed for the outdoor pool. Charlie could see steam rising from the water in the cold air.

"I didn't think the pool would be heated yet," he said.

"I called Grant and made sure it was turned on as soon as I got back to the hotel." She quickly stripped and dove into the pool.

Charlie struggled with his second boot. "I'm always amazed at how fast ya git naked and into the pool. I don't think I could get off and picket Tony as fast. I'll be there in a minute."

They enjoyed a few laps and then climbed out and went inside to eat dinner and enjoy the Cabernet.

Susan sat on a large blanket they had brought from the hotel, snuggled in their warm robes. "Charlie, you're the best at problem-solving. I decided to wait to respond to what you said back at the hotel, but I think it is one of your strengths. I don't need nor want to discuss it any further right now." She grinned. "Let's focus on each other."

She winked and took a sip of wine.

Charlie wrapped his strong arms around her. "Thanks, Sweetheart, and you're right; we need to focus on each other this evenin'."

Chapter 9

Security Planning

November 1919

CHARLIE SAT ON THE edge of the bed in the hotel. He leaned over and kissed Susan's cheek. "Mornin' Sweetheart. I sure enjoyed our new place last night."

Susan's eyes fluttered open. She looked over at her man and smiled. "Me too. I love our new home; aren't you glad it's ours?"

"Yep, we now have three wonderful places to get away to and leave all the worry back at our office."

Susan scooted over, embraced Charlie, and whispered, "Can we go back there again tonight?"

"It will be better when we git some furniture there, but I think we should. Now, we better git goin'. We've gotta meet Rice and Bailey for breakfast in a little while."

***

Charlie and Susan met Rice Coburn and Bailey Muldoon in the VIP dining room at the Hotel Tulsa. Pleasantries were exchanged as they all got their coffee and food.

As Charlie raised his coffee cup to take a sip he was surprised to see Hank Thomas enter the room. He put his cup on its saucer. "Hank, buddy, what are ya doin' here? I didn't expect to see ya today."

"Charlie, I'm sorry to barge in on your meeting," he nodded at Coburn and Muldoon and each nodded back in greeting. "I've got some great news. I just come from down in Garvin County."

"What were you doin' down there? You've got things to be doin' in Burbank, Cushing, and who knows where before ya go to California."

"Now settle down. I stopped by and made sure things were

goin' fine at those places. But I believe I told you some folks were likin' Garvin County for oil some time back, didn't I?"

"Yep, and it didn't surprise me when Getty had some holdings there."

"Hank," Susan said. "Please have a seat." She turned to Rice and Bailey. "I hope you gentlemen won't mind this brief interruption."

"Not at all," Rice Coburn said. "As excited as Mr. Thomas is, this might impact the construction business."

Hank sat down and poured himself a cup of coffee. "It might, Mr. Coburn. Getty owned, and it now means we own some prime property for oil in Garvin County. I couldn't wait to go check it out since we purchased it from Paul. Now, I've already picked out where we need to drill and contacted the crew wrappin' things up in Burbank. They'll meet me in Elmore City. I'll take them out and get them started."

Charlie said, "You think it's that good?"

Hank nodded. "I know it's that good."

Charlie leaned back. "We were just gittin' ready to talk security and our overall plans with Bailey and Rice."

Hank looked over at the two men, "Charlie, I'm glad to listen and help where I can. But things are busting loose in oil right now. I should talk with Rice here at some point about construction needs, but it will take me at least a week to hire another crew I need. We can drill more wells up in Osage County. Frank Phillips hit another big gusher up there last week. And we'll need to drill several wells in Garvin County. Charlie, I still think it will be bigger down by your ranch than anything we've seen."

Charlie held his cup a little below his chin with both hands as he mulled over what Hank had said. "Do ya still plan to go to California?"

"I sure do. My daddy had a friend who was out there twenty years ago. He described petroleum oozing out of the ground in parts of Los Angeles County. I can't wait to see it. I hear there have been more big strikes recently around Huntington Beach."

Susan said, "You seem a little restless. What's wrong?"

Hank shifted in his chair and reached for the cinnamon rolls. He took a bite and a sip of coffee. "I've got to get somethin' off my chest."

"We should step out of the room," Muldoon said and started to get up.

"No, this is business," Hank said. "You are part of the company, so you'll hear this eventually."

Charlie said, "Speak up, buddy."

Hank took another sip. "As our Landman, I've got to spend my time as wisely as possible. We have so much we can and must do here in Oklahoma, I think I need to stay here for several more months. This is more important than potential in California."

Susan said, "Are you sure, Hank?"

He looked at Susan. "I've got enough already going here and more that I should start, so I should wait to go to California. I want to get things settled here first. And one more thing. A couple of geologists have mentioned interest in West Texas and Southeastern New Mexico, but no one's hit anything there yet."

Charlie leaned forward. "Then stay here and go do what you think best. It sounds like Oklahoma, Texas, New Mexico, and California are all good possibilities and we need to explore them all. Work them in whatever order you think best."

Hank smiled and took one more sip of coffee. "I'll do that." He stood up to go.

"It does sound like we should talk, Hank," Rice said. "This amount of growth might strain our refining capabilities, and we might need more pipelines built. Please reach out to me when things settle down a bit."

Charlie said, "Hank, let me know how things go down in Garvin County."

"I'll do that. Gentlemen. Susan." Hank made his good-byes and walked out of the dining room.

"I will need to talk to Mr. Thomas about site security as well," Muldoon said. "I've heard a lot about problems with sabotage in the oil patch."

Charlie said, "You have both started talking about exactly what I wanted to discuss today. Rice, as you start the remodel, or whatever we call it at the refineries and pipeline operation in Cushing, we want to address security as part of the effort."

Bailey said, "Our basic security should include fencing, gates, special locks, and a staff of guards, but do you have any specific requirements?"

Rice answered, "Maybe Hank should have stayed. This is all so new to me. I heard about Sapulpa's damage, and it reminded me of what we've dealt with in Cushing and Kansas City. Charlie, what do you think?"

Charlie rubbed his chin. "Bailey, we need to hire some guards to protect the construction sites and the crews. We had a member of a construction crew in Kansas City shot and killed last year by some of these mob types. You and I need to create a plan for how we address this threat."

Bailey said, "I haven't developed my master plan for the

company yet, and we already have threats and actual attacks happening. I haven't created a budget for the startup work yet."

Charlie interrupted Bailey. "I'm confident you know what we need. It's people and an initial plan of attack for dealing with the specific threat created by the Chicago bunch we work out first, right?"

"Yes, if we are, as you said, dealing with the Chicago Outfit, or remnants of the Black Hand, we need to focus on it right now. I can develop a basic plan to respond to these guys in a few hours. I wish I had time to give you a detailed budget."

Susan said, "Bailey, would you agree we need some good solid citizens to protect Rice's crews and some very experienced and specialized individuals to address the mob types?"

"Yes, Susan, mob types create an entirely different problem."

She replied, "Do you know where you can get those special people we will need?"

Bailey nodded. "I do. I have about a dozen men I was in the war with who would be perfect for addressing this threat. The basic security staff members need to be trustworthy but not trained the way my old Army buddies were. We worked on the most difficult and dangerous operations of any soldier. Those experiences will be required to address these thugs threatening you two and the Kramer Group."

Charlie said, "Go hire as many of those old Army buddies as you can. And also, let's get the refineries protected as soon as we can."

Bailey nodded. "I will also need to hire men to protect Mr. Thomas' drill sites. Oil field sites were already on my list of assets to protect along with banks, stores, new construction sites, and refineries. But with Mr. Thomas expanding already I will need to get that risk addressed soon.

Susan leaned forward. "Bailey, go hire men who can't be intimidated, who are highly trained and can be as ruthless as required and..."

Charlie slapped the table as he stared at Bailey. "We need people who will stand their ground and take someone else's life if need be. I hear these guys in Chicago have wars between themselves. We don't need to, nor do we want to take over their brothels, their bootleggin', or any other illegal business they have. But we won't be run over by them either. They need to fear us if it's necessary."

Bailey stood and picked up his coffee and drained it. He looked at Charlie with his brow furrowed and spoke with a steady tone. "I do get the picture, and as I said, I know the people we need for this job. They're all working as bodyguards, or they are mercenaries. A couple are with the Federal government doing investigations and undercover work. It will take some money, but you'll have people you can trust with your life, and they'll get any job done. And as we build out the security business, some of them are true leaders who can run a significant part of the business."

Susan said, "Then, go get them now."

Bailey turned to leave. He stopped, looked back, and grinned. "I'm glad we're in a fancy hotel with phones in private rooms. I'll go upstairs and start calling right now. Thanks for your support."

Charlie stood, walked over, and patted Bailey on the shoulder, "Yep, like Susan said, go git 'em." Bailey walked out of the room.

Charlie turned back to Rice and asked, "I know you're planning to leave for Cushing today. Will you meet with Abrams?"

"I'll see him tomorrow morning. We'll be going to Shawnee to look over the location where we may build the next store."

"When are ya meetin' with the refinery folks?"

"I'll see them on Monday. I hope to get all their requirements then, allowing me to start to hire and mobilize the people and equipment needed to complete the work."

Charlie said, "Give us an update. Where are ya in gettin' an office established in Tulsa?"

"I've not spent any time looking for a property. I've got two of my guys from Kansas City down here interviewing for crews to work at the refineries and the stores. We have hired all the store construction crew, but we won't finish the refinery crew until after the Monday meeting. We have the basic craftsmen hired, but I don't feel we know enough about the skills needed regarding the modifications to the refinery equipment until then. I hope to have my Oklahoma operation in place by the end of the next month."

Rice left, and Charlie and Susan stayed to discuss the various issues they were facing.

Susan said, "Sweetheart, security is a top priority, but we have a lot happening. Can we go over some other things while we have time and this quiet place to talk?"

He looked at her and smiled. "Sure, what's on your mind?"

"Well, let me get my notes. I've made a list of tasks I know we need to finish over the next several days and weeks." She adjusted her chair, so she was facing Charlie. "We meet with Jim and Zane tomorrow regarding the quarry damage and the oil field service acquisition, and the training starts in Duncan for the oil field service crews on Monday. After we're done there, we need to get back to the ranch to sign the paperwork for the new property we are buying in Earlsboro and the Meehan ranch."

Charlie said, "That does cover our meetings already planned, and we have actions goin' in banking here in Tulsa and down in Texas designed to expand and grow our holdings there. I heard from Harry Sinclair. He asked that we meet with him and some men from here in Tulsa tomorrow morning regarding a banking possibility. Curt and someone from our banking business should arrive this evening on the train. Speaking of trains, we also have new things happening with Owen and the railroad. And we also need to make some decisions regarding the overall structure of The Kramer Group."

"As I said, Sweetheart, we have a lot on our plate. I look forward to seeing Uncle Curt in the morning."

Charlie nodded. "Okay, I'm ready to go back to our suite and make some calls."

Susan took her final sip of coffee. "I know I want to talk to Uncle Curt about the restructuring idea while he's here. And let's go out to the house at twilight for a swim, and a bottle of wine. Okay?"

Chapter 10

A New Opportunity

November 1919

THE NEXT MORNING, CHARLIE and Susan rode the elevator down to the lobby where Harry Sinclair would meet with them. On the way down, Susan asked, "Did Harry say exactly what this meeting was about?"

"He didn't give me specifics. Just that this meeting was to discuss a potential business expansion for the Exchange National Bank."

As they arrived at the lobby, Charlie said, "It was great when Curt called the suite last night and said he and Johnathan had arrived. He has all the paperwork with him."

Curt and Johnathan were waiting outside the Topaz when Charlie and Susan arrived.

Susan said, "Uncle Curt you're looking good. And Johnathan Mitchell it's good to see you. It's been a while. I remember when you came to work for my father right out of the Wharton Business School at Penn."

She put her hand on Charlie's arm. "After a few years as Father's assistant, he moved into our banking business. Now he's Gordon's right hand. Johnathan led the negotiations for the acquisition of the Texas banks. If we decide to do this deal Harry has in mind, we'll need him to finalize it and stay on in Tulsa for another six months to secure our interest and lay the groundwork for further expansion."

Charlie extended his hand. "Johnathan, it's good to meet ya." He turned to Curt. "It's good to see you again."

Johnathan replied, "Yes sir. I look forward to spending more time with you."

"Me too. Let's go in."

The maître d' took them to the VIP dining room. "Mr. Kelly, I understand, you're expecting another person in about an hour and a half?"

"Yes, you'll recognize him. It's Harry Sinclair and he may have others with him."

"Oh, of course. I'll bring him back as soon as he arrives."

"Thanks, Pierre."

Before he took his seat, Curt asked, "How do you want the table and chairs arranged?"

Charlie smiled. "Good question, Curt. "We're here to listen to all of Harry's ideas, and I want to be eye-to-eye with him. But I don't want it to appear confrontational."

Susan said, "Harry told us he wanted to discuss a banking proposition. The Exchange Bank is doing well according to what I've seen in the reports."

Still standing, Johnathan said, "Yes, Gordon and I are pleased with the reports. Harry hasn't indicated he has seen issues, so I don't know what he has in mind."

The waiter entered the room and asked for their orders. He provided them coffee cups with saucers and poured their first cup.

Before the waiter left the room, Susan waved. "Please bring two carafes of coffee as well as some additional coffee cups and saucers for the table with our meal."

Charlie regained everyone's attention. "Back to our arrangement; let's spread ourselves around this table, so Harry is not the only one on the side opposite from Susan and me. We should move into place now. Susan and I will stay where we are. Curt, you move to my right and sit at the end of the table. Johnathan, you sit across from Susan. We leave one chair vacant straight across from me and to Curt's right. Comments?"

Johnathan said, "I think that will work. He should feel part of the conversation, not the focus of it."

Susan leaned forward on her elbows. "I agree, and I'm glad you're concerned about the environment we're putting Harry in. He is important to our oil business beyond his role at the bank."

Curt added, "I wonder if he's thinking of acquiring something? We're still doing a lot of organizational structure rework with all the acquisitions we've already made. Things like electing boards of directors and creating strategic plans. Negotiating the purchase and or starting a company from scratch is just the first step. But paperwork and crucial decisions must be made as soon as possible to give the new business an identity and its focus."

Susan said, "Right you are, Uncle Curt. And I need to get with you to help in creating those documents. Charlie and some of our subject matter experts, as Father always called them, will need to comment on the documents we create. And I want to help create the first drafts."

A few minutes later their coffee service arrived as they anticipated Harry Sinclair's arrival.

After the group finished their discussions and as the waiter cleared the table and refilled the coffee cups, Pierre come into the room to check on the service. He looked over at the doorway. "Mr. Sinclair is here to join you, Mr. Kelly. I'll bring him to your table."

"Thank you, Pierre." As Charlie stood, it was apparent Harry was not alone. "How are you doin' Harry? Who's with you?"

"Charlie, Susan, and the rest of you folks, these distinguished gentlemen are the leaders of the Negro community, called Greenwood, here in Tulsa." He stepped aside and indicated the men with his right arm, "Allow me to introduce, O. W. Gurley and J. B. Stradford."

Sinclair turned and faced his guests. "Gentlemen, let me introduce you to Charles and Susan Kelly. They are the sole owners of the Kramer Group and the folks I wanted you to meet."

Charlie nodded and smiled as everyone shook hands. "Welcome." He looked at Pierre. "We will need those additional cups and saucers for our new guests and more coffee. Oh, and bring some chairs, too."

Harry said, "Thanks, Charlie. It looks like I have some new faces to get to know."

"Harry, you have met Curt Schlegell by phone. We had him come in from Kansas City to assist us in gettin' recent contracts completed. We wanted you to meet him."

"Well, hello Curt, it's nice to be able to put a face with the voice."

Charlie added, "And to your right you know Johnathan Mitchell from his work with the Exchange Bank. He'll be here in Tulsa for a while as we continue our acquisition and expansion projects. We've also asked him to be here, in case we needed him."

Harry turned to Johnathan and offered his hand. "Good to see you, Johnathan." He grinned. "I'm a little curious. Are you fixed, as in permanent in the Kramer family?"

Johnathan looked at Sinclair and smiled. "I am, Mr. Sinclair. Susan's father hired me right out of college, and they pay me way too much money now. I don't think anyone, but the Kellys, can afford me."

Everyone laughed. Then Charlie said, "Harry, what's on your mind, my friend?"

"I don't think it's a surprise I consider you folks experts in banking and finance. These gentlemen are successful businessmen in the Greenwood section of Tulsa. They are the creators of what the nation now calls Black Wall Street. At this time, they have grown about as far as they can with the resources they have, but more could be done with additional financial support."

Susan put her coffee cup down and turned to Harry. "Why? What information has convinced you that's the case."

Harry squirmed in his seat. "I'd be happy to share it, but it would be best if Mr. Gurley gave you the details." He turned to one of the men and gave a nod.

"Tulsa has grown by ten times over the past decade. We now are a city of over 70,000. Ten percent of the population is Negro and living within or nearby Greenwood Avenue. We have invested in close to 200 businesses of various types, including a library, two schools, a hospital and two newspapers. I myself own several properties including the Gurley Hotel. My companion here, Mr. Stradford," he gestured at the man, "has similar holdings and owns the Stradford Hotel—"

"The grandest Black-owned hotel in America," J. B. said with pride.

"But what we don't have is a dedicated bank," Gurley continued. "J. B. and myself have functioned as financiers for several other businesses, but I believe we can offer the community better support as it grows by opening a branch of Exchange National in Greenwood."

Charlie leaned back in his chair and shook his head. "Wow, you've given us a lot to take in, Mr. Gurley."

Susan looked at O. W. and smiled. "It sure is, and I'm interested in getting to know more details about Greenwood and these men. It is clear to me, Mr. Gurley, that you have an amazing vision for your business, and Greenwood as a whole. You remind me of my father."

Johnathan raised his hand. "May I ask a question or two?"

Charlie said, "Of course. Ask anything you want."

"Mr. Gurley, of the 200 businesses, how many have been in existence for at least two years? And how many have you invested in yourself?"

Gurley nodded as he turned to Johnathan. "I would say close to eighty percent of the businesses are at least two years old and

I've loaned money to eleven of them. And I've continued to invest in my grocery store and hotel."

Johnathan looked at Charlie and Susan. "This is very interesting. I also would love to learn more. I believe these gentlemen are on to something."

Charlie nodded. "I agree. Gentlemen, do you have a few hours to devote to some discussion?"

Stradford reached out with his hands palms up. "Sir, the afternoon is yours for the askin'."

The next several hours were filled with questions on business philosophy, experiences, and getting to know each other personally.

After Harry and his associates were gone, Johnathan said, "Impressive. Charlie, you did a wonderful job of leading them through deep discussions and some tough decisions."

Curt smiled. "I've already learned to keep quiet until Charlie asked for something. He's a natural negotiator."

Susan said, "I know he's not perfect, but I've seldom seen him fail to get what he wanted. This discussion was great because we got plenty of information we'll need to determine if we want to explore putting a branch of Exchange Bank in Greenwood. And Harry also got what he needed to know so he can decide whether to locate gasoline and automobile service stations in northern Tulsa."

The Kramer folks talked for a while about plans for more banks around Tulsa and across the state.

Chapter 11

Quarry Plans

December 1919

CHARLIE AND SUSAN DROVE to the Sapulpa quarry to meet with Missouri Concrete President Jim Townsley and Zane Krebs. Jim and Zane were to update them on the damage at the new quarry and the oil field service training scheduled to begin in a few days in Duncan, Oklahoma. They arrived several minutes before the meeting, entered a conference room, and saw a table ready with a carafe of coffee and Danishes.

As Jim and Zane walked in, Charlie said, "Good to see ya guys. Thanks for the coffee and sweets. Get yourself something before ya sit down."

Jim offered a big grin, "Yes, we will. Like I've heard you say, Charlie, I'm still a quart low on coffee."

Susan pointed. "We found a full carafe on this table. Help yourself."

Zane sat across from Susan. He poured coffee for himself and Jim. "What's the latest you hear from the authorities on our break-in here at the quarry?"

Charlie shook his head. "We haven't heard a thing. But we had a meetin' two days ago with Bailey Muldoon, our new security company lead, and he is puttin' together a team and a plan on how we'll respond as a company to it."

Jim asked, "Do you still think it's someone out of Chicago? I know it's what the message on the wall implied, but would they be foolish enough to mess with you? After the incident in Kansas City the gangsters went quiet after the AG started making threats."

"The short answer is yes. It might not be the same people, but they are part of the Chicago mob world. There are other

Chicago mobsters, but the organization known as the Outfit, according to Bailey, has spread across the Midwest and out to California."

Zane looked at Charlie with concern written on his face. "I hear they're killing each other in gang wars up there. Do we have that to look forward to?"

Susan placed her cup down. "Zane, at first, I was worried. Charlie and Bailey convinced me we must be direct and firm with this bunch. So, we gave Bailey directions to hire people with the skills and experience to address anything they may throw at us. Charlie and I feel we can't let this organization of hoodlums roll over us. We'll stand up to them and end any threat they may be to the Kramer Group and our employees."

Jim's eyes grew large. "What do you mean by people with skills and experience? Is he going to hire ex-cons?"

Charlie stifled a laugh, "Jim, of course not. He'll go after some folks he knew in the Army during the Great War who are now employed as security folks. Bailey was a leader in some special units in Europe during the war. The guys he hopes to bring to the Kramer Group were with him. They will have skills even the mobsters will fear."

Susan added, "We have no plan to break the law as part of our response, but we will use surprise, direct force, and whatever it takes to create fear and uncertainty in the minds of the kingpins of this Chicago Outfit."

Charlie nodded, "It could include, in my mind, goin' right into their backyard in Chicago and doin' everythin' but kill 'em."

Zane shook his head and slumped back in his chair. "I'm glad I'm on your side. I hear no fear from you, just a lot of anger and determination."

"I can get mad, even furious, so I try to control myself. But, when our people and property are jeopardized, that's where I draw the line."

Susan said, "Zane, when Willard kidnapped me, I saw Charlie mad. With help from another guy, Bailey had to pull Charlie off the man threatening me. These people don't want to mess with us. They don't know it yet, but they'll learn it."

Charlie said, "If what they did at this new quarry is the last we hear from them, I'm willin' to let it go. If it's the first in a series of similar things and maybe worse, we'll go back at them in ways they could never expect."

Jim grinned. "I guess I agree with Zane. I'm glad I'm on your side. I'll let you all handle it. Just let me know what I need to do to stay out of your way."

Charlie wiped some sugar from his Danish off his cheek. "I hear ya, Jim. We've covered what we need to regardin' the damage to the quarry before. But I do have one question. Is the quarry back operational? Did the damage cause ya to shut somethin' down?"

Jim nodded at Zane. "You can answer."

"Everything is back to normal, but we had to move some support functions into other structures at the site or over to the old site. The damage stopped normal operations for a day, maybe two. But we're back to normal now."

Susan said, "Under the circumstances, that's great news. Let's talk about the training."

Jim said, "Yes. And this should all be good news. I've selected five men to lead the five crews to operate the oil field cement or mudding equipment. I'll send fifteen men to Duncan for the class at the Halliburton Company, along with Zane and me." He looked at Zane. "He'll manage the five crews, and our long-range plans are for him to run our Oklahoma operation. I'll return to Kansas City and work to find my replacement. I know I said I would give you three years, and I will, but someday, there'll need to be a new Missouri Concrete President."

Charlie said, "Hey, my friend, we aren't ready to start talkin' about Missouri Concrete without Jim Townsley. I agree, though you gave us good news regardin' the trainin', and we know you'll retire someday, and we'll work with you to make it happen."

Susan said, "Gentlemen, Charlie and I have an appointment at our new house in a couple of hours, and I have some things to do. We'll leave you now. It's been good to see you and travel safe to Duncan."

***

In their suite, Susan sat on the sofa next to Charlie. "Sweetheart, we've gone to the house every evening since we got the keys. Do you want to spend the evening there again tonight?

"Yes, I would love to. We can git some food, wine, and loungers like at the ranch. Then, after the decorator leaves, we can be alone."

"Well then, I'm going to change what I'm wearing to something more casual and I know you'll love. You're ready for tonight with what you have on. I know we're meeting Emilia, and she'll not even notice what I have on. I saw how she looked at you the other day."

Charlie grinned, "Really? I hadn't noticed."

Susan returned his grin with a sly smile. "Of course you hadn't."

***

They met their decorator at the house at 1:00 p.m., and she had her arms full of catalogs, drawings, and a complete plan for them to go through.

Emilia said, "It may take all afternoon to show you room by room what I recommend we do in this beautiful home."

Susan looked around the room. "Fine, we have the time."

Emilia gave the Kellys a thorough tour of their new home and provided details of her plans. Charlie looked at Susan. "Do you like what you've heard?"

"I love her ideas. I wish we could move into it tonight."

He turned to Emilia. "We'll take it just the way you described it."

They were standing in the living room. Emilia looked at her watch and said, "It's after 4:00. I hope this hasn't been too much for you. Are you sure you're happy with what we've discussed?"

Susan reached over and patted her shoulder. "I appreciate your thoroughness. I'm amazed at how you've captured what we discussed before. I wanted elegant but with a homey, cozy feeling. I agree with Charlie we can approve your plan as it is. If I'm not pleased with it, I might want to change a piece after it's in place."

"Absolutely Susan. All I need is your signature."

Susan said, "Where do I sign?"

Charlie raised his hands palm out, "Whoa now. What is this costing us?"

"Oh, of course, the costs are $10,354.27 to be thorough."

Charlie had a devilish grin. "Now, Sweetheart, you can sign her paperwork."

***

They had decided to wait to get set up for the evening. So, after Emilia left, they purchased two loungers for their patio and two matching side tables. They also brought back food and wine. It was dark when they were in their backyard on their loungers for the first time.

Susan was taking her clothes off. "Charlie, I can't imagine being happier than I am now. This house is the first home where we are the original occupants. If the furnishings turn out anything close to what she described, our home will be beautiful while still having a welcoming feeling and maybe even cozy in some places. What do you think?"

"I agree, and I'm excited to git moved in. This pool area and patio are perfect for us. Our bedroom has doors opening onto this patio, like the ones on Westover Road and at our ranch. The office is wonderful. The whole house is great. Cleta and Attie will have rooms they should love."

Susan scrunched her nose. "Are you planning to stay in your clothes all night?"

"Oh, no, I was havin' fun watchin' you gittin' naked. I also loved how you teased me every chance you could this afternoon. I don't think Emilia ever saw anythin', but I sure did." He was out of his clothes in no time. He walked over to Susan, and they embraced. They dove in after walking with their arms around each other's waist to their heated pool. They added another night filled with good food, wine, and passion on Madison Avenue.

Chapter 12

A Visit to Black Wall Street

December 1919

THE WEATHER HAD TURNED cold and blustery as Charlie and Susan arrived at the Exchange National Bank to attend the staff's Christmas party. Johnathan welcomed them as they entered the lobby. "I know it's the 12th, but Merry Christmas anyway. We all appreciate you coming and being a part of this afternoon. It's about time to lock the doors, and after everyone has finished their work, we'll start celebrating."

Susan looked at Charlie and then back to Johnathan and patted his shoulder. "We are proud of you and everyone here. We were thrilled when you invited us to join you."

Charlie looked at Susan, and back to Johnathan. "You're right, Sweetheart. Johnathan, before I forget to ask, have you an update on anything from Greenwood?"

"Yes, I have. Since our initial meeting about a month ago, I've stayed in touch with the Greenwood leaders. Yesterday, Mr. Gurley called me and offered to provide us with a tour around the area. He will introduce us to several business owners. He said the place is a real beauty at Christmas time."

Excited, Susan said, "When can we?"

"How about early next week?" Charlie asked.

Johnathan smiled. "I had hoped you were available because I agreed to Tuesday afternoon."

Charlie clapped. "Perfect. We don't have anything planned we can't reschedule."

Johnathan said, "How about I come to pick you up at noon on Tuesday? And I told Mr. Gurley we'd meet him at the *Tulsa Star* newspaper office."

Susan said, "Thanks. We can finish everything we need to do

by lunch and be ready for you."

***

As Johnathan drove the three along Greenwood Avenue toward the newspaper office, Charlie said, "I'm seeing what I'd call luxury shops. Fine furniture and clothing establishments. I'm impressed."

Susan said, "Yes, and I see restaurants, movie theatres, and a library. And aren't the Christmas decorations beautiful?"

Johnathan laughed. "They sure are." He chuckled as he looked over at Charlie. "And don't forget there was a pool hall and two nightclubs, too."

Charlie rubbed the back of his neck. "I saw them, buddy. All these businesses tell me people are doin' better than just gettin' by. I look forward to seein' and hearin' more about Greenwood."

Susan pointed. "Me too. And there's the *Tulsa Star* office."

Johnathan parked, and they got out and walked to the entrance.

O. W. Gurley opened the door as they approached. "Good afternoon, and welcome to Greenwood, or Black Wall Street as many call it now."

Charlie offered his hand. "Thanks, Mr. Gurley, and we're excited to visit here. We have looked forward to today and what you plan to show us."

"Yes," Susan said as she also offered her hand. "Greenwood Avenue is very impressive with its mixture of businesses."

Another man walked up, and Gurley nodded in his direction. "Let me introduce Andrew Jackson Smitherman. He's our host here at the paper as owner and editor of the *Tulsa Star*."

Smitherman showed no warmth. He spat, "I hope you find what you need this afternoon. We are proud of what we in the Negro community have built."

Charlie bit his tongue. *Your message is received, Mr. Smitherman.*

The chill in the air made it obvious to everyone it was time to depart on the tour. Gurley cleared his throat. "We'll go now, and thanks for letting us meet here, A. J."

Smitherman nodded. "Sure, O. W, and we'll talk tomorrow."

As they walked down the street, Gurley said, "A. J. is a brilliant man, but he has a real problem trusting a white person. Over the past few years, there has been some violence aimed at Negroes around the city. It included more than one lynching. He is an attorney as well as a journalist who advocates strong resistance to those activities and the folks behind them. He has influenced some in our community to share his views. My hope for today is you'll see and focus on those who'll welcome your interest and support of Greenwood as we visit several of our businesses." He smiled. "But I know you'll also sense some coolness in the air."

The group stopped as Gurley pointed to the entrance of the business next door to the newspaper. "This is my hotel. Well, to be honest, it's Emma's. My wife runs this, and I just do whatever I'm told." He was grinning with obvious humor and pride as he said this.

Susan placed her hands on her hips and stuck out her chin. "And Emma and I know that's as it should be!" They all laughed and then walked into the lobby.

As Charlie gazed around the room, he said, "Can we go back to what was said about Mr. Smitherman and the violence? Are you referring to what has been called the Red Summer? Susan and I are very aware of mob scenes across the country, even in places like our nation's capital. I hope you already understand. We do not agree with what went on there and will do whatever we can to avoid it here in Tulsa."

O. W. turned and offered his hand. "I believe our being here and me introducing you to our Greenwood citizens should prove it."

"It does," Susan said. "And we hope there will be a future collaboration between The Kramer Group and the businesses here in your community."

Gurley said, "I hoped Emma would be here in the lobby. But she's busy somewhere else. Let's keep going."

Over the next several hours, Charlie, Susan, and Johnathan were guided through several businesses, meeting the owners and managers. At their last stop, J. B. Stradford met them at the entrance of his hotel. He ushered them into his coffee shop, where they sat around a table and enjoyed coffee and pie as they discussed the possibilities.

J. B. said, "Well, what do you think of what Mr. Booker T. Washington called Black Wall Street?"

Johnathan looked at Charlie. "May I answer?"

Charlie nodded. "Go ahead."

"People at the bank had told me you had created a self-contained set of businesses and support organizations here in Greenwood, but this exceeded everything I imagined. You should be proud of this place."

O. W. leaned back with his chest puffed out. "We are. And I

think we have a right to be proud. But we could do more with more resources. Charlie, what do you have to say?"

Charlie leaned forward and placed his elbows on the table. "I see a lot of potential here. But I also saw glares aimed at me, Susan, and Johnathan as we walked the streets. The tensions caused by the racist laws in the southern states, and even here in Oklahoma, I'm sure, contribute to those feelings. But as my late father-in-law shared with me during our long discussions, good jobs, respect, and financial stability create more goodwill in a town than almost anything else. If we invest here, our goal is to create jobs, leading to self-respect and financial stability for your citizens here in Greenwood.

Stradford said, "We'll do our part to make sure our local folks know how you are doing good by placing a bank here in our community."

Susan cleared her throat. "I think we need to do all we can to have a member of your community manage the Greenwood branch. That would be a strong indicator of our commitment. Do you have a candidate in mind?"

Gurley stood and walked to the sideboard and filled his coffee cup. He turned and said, "Yes, I have a person in mind. His name is Ralph Nelson. He's about thirty years old and a graduate of Howard University. His degree is in business management. I have him keeping track of my business. But his skills would better serve Greenwood as head of our bank. What do you think, J. B.?"

"Ralph would be a solid choice. My concern for you is how do you replace him in your organization?"

Gurley raised his hand palm out. "I understand. But I have a young man who graduated from Oklahoma Colored Agricultural and Normal University over at Langston, Oklahoma, back in the spring who's as sharp as a tack. He's been supporting Ralph since he got here, and I think he can step in. Charlie or Susan, I'm sure we're weeks or months away from getting a branch here if we decide to do this, aren't we?"

Charlie said, "Yes, I'd say so. For it to be as soon as possible, we need to find a location to remodel so we wouldn't need to build from scratch. I hope there's a vacant building in good shape we could remodel and use."

Gurley said, "Did you notice the empty building on Greenwood Avenue next door? It was a furniture store, and the owner died about six weeks ago. The family sold the merchandise to another store in Tulsa, and they want to get out of their lease with Stradford here."

Stradford laughed. "Telling my secrets, are you? He's right and I bet we could make everybody happy mighty quick."

Johnathan placed his arms on the table. "I'd like to put my two bits in here. All of this sounds too good to be true. It can't be this easy. My first issue is I need to interview this Nelson fellow. I'm sorry, your recommendation is not enough. He will work for me, and I need to learn more about him. The second issue is we must see this building and ensure we can locate a safe or maybe a vault into the structure. A bank has different requirements than a furniture store. Now, I'm excited we have a possible solution to the main issues beyond our determining we want to place a bank in Greenwood."

Susan smiled. "My goodness. Gordon has trained you well. I can't wait to tell him how you put this group on the right path." She turned to look at Gurley and Stradford. "Gentlemen, I see some real possibilities here. My instincts tell me a true business need is not being met here. With the Kramer Group's assets, I'm sure, Charlie and I can meet whatever the need is." She turned to Charlie. "What do you think?"

"Susan, I agree with what you said. Now, we need to let Johnathan work with these folks to put together a plan and bring it to us for our approval."

Susan said, "That's what we must do then." She looked at Johnathan. "Gather all you need from these folks and whatever you need from anywhere else and come to see us with a plan."

Charlie stood. "Gentlemen, any questions?"

Gurley said, "When do you think we can sit down and go over your proposal?"

Charlie looked at Johnathan as he answered. "Give us a month, maybe less."

Johnathan nodded his agreement.

As the Kramer trio rode back to the Hotel Tulsa in Johnathan's car, Susan said, "My biggest concern is what seems to be real tension throughout the community."

Johnathan said, "I hear there's the same thing in Kansas City, and fights are breaking out there over this prohibition thing, too."

Charlie sighed. "Regardless of all that, I think there's a ton of money to be made in the next decade, and we better be prepared to make it."

***

Later the Kellys decided to go down to the Topaz Room for a

Christmas party hosted by the hotel. Charlie agreed to leave the suite ahead of Susan and wait for her at the Topaz because she wanted to surprise him with something new.

Susan was a vision of sensual beauty as she walked into the dining room wearing a black dress that showed every curve of her body. The neckline was scooped, and the dress was backless to just above her hips.

Charlie stood bug-eyed with his pulse racing. "Oh, my goodness! Susan, when and where did you get this amazing dress?"

Susan grinned, "You like it? I ordered it from Paris. The French clothes designer Coco Chanel is becoming famous for her designs, so I had to have one. I know this may not be what you would expect at a Christmas party, but I was excited and wanted you to see it."

"Sweetheart, you look beautiful."

"Thank you, Charlie."

"Did ya git one in other colors?"

"You know me too well."

Chapter 13

Christmas in Maud

December 1919

CHARLIE AND SUSAN ENJOYED a walk along Cincinnati Avenue on an unusually warm December evening. As they approached the front entry to the hotel, Susan stopped and looked up at Charlie. "Sweetheart, we didn't see family at Thanksgiving, so we must go down to Maud for Christmas."

"You're right. We won't be gettin' back with the people in Greenwood for a few weeks, and it would be nice to see the folks and the Double Bar K while we're in Pottawatomie County. I'd like to see what Boss and Dan have done with the places since we bought those additional parcels."

"Yes, and Emilia won't have anything for us regarding the house until sometime well past the first of the year. Let's call and tell them to plan for us to be there. Christmas is next Thursday, and we can spend a few days at the ranch before going to their house if we leave tomorrow."

After getting settled back in their hotel room, Charlie called his folks. He held the receiver so Susan could hear.

A woman's voice answered. "Hello, this is the Kelly home."

"Anna?"

"Charlie, it's great to hear your voice. Yes, do you want to talk to Mom or Dad?"

"You sound so grown up. But of course, you should. I still sometimes think of you as my little sister from our days in New Mexico. Yes, please put one of them on the phone."

"Okay, I'll go get Mom."

Charlie squeezed Susan's hand. "She sounded grown up. My goodness, she'll leave the house and have her own family before we know it."

Susan laid her head on Charlie's shoulder. "We've got to see the family more often than just on holidays."

"I agree. We say we will. But we haven't changed anything, have we?"

A few moments passed, and they heard through the phone. "Anna, please keep an eye on the pot of beans for me."

"Yes, Momma."

"Hello, Charlie, this is Mom. Is everything okay?"

"Yes, we're fine."

Susan said, "Mom, we wanted to call and say we are planning to come to Maud for Christmas."

"Oh, lordy, Sweetheart. What wonderful news. It's been a while since we have seen you. We need to catch up on what you all are doing, and we have news down here as well." She hesitated and then said, "Jess is here and wants to tell you something."

After a few seconds, "Charlie... Susan, I would like it if you could come to Shawnee. Chester and I found the perfect lot to build the store on and bought it for a song. I think it was a great price anyway. We've broken ground already. You both have been to Shawnee, right?"

Susan stifled a laugh. "Yes, we have, where is the lot?"

"On the corner of Main and Beard downtown. I couldn't believe we got it. There was an old wooden building on it we removed. Stanley, our construction supervisor, had his crew start there last Monday. The lot is the same size as the one in Cushing. We'll use the same blueprints and materials for this store, and Stanley hopes to have everything done so we can open by the first of May."

Susan looked at Charlie and nodded. "Jess, we can be there tomorrow afternoon if you like. We were planning to go to the ranch anyway before coming to Maud."

Jess said, "Perfect. Chester, Stanley, and I should be able to meet you at the site. See you when you get there. I'll give the phone back to Mom."

"Charlie, be careful on the roads, and we'll see you next week."

***

Early the following day, they pulled onto Peoria Avenue and headed south. Peoria was a paved street running north and south and followed the Arkansas River. They would cross the river a short distance before getting to the town of Jenks.

As they entered Jenks, Charlie reached over and took Susan's hand. "It looks like you have nothin' under your flannel shirt."

She opened it. "See," She purred. "If it was June instead of December, because I know what my man enjoys, I might not have any clothing on above the waist. But, even in this fancy Cadillac, the heater is not able to keep me warm enough."

Charlie patted her leg. "Now, Sweetheart, I don't want you freezin', so use the blanket we keep in the car. I'm still in my coat."

"Yeah, but you're so hot-blooded you'll be out of it in a few minutes. I'm fine; I want you to have your favorite view."

Charlie grinned, "I love ya. I'll enjoy the view since I know it'll make the trip pleasant. Sometime soon, I need to teach you to drive."

Susan sat up straight. "I would love it. When can we start?"

"Maybe next week at the ranch. I'll first teach ya on a Ford truck in a pasture wherever we can find a smooth area. Then we'll drive on our long entrance road. And finally, use a public road."

Susan turned to face Charlie, "As my cowboy would say it. I'm gonna need to treat ya real good tonight." She giggled. "Of course, I would have anyway, but you know what I mean."

Charlie shook his head. "You almost sounded like a Sooner."

Even stopping in Sapulpa for a quick breakfast, they still arrived at the Shawnee store location by noon. Jess, Chester, and Stanley greeted them as they got out of the car.

Chester said, "You sure made good time. We haven't had lunch. Are you hungry?"

Susan said, "We could eat. We had an early meal. Where do you recommend, we eat?"

Chester said, "I've enjoyed the restaurant at the Norwood Hotel. It's a short walk from here."

Susan noticed Charlie hesitated to speak. She turned to Chester. "Well, let's go there then. I bet we can get a fine steak. I'm hungry."

Charlie couldn't stop himself from laughing. "Fellas, our ranch supplies the beef for the restaurant at the Norwood Hotel. We've eaten there often."

Jess chuckled. "Of course you do. When talking on the phone, you knew exactly where we were building the store."

Susan said, "We still wanted to be here and discuss everything with you."

Chester said, "I'm glad you're here. We think the location is perfect. We're across the street from the bank. Lehman's Hardware is two doors down Main Street, and we're a few blocks from Shawnee Mills to the south. This is the busiest corner in Shawnee. Let's go eat."

***

As the group finished their meals, Chester said, "We need to give you some news. It's not good news, but we'll work on the issue, and things will be fine."

Charlie sighed and leaned forward, resting his elbows on the table. "What's wrong?"

Chester took a sip of his sweet tea. "This morning, a city official stopped by the work site and ordered us to stop work. It seems someone has filed a complaint with the zoning commission because we'll impact his business. The building we removed was not used for retailing. It was a storehouse. We'll get this worked out. Every other building within two blocks of us is a commercial business, so I can't imagine we'll not be able to put our store where we want."

Charlie leaned back and rubbed the back of his neck. "I agree but keep us informed. We may have stepped into some local politics, but you should win this battle."

The group walked back to the work site, where Stanley provided details about the planned construction. Following more discussion, Charlie and Susan drove toward the ranch.

A few minutes' drive outside of town, Charlie patted Susan's leg. "It's gettin' dark, but you're still a beautiful sight for my eyes. We'll be home before too long, and I'm ready to enjoy some quiet."

"Sounds to me like you're in a romantic mood."

"Yup."

***

Later at the ranch, Charlie and Susan enjoyed their Cabernet while lying in front of the fireplace. Susan rose up on her elbow and reached over and gently rubbed Charlie's chest. "Sweetheart, we need to do some Christmas shopping. We can't arrive at your folk's house empty-handed."

He took her hand and kissed it. "You're right. Let's go to Seminole in the morning and shop at Sharpe's. Our buddy, Hank Thomas, has shopped there before. He told me they have several stores around the state. We should be able to find whatever we need. We could shop where Jess worked before, but we might run into family."

"You're right. Sharpe's is a good idea." Susan stood up and

put on her robe. "I want another glass of wine, maybe two."

"I still need to take care of our suitcases and unpack the car. I'm glad the girls came down to the ranch. They can have Christmas with their families too. Can you find Cleta and have her make me a roast beef sandwich? I'm still hungry. I'll join you in a few minutes."

Later, Charlie entered the kitchen and found Susan and the girls laughing. "What's so funny?"

Susan poked Charlie in the chest. "Oh, we're out of wine here at the house. And we've chosen you to go down to the barn to bring some bottles up here, so we have a supply here in the kitchen. Take something with you so you can carry back at least a half dozen bottles."

"Without my sandwich?" Charlie joked.

Susan poked him in the stomach. "I'm sure you won't starve before you get back."

"I'll have your sandwich for you when you get back," Cleta said.

Charlie smiled, turned, and went out the door to the patio. He lit a lantern they kept on a bench and used it as he wound his way down the hill to the barn.

Later they were back in front of the fireplace enjoying their second glass of Cabernet. Charlie set down his sandwich when Susan said, "I'm so glad we converted those spare stalls in the barn to wine storage."

"I'm even happier we have arranged a way to keep a supply for the future. The Volstead Act goes into effect a few weeks after Christmas."

"As a precaution, Uncle Curt set us up with Bishop Lillis in Kansas City to get wine through him if we funded the wine for the Church. He also has put me in contact with Bishop Meerschaert here in Oklahoma, so we'll be able to do the same down here."

"Good thing the politicians made an exception for religious wine," Charlie said.

Susan's eyes twinkled. "Isn't it interesting how our generosity with the Church allows us to have something giving us such pleasure?"

Charlie took another sip of wine and put the glass down. "Yep, and I also say it's another benefit of our hard work."

They completed their shopping the next day and enjoyed several days at the ranch.

***

They drove to Maud on Christmas Eve to have dinner with the family. As Charlie and Susan got out of the car, the entire family came hurrying out the front door of the house to welcome them. Jess was the first to hug Charlie and Susan. He stepped back and said, "Merry Christmas, you two. I have someone you need to meet." He turned and directed their attention to a lovely, tall, and very shapely brunette. "This is my fiancé, Diana Sue Lawson. Diana, these are my brother and sister-in-law, Charlie and Susan."

Susan gasped. "Jess, you've been keeping secrets from us. Diana, welcome."

Diana's eyes grew with excitement. "Jess has told me about you and Charlie, but you know a man never has any details." They laughed and nodded as if to say we'll talk.

Charlie asked, "Do ya have a wedding date set yet?"

Jess shook his head. "No. I only asked her a few days ago. When you guys headed to your ranch, I went to see her."

Diana added. "It'll be in June. I've always wanted a June wedding. And it'll be in Cushing at the First Baptist Church."

Dan walked up and pointed at the young lady coming out of the house. "I think ya know Tess. We're plannin' a weddin' for Memorial Day weekend. We're askin' if you'll stand up with us?"

Charlie and Susan looked at each other, and their faces lit up as they said in unison, "Yes."

Susan ran to Tess and hugged her. "Oh my, sweet girl. I'm honored. Where are you planning to have the ceremony?"

Tess wiped a tear from her cheek. "It will be in the main barn at the Meehan ranch where I grew up. Dad said he would make it beautiful, and Dan is happy with the idea of having the ceremony at the ranch."

After a few more minutes of conversation, Anna stepped up and said, "I have someone I'd like you to meet too. Charlie and Susan, this is Roy Stephens. Charlie, I believe you know his dad."

Charlie chuckled as he nodded. "I sure do. I wondered who this guy was. You favor Clay, and he mentioned you to me. My pleasure, Roy."

Susan stepped up next to Charlie. "We're enjoying the ranch you must have lived on for a lot of your life."

Roy replied, "It's nice to meet you. And yes, the ranch will always be home to me."

Anna took Roy by the arm. "We've been seeing each other for about three months. We met at Seminole College. When he learned I was a Kelly, he asked if I knew you, Charlie." She laughed. "I asked him, why should it matter if I knew you? It didn't make any sense at all to me."

Roy said, "I told her my daddy placed a lot of value on Charlie Kelly."

Anna said, "I told him you were my brother, and then he got mighty interested."

Roy said, "Hold on a minute now, I'm here because of you, Anna, not your brother."

Charlie laughed as he patted Roy's shoulder. "That better be the case 'cause she's a beauty, and Roy, you're probably a great guy, but I'm sorry you're not my type."

The crowd roared, and Charlie gave Roy a brotherly hug.

Joe and Ellie stood back with pride and let the kids share their excitement and news. Then Joe said, "Let's all go into the house. Momma's got dinner ready. Afterward, we've got a Christmas Eve present for everyone to open."

Everyone headed inside.

***

The women congregated in the kitchen to help prepare the dinner. After a while, Ellie said, "You girls can go on, I've got this."

Susan turned to Diana Sue, "Let's have a chat, okay?"

"I'd love to. Do you want to get our jackets and take a walk?"

"Sounds perfect."

They told Charlie and Jess they were heading for a walk.

As they left the front yard, Susan asked, "I assume you live in Cushing, how long have you lived there?"

"I was born there and have lived there all my life. Well, I did go away for four years to school in Edmond where I attended Central State Teachers College. I was happy when I graduated in 1918 there was a job teaching sixth grade open at the elementary school where I was a student about ten years ago."

"I'm sure you know Charlie and I have become very familiar with Cushing. It's a lovely town and is very important to us."

"I am, Susan. I can't imagine how you could be so kind as to call the place you were kidnapped a lovely place."

"Diana, Cushing didn't kidnap me. It was a terrible hoodlum who happened to follow us to Cushing. Your hometown is an exciting place to be as we enter the 1920s next month. Between the oil boom and the overall population growth we are happy to plant some of our future there."

They talked while they walked and were heading back toward the Kelly home when they heard Charlie.

"Hey, you two. Dinner's ready, c'mon."

***

Following a meal of fried chicken and all the fixins, Joe said, "Let's all go into the front room and find a seat. There should be something for everyone under the Christmas tree."

After everyone opened a present and all enjoyed a cup of Momma's cocoa, Charlie said, "Susan and I better call it a night and go to the ranch. We'll be back in the mornin'."

On the way, Charlie said, "It's great my brothers are getting' married. And Anna has a boyfriend too. I didn't get a chance to ask you this. How did your visit with Diana Sue go?

"It was wonderful. She is so sweet. And Charlie, she went to college too. I think we'll have a lot in common. She loves Jess and I think they are a good fit."

"Which reminds me, we'll be married a year come Valentine's Day."

"Charlie, you're thinking about our anniversary. How romantic. A lot of men would forget."

"How could I forget what was the greatest day of my life? I hope we can do somethin' special."

"Me too."

The sun had been down for a while when they parked behind the house at the ranch. Susan got out and closed the car door. "I'm going to get us a bottle of Cabernet, and you can get a fire going for us to snuggle to."

"Sounds perfect." He went to the living room and started a fire in the fireplace. In a few minutes, Susan entered the room carrying a bottle of wine and two glasses. She placed them on the coffee table. "Charlie, I love this room with the fire going." She dropped her robe, and with a flirtatious smile, she purred. "I'm ready. Interested?"

Charlie looked over and saw her naked body glimmer as the light from the flames danced across the room. He sighed. "Your beauty takes my breath away." He undressed, and the evening was full of their version of Christmas cheer.

Chapter 14

Vandalism

January 1920

SEVERAL WEEKS HAD PASSED and Charlie and Susan were still living out of their suite at the Hotel Tulsa. They were settled into a routine of focusing on business during the day and going over and spending evenings at their Madison Avenue house.

Early one morning the phone in their hotel room rang, startling Charlie and Susan from sleep. It was Sunday, and they had planned to sleep a little later.

Through the fog of drowsiness, Charlie gazed across the bedroom and could see the wall clock showing 6:30. He reached over to the bedside table and answered the phone. "Hello, this is Charles Kelly."

A frantic voice said, "I'm so sorry to call this early. I tried to call Bunk Severs, your leadman here, but he didn't answer at the number I had for him. Oh, this here is Ben Cornwell calling from Cushing."

Charlie uncovered himself and sat on the edge of the bed. "It's okay, Ben. How'd ya know to call me here? What's wrong?"

"You mentioned when you were here in Cushing recently you often stayed at the Hotel Tulsa. I decided to give it a try. We have had break-ins at our refineries, and there's some serious damage done at one site. One of our employees was beaten almost to death. He is in the hospital here in Cushing. What do you recommend I do?"

Charlie ran his hand through his hair. "Have you called the police?"

"Yes, sir, I just got off the phone with them. Without even seeing the damage, the officer said they would call Richard Murphy at the Oklahoma Bureau of Investigation to assist them."

"Good. I know Richard. He's a fine man and the police know he helped us back when Mrs. Kelly was kidnapped. Ben, give me your phone number, in case I need to call you back."

"It's Cushing – 0998."

"Thanks, I'll be callin' Bunk and Bailey Muldoon, our head of security, and we'll be there today. Thanks again for callin' me."

As Charlie said goodbye, Susan climbed out of bed. "Who was on the phone."

"It was Ben Cornwell calling from Cushing."

"I can see concern written across your face. Charlie, what's going on? How serious is it?"

"We've had more vandalism, but this time it's in Cushing. We have an employee in the hospital. I've gotta git ahold of Bunk and Bailey and we need to make a trip to Cushing today."

Susan's hand went to her mouth as she shuddered. "Of course, I'll start getting ready."

Charlie immediately called Bailey's room at the hotel, "Bailey, this is Charlie, sorry to wake ya. We've another bad situation crop up at one of our Kelly Oil sites."

"What's happened?"

Charlie told him what he knew and then said, "Susan and I are goin' to Cushing as soon as we can. I'm gonna call Bunk Severs next. I want you both to join us there today. It might be best if we take separate cars as I'm sure you'll need to stay longer. Let's meet at the Cushing Hotel at noon. I'll have the man who called me, join us at the hotel and we'll go together to visit our employee in the hospital before we see the damage."

After completing his call with Bunk, Charlie turned to Susan and said, "I think our next few months will be tough. I'm guessin' the folks in Chicago are pissed."

She put her arms around him. "You sound discouraged, Charlie."

"They won't go away."

"Are you sure this thing in Cushing is caused by the same guys who hit Sapulpa? Couldn't it be some small-time thug like Willard?"

"Well, yes, I guess it could be, but I'd bet about anything it's the Chicago Outfit."

***

Charlie and Susan arrived at the Cushing Hotel registration desk at 11:30 and signed for the Presidential Suite, which was becoming a familiar home base. Charlie had arranged for two additional rooms for Bunk and Bailey. Bailey had followed them from Tulsa and was just now walking into the hotel. Bunk had not yet arrived. Charlie asked the clerk for Rice Coburn's room number and called, "Hello, Rice, Charlie Kelly. Susan and I are here in Cushing because of vandalism at one of the refineries."

"My God, what happened? Was anyone hurt?"

"I don't have all the answers yet, but we have an employee in the hospital. I need you to come to a meetin' in the hotel restaurant in ten minutes."

"I'll be there."

"Thanks, buddy."

As they finished at the front desk Charlie said, "The bellhop is takin' our suitcases to our room. Let's get our usual table near the window if it's available. We can have the restaurant staff move another table over to accommodate the six of us."

***

Before he could take his seat, Charlie saw Ben come into the restaurant and he waved to get his attention. "Good to see you, Ben, but we hate the circumstances."

They shook hands. Ben said, "It's great seeing you too. I'm sure we'll get this all fixed." He turned and tipped his hat. "Good day to you, Miss Susan."

A big smile crossed Susan's face. "It's wonderful to hear someone in Oklahoma call me Miss Susan. Several people in Kansas City have called me that for years. Hello, Ben, and yes, we'll get this fixed."

As the three were settling into their places at the table, Bunk, Rice, and Bailey hurried through the restaurant door. Bunk took the seat next to Charlie and Bailey and Rice across the table next to Ben.

Charlie motioned for the waiter, and he came with coffee cups, saucers, and a carafe. He filled everyone's cup.

Susan said, "Thanks, and we're not ready to order food."

Charlie took a sip of coffee and looked around the table. "Alright, let's git started. We need to be on the same page, so, Ben share everythin' ya know."

Ben looked down for a moment and took a deep breath. "I received a call at 4:45 this mornin' from my night watchman, Whit. I had difficulty understandin' him and realized he was hurt. He sounded bad. I got dressed and drove to the refinery as fast as I could. I found Whit sittin' with his back against the office wall, bleedin' from his mouth, and the right side of his head. The office was trashed, and all the windows were broken. There were holes kicked in every wall. I haven't inspected the plant area yet, but the best I could tell, there were no explosions. Whit is in the hospital fightin' for his life."

Bailey let out a big sigh as he shook his head. "This has got to stop. Ben, did you see any messages? Maybe something written on the walls."

Startled at the comment, Ben nodded. "Yes, as a matter of fact, I did. There was one on the back wall of the office. I don't remember exactly what it said. Somethin' like, 'Greetings from Chicago. Get out of town or we'll be back.' It wasn't signed or anythin'."

Bailey grimaced. "I don't think we need a signature. Charlie, I'd bet it's the same people that hit the quarry. If we don't get this stopped soon it wouldn't surprise me if things didn't heat up at other sites."

Charlie scooted to the edge of his chair. His brow furrowed as he made eye contact with every face. In a steady low-pitched voice he said, "Bailey, I agree with ya. And we're gonna deal with this goin' straight at 'em." He took another sip of coffee. "We can't do anythin' about them right now and even though I'm hungry I want to go check on Whit and see the damages." He looked at Ben and Bunk. "Since it's Sunday, would ya be operatin'?"

Ben said, "We're slowin' down at this refinery to begin work on the modifications needed to tie into the others. So today, there are only a few workers at the plant."

Bunk said, "I was coming down here tomorrow to begin working with Ben and the others to get everything going. I'll be interested to see if there's a lot of damage done to the plant refining equipment."

Rice added, "I'm glad I'm here in Cushing, but was planning to go to Shawnee today to meet with Chester Abrams to discuss where we'll be building some new stores. But I'll stay and do what I can."

Charlie looked at Rice. "I'm glad you're here. We need your help to determine the impact to our modification plans at the refineries. The folks in Shawnee are havin' a challenge on buildin' at the site they selected. Once you're down there, let me know what you find out. But I'd like ya to stay here until we figure all this out. Let's go."

***

At the hospital, they learned Whit was stable and would recover from the beating he had endured. Bailey asked him a few questions about the men who attacked him. Susan spoke with Whit's wife and the doctor, making sure that the hospital bill was sent to the Kelly Oil office for payment. They then drove to the refinery.

As the group walked toward the office, Bunk saw the door had been kicked in on a pump house. He pointed at the door. "I'm going to see what's happened over there."

The rest of the group went into the office and saw Ben had not exaggerated his description. They also saw several uniformed men looking around and writing notes on pads as they talked among themselves.

A voice from the corner of the room said, "Charlie Kelly, what are you doing here?"

Charlie turned and saw Richard Murphy from the OBI. His thoughts returned to another crime scene a short distance away in Cushing. He gathered himself. "I'm here lookin' at my refinery damage."

Richard's mouth gaped. "You own this?"

"Yes, I do, or we do." He pointed at Susan. "My company, Kelly Oil, purchased four refineries and a pipeline company here in Cushing."

"Now, I would have thought you two would never step foot in this town again. I guess it shows I have little or no talent to predict anything."

Charlie gave him a grin. "Tell me, what do you make of all this, Richard?"

"I guess, pissing off small-time local hoods wasn't enough." He pointed to a wall behind Charlie. "We found this message on the wall. You've gone after the big boys in Chicago."

In red paint, the message read, "We said get outta Oklahoma, Your friends from Chicago."

Charlie shrugged his shoulders. "It was never my intention. One of Susan's businesses, a construction company in Missouri, had some issues in Kansas City with some mobsters before we were married, but I thought we had them settled."

Bailey joined them. "I guess we didn't. Good to see you, Richard. I want to see this handled fast before it gets further out of hand."

Richard's face showed a little annoyance at Bailey's statement. "We'll do what we can as fast as we can. But you know as well as anyone, we'll follow our protocols." His face softened. "I'm glad you're working for Charlie now."

"I am too. This and Sapulpa's incident are the first since I started."

Richard's eyes got big. "What incident in Sapulpa?"

Charlie nodded. "Back in June, we outbid some folks for a quarry near Sapulpa. With our venture into oil field cementin' services, we needed an additional quarry. It turns out they were trying to buy it for the Chicago mob. I guess they wanted the quarry and the cement business it supports. I'm sure it would have been used to launder drug and prostitution money. That's what they were doin' in Kansas City when Susan's father got the Missouri AG to shut them down over a year ago."

Richard rubbed his neck. "So, what I'm hearing is there have been two serious incidents here in Oklahoma within a very short period of time, and you think the infamous Johnny Torrio is behind it?"

Susan had walked over to the group. "Richard don't get too worked up. Whoever did this never said they were part of the Chicago Outfit, but they do say Chicago." She gestured to the paint on the wall. "We believe it is the Outfit because they were the ones who were causing trouble with my construction company in Kansas City."

Charlie added, "Their main guy in Kansas City was Tom Pendleton, and an unknown person killed him, but we had him on the run anyway. I have no idea who they have down here in Oklahoma."

Richard wrung his hands. "Nor do I. But Charlie, these guys are notorious for driving by and shooting people."

Susan looked serious as she said, "I know," but she didn't elaborate. "We understand who these hoodlums are, and we're not going to be pushed around by them."

Richard put up his hands and said, "Charlie, you need to talk to your wife. This situation isn't Willard and his goon. This may be Torrio or someone just like him."

Charlie shrugged. "Susan and I are in complete agreement here. We have Bailey creatin' a security company within the Kramer Group to, among many other things, address any weaknesses we have to somethin' like this."

Bailey put his hand on Richard's shoulder. "Don't worry, we'll not be creating a police force, but we'll be protecting the Kramer Group's assets and, of course, Mr. and Mrs. Kelly. We'll operate within the laws of the land, but the Kellys will not be intimidated even by these goons from Chicago."

Richard winked. "I know you don't intimidate these two. I've seen them in action, as you know. I have my team documenting everything, so we need to step outside before we corrupt this crime scene further."

Outside, Richard continued. "Charlie, I have all the respect in the world for you and Susan. In the short time we've known each other I think we have developed a friendship. I don't want either of you to get hurt again or killed. I have law enforcement friends who deal with Torrio and the Italians as well as O'Connell and the Irish, who run the criminal elements in Chicago. They are both expanding across the nation. I believe the message "from Chicago" we saw on the wall inside there is from Torrio. Can I trust you not to do something to put you and your wife in danger?"

Charlie gave Richard a long, sincere look. "I believe I can say this without sounding too foolish. Richard, life is filled with decisions, and some are easy, while others are hard. Some decisions are safe to make, and some put you at some level of danger. I believe as I address this situation, I will do the right thing, and you will support me in this, just as you did the night we met here in Cushing."

Bailey said, "Richard, we'll work hard to address this with appropriate respect for the adversary. You and I had a long talk a few weeks back about our experiences in the Great War. We had a healthy respect for the Germans, but we had a job to do. Charlie, Susan, and I have a healthy respect for this Chicago group, whoever they are, and we consider this incident and what happened in Sapulpa, acts of war. We'll put all our effort into finding a diplomatic way to end this. But the Kellys and the folks working in the Kramer Group are law-abiding citizens who have a right to be in business without dealing with illegal actions against them. We'll stand up to these people. We'll never run from this group of outlaws."

Susan patted Bailey's back. "Well said. We need to let these people do their job. Would it be reasonable to have a meeting tomorrow morning back at the hotel?"

Everyone nodded in agreement; they could be there. Charlie said, "Good. Then we'll see ya there. Susan and I will arrange to have the room we used as our headquarters last time."

Bailey leaned into Charlie and whispered. "Can I have a few minutes with you today back at the hotel?"

"Of course. We'll meet you at the restaurant in thirty minutes."

***

Susan and Charlie arrived at the restaurant ahead of Bailey. Susan called Uncle Curt and updated him on the day's activities. Charlie spoke to the maître d' and acquired their usual table near the window and ordered a plate of meats and cheeses to make sandwiches and a pitcher of sweet tea. He'd have preferred wine but felt that a clear head was needed now.

As Susan joined him, she said, "I hope Bailey has some ideas about what we need to do next."

He pointed. "Here he comes now. I guess we'll find out." He pulled out a chair. "Bailey, glad you wanted to talk, have a seat."

Bailey sat across from Charlie. "I wanted to give you guys an update on what I've been up to over the last several weeks and discuss some basic ideas I have."

Charlie nodded, "Great, we want to hear what you have and discuss whatever is on your mind. But first, I'm hungry; are you?"

Bailey grinned, "I'm starving, glad you asked."

As they made sandwiches and poured the tea Bailey began to talk.

"I've reached out to six of my old Army buddies. One is from England. We all managed to stay in touch because we're still using the skills we developed during our military careers working classified special operations."

"What does that mean?" Susan asked.

"Let's just say we were not your regular soldiers. I can't give you any details about the missions we were given, but we have a mixture of talents making us, when formed into a team, intimidating, dangerous, and often described as menacing. I found it interesting, Susan, when you said, we will not be intimidated. I agree, but we might intimidate our adversary."

Charlie said through a mouthful of sandwich. "Are you planning to offer jobs to your old friends?"

"Yes, I am. I believe they will be true assets. Some will be ideal for heading up some of the areas we'll want to address as we build our security company. But, right now, we need them here to help with this situation. Three of them were already planning on being in Kansas City by the end of the month. I'm going to contact them tonight to see if they can arrive in the next few days. Two others had commitments and hoped to be able to join us by mid-February. I'll also see if they can speed things up. My English friend is working tasks for the Crown and said he couldn't leave for another week. It will take him about ten days to cross the ocean and reach K.C.."

Charlie asked, "Can ya tell us what jobs they are leavin'?"

"I can. The three on their way now have been serving as bodyguards. The first one served former President Teddy Roosevelt until his death last year. He was recently protecting his son Teddy Jr. who is serving in the New York State Legislature. The second one was protecting William Vanderbilt III in Newport, Rhode Island. The third one is also coming from the east coast. He has been protecting John D. Rockefeller Jr. As you can see, their experience is in dealing with wealthy high-profile clientele. The Bureau of Investigation employs the two who originally said they couldn't leave until February. They're detectives working cases which will be helpful to our concerns. My English friend is serving King George V but I am not exactly sure in what capacity."

Susan turned to Bailey. "I would say your friends must be highly skilled and trustworthy to have those positions. We'll be lucky to have them."

Bailey said, "I have some things we should discuss, but I need to do some research. May I have some private time with you tomorrow?"

Charlie looked at Susan. She nodded. He looked back at Bailey. "Of course. You'll be at the meeting we set up in the morning, won't you?"

"I plan to be there. Maybe we can talk after the meeting."

Susan reached over and touched his arm. "Yes, unless we have another issue arise. See you then."

Bailey took his uneaten sandwich with him as he left to make his calls and get his new team together sooner rather than later.

Susan took another sip of tea. "Ever wish you were back working on a ranch, Sweetheart?"

Charlie leaned back and sighed. "Sometimes. But honestly, only because I loved bein' a cowboy, not because I'm not lovin' what we're doin' together. You make my life so wonderful. Dealin' with whatever challenges these Chicago assholes come up with won't be any harder than what those rustlers back at the 101 caused me and my guys."

"I know Father had his challenges too, but I don't think they ever included mobsters any more dangerous than Pendleton." She brushed his cheek and kissed him. "I love you Charlie Kelly and you make my life wonderful too."

Chapter 15

Addressing the Damage

January 1920

THE LARGE MAHOGANY PANELED meeting room in the Cushing Hotel was buzzing with anticipation. Charlie and Susan had gathered their team who were poised to address the latest threat to Kelly Oil, the Kramer Group, and them.

Charlie stood at the head of the conference table. "Everybody please take your seats. There's a lot to cover today, so let's git started. Bunk, please give us an update on the requirements Rice will need to meet as we start repairing the refinery and bringin' it back online."

Bunk set his coffee on the table. "We have a plan I have already discussed with Rice and my leads at the refineries and the pipeline company. We have all the refineries except the damaged one operating at their normal rates based on their current configuration. The first refinery to be prepared for integration was always going to be Ben's. Rice and I had planned it before the damage, but now it makes even more sense." He laughed and slapped his leg. "I have a little humor for everyone regarding the damage. The building and equipment where most of the damage happened was going to be demolished anyway." He laughed again. "Those Chicago fellas saved us a little time and some money. Do you think we should send them a thank-you card from the Hallmark Card Company?"

The room erupted in laughter. Charlie chuckled. "Do ya need someone to pay for the card? I'll be happy to cover the cost." He flashed a dollar bill to the crowd.

Bunk said, "I'll let Rice discuss the schedule and the costs, but we plan to have all the repair and integration work on the refineries done and have them operating as a refinery system fed by pipelines, trucks, and trains in about ninety to a hundred and twenty days from now."

"Thanks, Bunk," Susan said. "Rice, what do you have?"

"By the end of today, we'll have all the personnel and materials on-site to start tomorrow at the Cornwell refinery. And even with the help the vandals gave us," there were some more chuckles from the group, "we still have a lot to demolish before we start building. I think it's great they saved us several thousand dollars, but so far as I'm concerned, we won't tell them. At the end of the project, we'll have two refineries set up to produce gasoline and a little kerosene. One will produce light oils for vehicles and equipment requiring it. The final refinery will produce heavy oil products for commercial use such as trains and manufacturing equipment. The overall costs, if we have no further surprises, will not exceed $125,000. And Bunk was correct. We are targeting full operation by May or maybe June."

Susan said, "Rice, are you planning to be here the entire time?"

"I plan to split time with Roy Goddard. We'll alternate at two-week intervals. So he and I can stay aware of what's happening in both places. Bunk will be here full-time. Charlie, Susan, as you already know, I have hired an Oklahoman named Stanley Farley to be the lead on the Abrams project. Stanley was the Construction Superintendent at the Abrams site here in Cushing. We stole him from Sam Holder. I'll check on the Shawnee site and let you know what I find out. I'll continue to also check on things here from time to time."

Charlie said, "Thanks Rice, and now Richard, can you give us information from your team?"

"Good morning, everyone. We continued yesterday to work into the night, and we found dynamite was used where the worst damage was located. Then it appeared sledgehammers and crowbars or something similar were used in the office area and a few outbuildings. I called our main archives in Oklahoma City and described what we saw, and the damage at this site does not parallel with any other place, so with the message on the wall, we do feel it is someone from out of state. With what Strawberry Hill Construction experienced in Kansas City, you could be correct in assuming it's the same guys from Chicago. There were no usable fingerprints, and we're not good yet at using them anyway. We'll work with Bailey, the local police, and anybody with additional information to help get to the bottom of this."

Susan said, "I know Charlie and I want this to stop as soon as possible, and it appears these aren't inexperienced thugs. That's another reason we think it's the bunch from Chicago. Thanks, Richard. Bailey, what can you add?"

"I have made some headway since we talked yesterday. I will have two people here in a couple of days to help me. I also spoke with the two men coming to us from the Federal BOI. They were able to confirm Johnny Torrio in Chicago is probably behind these incidents. The Outfit is starting to move some operations into Oklahoma. As we see Prohibition begin, they want to own the bootlegging business. The speculation is that they were planning to use the cement business to launder money from booze and prostitution. I'll never know exactly how my source knows this because he is somehow working undercover inside the Outfit."

Richard raised his hand. "Bailey, how are you getting BOI guys to come to work for you?"

Bailey smiled, "Money and some of the best additional benefits you can imagine. The Kellys want to create a large, diversified security business, and my guys are among the best. They'll have the background to run some aspects of the business they'll help create."

Richard turned to Charlie and said, "I'm excited to see what you're building. Maybe someday, I'll come and be part of it?"

Susan didn't wait for Charlie and said, "Richard, you've only got two years, maybe less, and then you'll have your pension. Get it. Then, we'll find you a place with us somewhere."

Charlie nodded. "You have been, and I know you'll always be, a loyal friend. Susan is right. You'll have a place somewhere within the Kramer Group."

Bailey asked, "Richard, as I said, I'll have two guys here in a couple of days and five by this time next week. I want some time with you today and then later in the week to draw up a plan for addressing how we will put an end to this. Are you available?"

"I am today for sure. The more you can tell me about the reasons you are certain it's the guys in Chicago, the more I'll be able to justify to my boss that this needs to be a priority for me and my guys. I know the OBI does not want them to gain a foothold in Oklahoma."

Bailey offered, "You have me for the rest of the day and into tonight if needed. I want to give you whatever you need, and I want you to understand how my guys and I'll be operating when we are working as a team."

Charlie stood and said, "We jumped right into the meeting and didn't order food and I'm hungry. Order whatever ya want. I'm buyin'."

They all enjoyed their food and continued to work on the details of the refinery repairs, renovations, and the new security group well into the afternoon. Near the end of the day, everyone seemed satisfied with what needed to be done. Charlie and Susan had spent an hour with Bailey and Richard to discuss the specifics of the case against the Outfit. When the meeting broke up Charlie and Susan headed to their suite.

The Cushing Hotel, like the Hotel Tulsa, was beginning to seem like home. When they passed the registration desk, the clerk said, "Mrs. Kelly, I have a message for you." He gave a note to Susan. She read it aloud.

"I received a wire from the furniture manufacturer and your order was destroyed in a train derailment. Therefore, I will not have your custom furniture and other furnishings ready for you to move into your home until March or late February at the soonest. Emilia Monahan."

Susan smiled. "How did she know how to reach us? I guess she must have learned we were here from the folks at the hotel in Tulsa. Charlie, I'm sad. I wish it was sooner, but we'll get to move into our new home someday."

Charlie nodded. "There's nothing anyone can do about it. We'll still go over to the Madison house in the evening when we need to get away. Let's go upstairs."

They hadn't been in their room long when Charlie said, "Sweetheart, I had planned for us to be arrivin' at Medicine Park down near Lawton, Oklahoma tomorrow. It's a new resort Harry Sinclair told me about. I was goin' to surprise you for our first anniversary."

Susan walked over and put her arms around Charlie. "Oh, you wonderful man. I love the idea of getting away to someplace. I know we can't do it now because of what we're dealing with. But I want us to go there sometime soon."

"We will, I promise ya."

She hugged him again. "I want to get in our Cadillac and ride around Cushing for a while. Let me get out of this business outfit. I brought with me a pink silk blouse like the white one you like. I need to have some fun. We could go out to the city lake."

"It's a bit cold to take a stroll around the lake," Charlie said.

"I'm sure we'll be plenty warm just staying in the car," Susan said with a wink.

Chapter 16

Opening a Bank

February 1920

CHARLIE AND SUSAN RETURNED to Tulsa over the weekend after seeing their leaders were focused on moving forward. They settled back into their routine for a few weeks. It was early evening with Charlie sitting on the sofa in their hotel room reading the sports page when the phone rang.

Susan said, "Can you get it."

"Hello, this is Charles Kelly."

"Hello, Mr. Kelly. This is Johnathan over at the bank. I'd like to request some time tomorrow, if possible, with you and Susan. I have completed the study on a possible bank in Greenwood and would like to give you my report."

"We would love to hear it. Tomorrow is Wednesday the fourth, and we are free all day. How about we come to you at the bank? Can we expect Harry Sinclair to be there?"

"Yes, he returned to the office yesterday. He was in Casper, Wyoming exploring the possibility of getting in on the oil boom up there. I guess he has seen Rockefeller make a lot of money in Wyoming and he meant it when he said why he wanted to reduce his investment in this bank. I can make sure he's here for our discussion."

"We'll be there at 10:00. Have the coffee ready."

Susan rose from her pillow and placed her book on the side table. "Who was on the phone, Sweetheart?"

"It was Johnathan. The study about creatin' a bank in Greenwood is finished and he wants to give us a report tomorrow mornin'. We'll join him and Harry at the bank at ten."

"Did he say what he'll be recommending?"

"No, he didn't offer anything, and I didn't ask. We'll hear

what he has for us in person."

She now stood just inside the bedroom door with her hands on her naked hips. "Oh, you men never get the details. Women ask the important questions right up front."

Charlie looked up and saw her in his favorite outfit. "Now how can I argue with you. You're just not fair."

She turned and headed back to the bed. "We can discuss the problem in here."

***

The next morning the couple walked the block or so from the hotel to the bank, arriving at 10:00. Harry Sinclair met them in the lobby and escorted them to a conference room. Johnathan was already in the room and ready for everyone.

Charlie said, "I see the coffee is waiting, and I hope it's still hot."

Susan said, "Oh, Charlie, I'm sure it is. I'm more interested in the report I see lying in front of each chair."

"Geez, can't a guy have a little fun needlin' one of our best people. Johnathan knows we appreciate him. And yes, I can't wait to hear what he's got for us."

Harry held Susan's chair for her as she took her seat. She looked at Harry as he said, "Johnathan wouldn't tell me anything this morning, so I'm anxious to hear his report too."

After everyone had taken their seats Johnathan cleared his throat. "Please open your packet to page one. There you'll see some basic financial and demographic information about Greenwood. Some of this Mr. Gurley shared during our tour in December, but we have now verified it through examining several Greenwood businesses and their books and we also met with and gained information from the board of directors from the Tulsa Chamber of Commerce."

Harry said, "Did you find any discrepancies with what Gurley provided us?"

Johnathan lifted his head to make eye contact. "We found Mr. Gurley and Mr. Stradford to be honest and if anything, undervaluing what has been created in Greenwood. There are about 200 solid businesses in Greenwood covering virtually every aspect of what consumers want and need. There is also a library, two schools, two newspapers and a hospital. With the resources of this bank, we can provide stability for continued growth by offering our services to what is already an excellent economic foundation."

Harry leaned back as he said, "I can attest to the fact Gurley, Stradford, and maybe one or two more businessmen have been able to get loans or some form of backing from us and some other banks here in town. But others have not, and at this point, the Greenwood general population is certainly being overlooked as potential banking customers."

Johnathan went over more of the numbers and demographics he had put together. The more in-depth he went the more it became clear that the thing that the Greenwood community was missing was access to capital so that the community could continue to build wealth on its own terms.

After going through most of the report Susan smiled, reached for her coffee, took a sip, and thought for a moment. "I'm very curious about all of this. My father would have wondered why no one was supporting what obviously, is a group of solid businessmen and a growing community. Charlie, you've something on your mind?"

He leaned forward, arms folded across his chest. "I hope it's not because they are Negroes. Bill Pickett is a Negro and is the best cowboy I've ever met. I also consider him a good friend. But that's not why I think we should do this. It's clear from Johnathan's research that there are a lot of opportunities for the citizens of Greenwood to build wealth if given the chance. And from what I have learned from Susan and Harry is that if a bank's customers are buildin' wealth, so is the bank. I'm inclined to say let's invest in Greenwood using our typical criteria for doin' so with no special concern these businesses will not continue to be profitable."

Susan tapped her chest. "I agree with my husband. Let's put together a plan to create a branch of Exchange National in Greenwood."

Johnathan stood. "That was going to be my recommendation. I'm excited to hear your support before I had to make my pitch."

Harry said, "Me too."

Susan stood and shook Johnathan's hand. "Look for a building we can remodel. We talked about it during the tour. It will be our fastest and cheapest way to get a branch open."

***

A week passed and things seemed to be progressing well in Cushing and Tulsa with the refineries and banks. Charlie and Susan were walking back to the hotel after an evening at the

Dreamland Movie Theatre watching the latest Mary Pickford movie, *Pollyanna*.

Susan hugged Charlie's arm. "I love Mary Pickford. And Charlie, she's a good businesswoman, too. *Pollyanna* is the first movie from her new company United Artists."

"Susan, I admire her too. Don't forget she has three partners. Her honey, Douglas Fairbanks, D.W. Griffith, and Charlie Chaplin."

"Okay, but she is a millionaire herself, and they need her money as well as all of her acting talent."

"Agreed, Sweetheart. Can we change the subject?"

"Of course. What's on your mine?"

"Things are going well, so let's take a few days and go down to Medicine Park and celebrate our anniversary. It is the day after tomorrow you know."

Her face lit up as she turned and faced him. "Yes, let's do it! We can leave in the morning and arrive at the resort on our anniversary."

***

As their Cadillac began its climb into the foothills of the Wichita mountains just north and west of Lawton, Oklahoma, the couple had seen and marveled at the many different landscapes that made up the Sooner state. From the rolling hills around Tulsa to the drier almost arid, rock-covered mountains of the Lawton area in southwestern Oklahoma.

Susan said, "This scenery is a lot different than what we have in Tulsa. And nothing like what I see when we visit Cushing, or even down at the folks' house in Maud."

Charlie patted her leg. "You're right. I saw those changes as a kid as my family moved from Oklahoma to New Mexico and back. This part of the state is more like the panhandle of Texas, and Tulsa is a lot like what you'll see in Arkansas, Missouri, and western Kansas."

"True. Tulsa and Kansas City are similar, although the west side of Kansas City as you get into Kansas is even more hilly than around our home in Tulsa."

As they arrived at the Medicine Park Grand Hotel, Susan said, "Sweetheart, this is wonderful. I love how rustic it is with the rock porch and pillars and just look at this setting along a lake."

"It is. According to Harry Sinclair, they call it Medicine Park Bath Lake. There's supposed to be a swingin' bridge across part of it. I've got us a cabin with a kitchenette overlookin' the lake. It'll let us enjoy some privacy, and we'll still have most of our meals here at the hotel's Inside Inn restaurant."

"Charlie, thank you for getting this arranged. Again, my darling, this is wonderful."

They stayed a week and filled the days going on hikes up Mt. Scott, enjoying evenings by the fireplace, and relaxing away from their typical daily grind. Charlie seldom called for updates from their staff.

As they drove away from Medicine Park, Susan said, "Well, my dear, you were very impressive."

"Whattaya mean?"

"I only caught you calling Uncle Curt or any of our other leaders twice. It meant to me you were trying hard to focus on us the week. I'm a happy and refreshed lady."

"Oh, and here I thought I got away with it." He laughed. "I was checkin' on the status of our house, hopin' to surprise ya with news on the way back we could move in when we git to Tulsa. It's still gonna be a few more weeks."

She smiled as she unbuttoned her blouse and popped a couple of snaps on Charlie's shirt. "I'm in no hurry to get back to Tulsa, even if our house is ready."

Chapter 17

Bank Hit!

March 1920

IT HAD REMAINED QUIET at all the Kramer Group business locations since the damage to the Cushing refineries in January. Progress was being made at the refineries and all the other business concerns in Oklahoma were running smoothly. As Charlie and Susan returned from a morning walk, they were called over to the hotel's registration desk. A clerk handed Charlie a note. "Mr. Kelly, Mr. Sinclair asked you to call him at the bank."

Charlie took the note and saw the bank's phone number on it. He went to a phone in the lobby and called. "Hello, this is Charles Kelly."

"Yes, Charlie, this is Harry. We've got major damage here at the bank."

Charlie turned and leaned against the wall as he looked up at the ceiling. "You've gotta be shittin' me, Harry. Are ya there now?"

"I wish I was shittin' you, my friend. And yes, I've been here for about thirty minutes."

"Okay, what happened?"

"All the front windows are broken out. It doesn't appear they stole anything. We were lucky some police were nearby and arrived during the vandalism. They have two guys in custody, but some others got away."

Charlie sighed. "I can't believe I'm askin' this. Is there a message on the wall?"

"Yes, there is. How the hell did you know? It says, "From your friends in Chicago."

"Of course it does. Is there anythin' else? Have the two guys talked? Is there anythin' else you've learned? Maybe, who do they work for?"

"It appears they were using this truck parked out front. It has faded lettering which reads Pendle… something Con… something."

Charlie said, "Harry, might it be Pendleton Concrete?"

"That's it. It's faded, but that's it."

"Here's what we'll do. I need to make some calls and git some people here as fast as possible. You gather as much information as ya can and come to the VIP dinin' room here at the hotel at 2:00 for a meetin'. Tell the cops they need to be here too. I know who did this. I'll see ya this afternoon."

"You know who did this?"

"Yes, be here at two."

"Sure, Charlie, see you then."

Charlie walked over to Susan and told her what had happened.

Susan asked, "Do you have a plan?"

"I'm callin' Bailey and have him come here as fast as he can. I have Harry and the police coming here at two."

***

Charlie went to the suite and called Bailey at the Cushing Hotel.

"Hello."

"Bailey, this is Charlie. There has been more vandalism. This time it's the Exchange National Bank here in Tulsa. I need ya here at the Hotel Tulsa for a 2:00 meeting with me, Harry Sinclair, and the police. The police have two people in custody, but there were more involved."

Bailey said, "I can be there in a few hours. I have two of my guys here, and they'll come with me. Anything else?"

"No, and I'm glad ya have some help. I'm sure this is the Chicago Outfit, and they are not goin' away. If anythin', it's getting hotter. Oh, can you call Richard?"

"I think so, he was working on another crime in Drumright yesterday and was planning to leave for Oklahoma City today, but he should still be here. I'll call his room and check. If he's there I'll update him. Do you want him in Tulsa?"

"Yes, if he wants to come, he is welcome. We'll be in the Hotel Tulsa VIP dinin' room."

***

Susan walked into their suite's living room and placed her hand on Charlie's shoulder. "Did you reach Bailey?"

"I sure did. He'll be here this afternoon at 2:00 with two of his guys. He may also have Richard with him. I need to arrange to use the dinin' room."

Susan said, "Someone else may have it scheduled."

Charlie said, "Could be. If so, I'll work somethin' out."

The room was available, but Charlie learned he could use several other conference rooms on days when the VIP room is not available.

As Charlie put the phone on its cradle, Susan asked, "Did you get the room?"

"I did, and I need to go down and talk to the maître d'. We didn't git our breakfast, do ya wanna come down with me?"

"Let me freshen up, then I'll join you."

He went down to the restaurant and talked to Pierre. "I need coffee and snacks brought to the VIP dining room this afternoon by 1:45, and dependin' on how my meetin' goes, I may need to arrange to keep the room or a room like it for a while. I'll be back in touch later today on that. Susan and I missed our breakfast. Can ya have our usual brought to us?"

"Of course, Mr. Kelly. I hope you don't mind me asking, how is your wife doing? We'll never forget her ordeal in Cushing a few months ago."

"She's pretty much back to her old self. Once in a while, she'll have a bad dream, but they are gettin' fewer and farther between all the time. Thanks for askin'."

Charlie went to their usual table and waited for Susan.

***

When Susan joined Charlie she said, "I assume you have the VIP dining room. Since we can't do anything until everyone gets here let's go over some of our other business."

Charlie nodded and poured coffee for them both.

"Emilia called me a few minutes ago. Our furniture arrived and she will have everything in place so we can move into our home on Friday. After I eat I'm goin' back up to the suite and call Cleta and Attie. I want them to come up here no later than Thursday. We can get them a room here at the hotel. If we're moving on Friday, we need to be able to sleep, shower, and eat at the house. I want them to see where they'll be living, and they can go grocery shopping and shop for linens, towels, and all the necessities and stock up the pantries. I'll come back down and eat lunch with you at noon, okay?"

Charlie said, "Perfect. I'm so glad you're handlin' the logistics of the move. I knew the move-in day was getting' close, but I hadn't given it much thought."

"Charlie, you've enough on your plate. I'll get us moved into Madison."

***

Charlie and Susan had a light lunch but neither had much of an appetite as they wondered what the news about the bank would be. The VIP room had been set up as requested when they got there just before 2:00. Harry Sinclair was the first to arrive and sat opposite Charlie at the table. Charlie noticed he looked haggard.

Susan said, "Harry, it's good to see you, but I wish we weren't here because of trouble."

Charlie put his coffee cup down. "I can see anxiety written on your face. I want ya to know; we'll git this handled, and soon."

Harry rubbed his chin then said, "How do you know this group is from Chicago, Charlie? The police say this is a gang from Kansas City."

Charlie nodded and took another sip of coffee. "Harry, I git you're concerned, maybe even a little scared, but we've dealt with this bunch before, and it's not you or even the bank they're after."

Susan looked Harry in the eye. "We won't be pushed around by these guys. They operate using fear, and it works on some people most of the time. Not us. We beat them in Kansas City, and we'll do it again here."

Harry sagged back into his chair. "Well, if you two say so."

Bailey came into the room followed by two guys that appeared to be in their late twenties. One was burly with a stubble of a beard. The other was a tall, rangy redhead. They walked straight to Charlie, who had come around the table to meet them.

Bailey offered his hand. "It's good to see you, Charlie. Let me introduce Karl Wagner and William "Red" Coyler. These are two of your newest hires. Karl was with the Roosevelts in New York. Red was working for the Vanderbilts in Rhode Island. They both are experts in several areas, including protecting high-profile assets."

Charlie smiled at each of them. "Welcome, it's great to have ya here. I want your input as we discuss our current situation. Bailey, please sit next to me, and you guys sit across from us, maybe next to Harry." Charlie pointed to Sinclair.

Harry nodded. "Good afternoon, I'm Harry Sinclair."

Charlie said, "He owns Sinclair Oil Company, and he is involved in running the Exchange National Bank as well. He discovered the vandalism at the bank."

Karl and Red smiled as they took their seats.

A young man walked into the room. He looked over six feet tall, medium-built, and around thirty years of age. He walked with confidence straight to the group. "I'm Lt. Lindsay McGregor, Tulsa Police Department."

Before they could make additional introductions, a shout came from the doorway, "Mr. Kelly," called a bellhop, "hurry outside, we have someone hurt asking for you."

Chapter 18

Creating Focus

March 1920

CHARLIE LED THE GROUP out of the room and through the lobby. Outside on the sidewalk lay Richard Murphy, dazed but coming around to his senses.

Charlie bent down next to him. "Can ya hear me? Are ya okay?"

Richard shook his head, blinked his eyes a few times, and then said, "I hear you, and I've been better. I asked a bellhop if he knew you and where your meeting was. I then heard this growl, "You're with that asshole Kelly. And wham, I'm seeing stars."

"Did you see who it was?" asked Bailey.

"No, I didn't get a look at the guy. Help me up. I'll be alright."

They all walked with Richard into the meeting room, including a bellhop, the desk clerk, and even a couple of hotel guests, and he found an empty chair.

Susan said, "Richard, are you sure we don't need to call a doctor? The hotel must have someone they call."

"No, I've been hit harder. I wish I could have got my hands on the bum, though. I might have needed some help, but we would have him here."

Charlie said, "What about somethin' to drink?"

"Not water."

Susan giggled, "Okay then, what?"

"Bourbon, neat. Make it a double."

"Too bad that's been outlawed," Susan said with sympathy.

"Don't I know it," Richard said.

Charlie noticed the bellhop that had followed the crowd into the room. He pulled out his room key. "You know where our room is?"

"Yes, sir," the boy gulped. "The Presidential Suite."

"Good. Please go up to our room. I have a bottle of medicinal bourbon on a table there. Please bring it down for me." He handed the young man five dollars.

Richard said, "Thanks, I'm goin' to be fine, but I have questions, many questions."

Charlie raised his voice to be heard throughout the room. "I need everyone out of here except those invited to my meeting. And all meeting members, let's git to our seats at the table."

With the help of the maître d' the room emptied, and Charlie walked over to close the door. He saw the bellhop coming with the bottle, so he waited.

Charlie took the bourbon and said, "What's your name, son?"

"Sam, sir."

"Thanks, Sam."

Charlie walked over and poured Richard his drink. "We'll need to pass this around since I believe Richard isn't the only one who needs a stiff drink. Now let's git this meetin' goin'."

Everyone scooted their chairs as needed to position themselves to see and hear best.

Charlie surveyed the faces around the table. "I don't think we all know who we are sittin' with, so I want us to go around the table, and each of us introduce ourselves and provide a short statement of our background. I'll start. I'm Charles Kelly but everyone can call me Charlie." He turned his gaze to Susan. "My wife, Susan, and I own the Kramer Group, which includes banking, oil, railroads, working ranches, construction, retailing, and security. At my request, we're here today due to the vandalism at the Exchange Bank. Susan, you're next."

Susan smiled as she stood. "As Charlie said, I'm his wife and proud to be. I was kidnapped, as a few of you know." She looked at Lt. McGregor. "Law enforcement caught the people responsible. Well, one was killed and the other is in jail." Her face grew stern as she continued. "Charlie and I are tired of us and our business assets being the criminal element's targets and want a strong, clear message sent saying messing with any part of the Kramer Group will not be tolerated and future activities will come at a high cost."

Charlie said, "Thanks, Susan. Richard, if you're ready, tell us about yourself."

Richard raised his bourbon, "First, let me thank everyone for your response to my situation a few minutes ago. I appreciate it. I'm Richard Murphy, Captain, Oklahoma Bureau of Investigation.

I got to know the Kellys when Susan was kidnapped. I also was in Cushing with them in January when they were dealing with damage to their oil refineries. I am here to offer the complete support of the OBI in finding, arresting, and prosecuting whoever is behind these incidents."

"Thanks, Richard. Lieutenant, you're up."

"Thanks, Mr. Kelly."

"We're fellow Irishmen, and for that reason alone, you can call me Charlie."

"Sure, Charlie. And please call me Lindsay. I'm here representing the City of Tulsa's Police Department. I was the on-scene commander at the bank this morning. I will be heading up the team of detectives working to locate and arrest those involved."

"Harry, you're next."

"I'm Harry Sinclair. I own the Sinclair Oil Company and am the President of the Exchange National Bank. We had vandalism at the bank last night. The police captured two of the individuals involved." Harry smiled at Susan, then continued, "I never expected getting into business with the Kellys would bring this kind of excitement."

Charlie smiled and shrugged. "Harry, we didn't expect it either, but Susan and I sure hope ya still would've joined us. Karl, it's your turn."

He nodded. "Thank you. I'm Karl Wagner. I've just arrived here in Tulsa. This is my first time in this city. As of last month, I worked for Teddy Roosevelt Jr. as his Chief of Security. I had worked in the same role for his father. Before him, I worked special operations for the U.S. Army during the Great War."

"Welcome, Karl, we look forward to workin' with ya. Red, you're next."

"I'm Red Coyler. As of last month, I was Chief of Security for William Vanderbilt III, living in Newport, Rhode Island. I was in the same unit during the War as Karl and Bailey, who I'm guessing is up next."

Charlie raised his coffee cup as a sign of recognition. "We welcome ya to the Kramer Group too. We look forward to gettin' to know you and Karl. Well, our last person is Bailey."

"Thanks, Charlie. I'm Bailey Muldoon, President of the Kramer National Security Company. I was Regional Manager for Pinkerton. I was responsible for the area from Chicago south to New Orleans on the east and Denver south to El Paso on the west. Before that, I was the commander of the unit Karl and Red mentioned during the war. Now I work for the Kellys."

Susan placed her hand on Charlie's arm. "Charlie, and I want to thank each of you for your time. Three of you work for us, and we are meeting two of you and the Lieutenant for the first time." She looked at everyone individually. "Again, thanks for being here."

Charlie said, "She's much better with words than I'll ever be. We are grateful. Okay, Lindsay, share whatever ya can with us regarding what your team has learned about the incident at the bank."

Lt. McGregor stood up. "Two of our officers were on patrol in the downtown area and saw four men at the corner of Third and Boston as they got out of two trucks and began breaking windows at the Exchange Bank. By the time our officers got to the building, two were inside, and the other two saw the officers coming and fled in their truck. One of the men inside was painting a message on a wall, and the other was destroying whatever he could. We have them both in custody. The message on the wall said, "Greetings from Chicago." The men hadn't divulged anything when I left to come here. But there were fading letters on their truck doors that read Pendleton Concrete Kansas City, Missouri. Does the message on the wall or Pendleton Concrete mean anything to anyone?"

Susan said, "The Kramer Group owns a construction company in Kansas City which was in competition for business with the Pendleton Concrete Company. The Black Hand in Chicago owned Pendleton. They used the concrete company to launder illegal money. We managed to get the Missouri Attorney General involved and ended up shutting down their K.C. operations. After that, Tom Pendleton was killed. Not by us, the AG thinks it was the mobsters turning on their own man. They have been operating at a low profile in Kansas City since then.

"And how did you know there was a message on the wall at the bank," the Lieutenant asked Charlie. "Mr. Sinclair mentioned that you knew what the words were when you called him this morning."

"Since what happened in K.C., we have had vandalism or some form of damage in two other locations here in Oklahoma. One employee was almost killed. The locations are a quarry we bought over in Sapulpa and oil refineries in Cushing. In both locations, the message, 'Greetings from Chicago' had been painted on the wall. That's how I knew a similar message was at the bank."

Bailey said, "Lt. McGregor, my sources have indicated that it is reasonable to attribute all of these attacks to the Chicago Outfit."

"Who are they?" Harry asked. "I don't follow much news about Chicago unless it's the commodities market."

"Their new leader is Johnny Torrio," Bailey said. "I can't say how or when, but I've met the man, and I don't consider it a privilege. He's ruthless. They operate using intimidation when they can. But I'll tell you from observation; you do not intimidate Charlie and Susan Kelly."

Richard added, "It doesn't appear to me that Torrio is trying to hide who's behind this."

Bailey said, "He won't. Torrio is a very confident bully and he's very cunning. He moved to Chicago from New York about ten years ago. The information I have is that he was invited to Chicago by "Big Jim" Colosimo to be his muscle and Torrio worked his way up in Colosimo's organization. Up until a month ago, Colosimo ran things. He has always been less inclined to get into violence when he didn't need to, which may be why things have been quiet in the past year."

"What changed?" asked Harry.

"We're not sure. My informants in Chicago think that Colosimo may be going through a divorce of all things, so maybe his attention has wandered, and this has given Torrio a chance to flex his muscle."

"Or maybe he's making a move on his boss," added Richard. Bailey acknowledged that with a nod.

Karl asked, "Bailey, how hard would it be to meet with Torrio face-to-face?"

Bailey thought for a minute, then said, "I doubt he would agree to a scheduled meeting. But we might be able to surprise him somehow."

Charlie said, "I say face-to-face sounds like somethin' he would never expect. I want the unexpected, and I want it at a place, and at a time he would never think possible."

Red added, "I like what Charlie is describing. I'm sure that would intimidate even someone like Torrio. When Briggs, Wyatt, and Josh get here, let's sit down and come up with something we can offer our new boss."

Richard said, "Are you planning on—"

Charlie interrupted him, "I'm not sayin' we kill the guy. We at the Kramer Group aren't mobsters. But if we do this right, he'll know he's alive only because we don't use murder as a weapon, like he does."

Harry asked, "Are you saying you want to go to Chicago yourself and be part of this?"

"Exactly. I want... No, I would love to go into Torrio's home and stand over him in his bed at 3:30 in the morning with a lantern in his face and say, "Stay the hell away from me, my family, and my company."

Bailey said, "Damn, Charlie, that would put fear in anyone."

Lindsay said, "I doubt there is a police force anywhere dealing with people like Torrio who would arrest you for breaking and entering. I know I wouldn't. I agree it might work. The sooner you can do it, the better. We don't want drive-by shootings with machine guns like they have in Chicago."

Bailey asked, "Charlie, a nighttime mission like you described is one of the things my guys and I have done for the Army. Do you want us to develop a plan to execute what you described?"

"If there are no objections from our law enforcement folks, yes, it is what I want you to do."

Richard said, "I'll be happy to help plan it."

Lindsay said, "I support it, and we'll make the perps we have in custody available to you."

Harry said, "Charlie, you are not the sweet, brilliant young businessman I thought you were."

Susan said, "Oh, yes, he is. But you don't want to get him mad at you."

Sinclair laughed. "I'll not be one to mess with him."

Charlie replied, "Let me make this clear to everyone. To some extent, I can tolerate messages on walls, broken windows, and most damage to real estate, but when ya put one of my people in the hospital, or kill someone as they did in Kansas City, you have pushed me too far. I don't plan to kill anyone or even put them in a hospital, but I will defend myself, and I expect all my people to defend themselves when they are in jeopardy." He stood, smiled, and said, "I think this meetin' is over. We are as far as we can go today. Bailey, once all your new hires are in Tulsa, let's get together. Do any of you from law enforcement want to continue to participate in planning meetings?"

Richard and Lindsay both said they would. Charlie closed the meeting. Before getting out of their seats Susan leaned over to her man. "I'm proud of you. You are a great natural leader."

Charlie said, "Thanks, Sweetheart, I appreciate it."

Chapter 19

News, Good and Bad

March 1920

CHARLIE AND SUSAN WERE almost dressed to go to breakfast when the phone rang. Charlie answered, "Hello, this is Charles."

"Charlie, this is Hank."

"Hey Hank, good mornin' to ya."

"And to you too. Last night, we began gettin' those sounds and tremors signalin' somethin' is about to happen at our drillin' site here in Garfield County. I'm in Elmore City now, but I'm headin' back to be with the crew when we finish talkin'. I wanted you to know what was happenin'."

"Thanks, buddy. Call me this evenin' with an update. Leave a message at the front desk if you miss me."

"Sure will. I gotta go. Goodbye."

Susan stuck her head out of the bathroom. "Was it Hank? Which one? I thought I heard you say, Hank."

"It was Hank Thomas callin' from Elmore City. It sounds like we'll have another producin' well sometime soon. He thinks they'll hit oil maybe as soon as today."

Susan returned to the mirror above the sink. "Great, Honey. He's on a winning streak. He can't get it right every time, but that's wonderful news."

"I agree he can't git it right every time. But he sure does has a winnin' track record. His phone call was a much better way to start the day than what we've had way too often lately. I'm ready to go to breakfast."

"Me too." Susan stepped into the room wearing gray trousers and a light blue shirt. "I'm prepared and determined to put a smile on your face all day." Her cleavage was in view for

Charlie to enjoy.

"I love ya, Sweetheart. You look beautiful as always. I'll try to focus on business for the next several hours and then this evening let's go over to the house."

"Thank you, Charlie. And what a beautiful way to end the day."

***

As they walked across the restaurant toward their table, Bailey spotted them. He was sitting at a table with a stranger. He waved at the couple to join them.

As they neared Bailey's table Charlie asked, "Who is this here with ya?"

Bailey and his companion stood. The new man was nearly Charlie's height. Bailey said, "Charles and Susan Kelly, this is Briggs Collins, another of our new hires. He came in on the midnight train. This only leaves Wyatt and Joshua to arrive. They should be here this afternoon."

Charlie offered his hand. "Welcome to the Kramer Group. Susan and I look forward to gettin' to know you. Bailey, I mentioned as we were endin' the meetin' yesterday, we should get together after everyone arrives. I'll get the hotel to get us a room for us to use tomorrow evenin'. We'll have steak dinners, and everyone can order the beverage of their choice."

Briggs said, "It's great to meet you, folks. I also look forward to getting to know you. It's generous of you to provide such a fine welcome meal."

Bailey said, "You thought you had a good situation with the Rockefellers, which you did, but coming to the Kramer National Security Company will be the best move you'll ever make."

Susan nodded. "Thanks Bailey. We do our best to provide a good experience for the people who work for us." She held out her hand to Briggs who gave her a gentle shake. "Mr. Collins, we hope you have found a home with us. Welcome."

As Charlie and Susan continued toward their table Susan looked back over her shoulder at Briggs. "Bailey has indicated he knew these men in the Army. How much has he shared about them and what they did?"

They arrived at their table and took their usual chairs across from each other.

"He said they worked together, and they did special missions. I don't know any more about them."

With her back to the room, Susan tilted her head as her eyebrows furrowed. “I’m happy we have them, I think, but I would like to know more about them and what they will do for us.”

“I agree. Remind me to ask them as they’re leaving now.” He spotted their waiter heading over. ”Looks like our waiter is Jeff today.”

Susan adjusted her shirt. “How do I look?”

Charlie winked. “Perfect.” He looked up at Jeff. “Oh, hello Jeff, how are ya today?”

Susan faced the waiter. “Yes, how are things?”

Jeff looked down at Susan, gulped, and immediately looked to Charlie. “Oh… I’m g…great. Can, uh, I get you, folks, some coffee? And, uh, do y… you want your usual order?”

Charlie replied, “Yes to both of those.”

Susan flirted, “We’re so sleepy and starved this morning, please hurry back.”

“Uh… I will, Miss Kelly.”

After Jeff walked away, Charlie smiled. “Susan, you’re so bad.”

She put her hands on her hips and tilted her head and shared a coy smile. “Hey, I’m just doing what you said you wanted.”

“I guess ya got me there. I love ya, Sweetheart, more than words can say.”

They enjoyed their teasing and banter with each other through breakfast, and Charlie noticed Bailey was walking back into the restaurant. “Here comes Bailey,” he said. Susan checked her blouse and closed one of the buttons.

“Bailey, what’s up?” Charlie asked.

Bailey stopped next to their table and stood where he could see both of their faces as he talked.

Susan added, “Yes, Bailey, is there something wrong?”

“No, I just got a call from Wyatt and Josh. They were delayed out of Chicago, and they just arrived in Kansas City. They have a two-hour layover and will be arriving here tonight around 9:00.”

Susan dabbed her mouth with her napkin. “Good. Get them settled in rooms and make sure they have anything they need.”

Charlie said, “I want tomorrow’s dinner meetin’ to be just you, your guys, and the two of us. We want to get better acquainted with your team and them with us. We want you and your team’s first thoughts on what we must do to win against these Chicago assholes.”

Bailey nodded at Susan then looked at Charlie. “We’ll have a solid plan when we meet with you tomorrow night.”

Susan smiled. “Great, Bailey, see ya then.”

As Bailey walked away, Susan looked at Charlie and winked, "He's a handsome guy. Don't you think, Sweetheart?"

"Sure, and he knows I'm a lucky man. I think he and all his men are single. That would be somethin' to ask about tomorrow evenin'. It doesn't matter. I'm just curious."

Susan asked, "Jealous?"

"No, just curious."

"Okay. What do we need to do today?"

Charlie said, "We need to make sure the telephones are installed in our house where we asked and ready for use when we move in on Friday. I thought I might spend the afternoon getting updates from Rice, Bunk, Jim, Zane, Gordon, and Owen. Each of them has a project they should have made some progress on since I last heard. By the time I'm through with them, we could start preparin' for tonight at the house."

Susan put her coffee cup back on its saucer. "I would like to be part of those conversations. Why don't we do those calls from our suite which will allow me to hear what is said."

"Of course, Sweetheart, I did not intend for ya not to be part of those updates. They're not expectin' a call, so I may not catch all of them. A call to Uncle Curt might be smart too. I don't expect these calls to take all day. We might go to Bishop's for lunch, whattaya think?"

"We can. Let's go upstairs and start now."

***

The calls that morning went well with nothing unexpected from Rice or Bunk. Jim Townsley had been out of the office so Charlie and Susan had enjoyed some 'play time' on the couch in their suite before heading for lunch. As they walked into the suite after returning from Bishop's, the phone rang.

Susan walked over and answered it. "Hello, this is Susan Kelly."

A voice screamed so loud she had to hold the earpiece away from her head. "Hank, Hank, settle down, and I'll get him." Her heart raced as she turned to Charlie. "It's Hank Thomas, and he's going crazy."

Charlie took the phone from her. "Hank buddy, what's up?"

Hank said, "We have a gusher!"

Charlie's eyes widened. "Git outta here."

Hank then shared the bad news.

"Are ya on the level with me? It can't be. Really?"

Susan asked, "Charlie, what is it?"

"Hank says the well came in and blew so hard it destroyed most of the derrick. It's gonna be a big producer. But in the explosion of oil and collapse of the derrick we lost two roughnecks. Our Toolpusher, Seth Spaulding and a Worm. I don't know the name of the Worm."

Charlie flopped down on the sofa. "Whatta we do, Hank?"

Hank said, "I'll handle it. Seth had been with me for years. He has a family. The Worm, I think, is an orphan and new to the crew. I'll do some checking before I say what's next."

Charlie sighed. "Hey buddy, I better let ya go so ya can git back out to the site. I know ya can handle everything, but Susan and I will come down there tomorrow. She needs to see what we risk every day at a drillin' site. Call me in the mornin'."

Susan reached over and placed her hand on Charlie's cheek. "People died at our well site?"

Still holding the phone, he turned to Susan and nodded. "Yes, I think we need to go to Garvin County. The well site is west of Elmore City. That's where we met, ya know?"

She smiled. "Oh, I remember, my Darling."

He said, "I'll contact Harry, Bill, and Bailey. We need to postpone those meetings."

She patted his arm. "I agree, Sweetheart."

He returned to the phone call. "Hank, we'll come tomorrow. I'll let you go for now, goodbye."

The couple took a break and went for a long walk to allow themselves to recover from the bad news. As they rode the elevator up to the twelfth floor Susan said, "If you're ready, let's get back to our phone calls. We need to get our minds on something positive."

"You're right. I was waiting to let you say something. Let's make the calls but keep them brief so we can prepare to leave tomorrow morning."

***

Their calls in the afternoon went better than the call from Hank had. The only significant news was that Owen McGill mentioned they had an opportunity to purchase part of the Rock Island Railroad. The three decided it would be good for Owen to pursue that purchase. That had lifted their spirits some, though the news from Hank was still in their thoughts. They arranged for the hotel to pack them food and headed to their house. They arrived at their Madison Avenue house at about 6:30 just as the sun was setting. Emilia and her workers were gone.

Susan said, "Charlie, let's have a look around. I want to see what the house looks like furnished." They entered the house from the patio. She said, "Oh, this is beautiful; it's just how Emilia described it and what I pictured in my mind."

Charlie said, "The furniture is nice, and it fits the house so well."

They spent enough time looking around that it was full dark when they got back to the patio. They turned on the lights and Charlie started a fire in the fireplace before they removed their clothes and dove into their heated pool.

Susan swam a few laps, then climbed out and said, "Sweetheart, let's open one of our bottles of wine we stashed away and lay back and relax."

Charlie looked at her, enjoyed how the water gave her body a glow, and replied, "You're right." He climbed out of the pool. "Let's end today with good food, good wine, and each other."

Chapter 20

Elmore City

March 1920

CHARLIE WAS OUT OF bed, showered, and dressed early the next morning. He called the Leland Hotel in Pauls Valley where Hank was staying and arranged a room for Susan and him.

Susan joined Charlie in the living room of the suite as she dried off from her shower. "Did you get us a room?"

"I did. I also spoke with Hank. He knows we'll be there around lunchtime. I asked him for the latest on the two who died. He met with Seth's family and told his wife we would cover the burial expenses. He also recommended we provide a financial package for the Spaulding family. Some amount to help his widow for a while."

Susan said, "By all means. But, what about the other guy?"

"He couldn't find any family or anyone who knew him. So, he'll be buried in the Elmore City graveyard at our expense."

"Okay. We need to talk with Uncle Curt and see what he recommends we offer the widow. Maybe an amount equal to Seth's annual salary plus enough to educate his kids. If she agrees to accept that, then Uncle Curt can send us a check for her and some standard forms for her to sign accepting that as a settlement."

"That makes sense. We can get an update when we arrive down there and call Curt for some guidance. Hank will meet us at the hotel and take us to the well site. He also said to have an appetite when we get there. He wants to eat lunch at the Badger Den Café in Elmore City. He eats every meal he can there."

Susan turned to go to the closet, stopped, and looked back. "Well, I guess that's what we'll do."

***

The car ran perfectly, the roads were decent, and the weather was good. They arrived at the Leland Hotel before noon. As Charlie signed the hotel's registration ledger, he said, "You have a Hank Thomas stayin' here. What room is he in?"

The clerk replied, "We don't give that information out. But he is in the coffee shop, sir."

"Thanks." He turned to Susan. "Let's tell Hank we're here." He turned back to the clerk. "Can you have someone take our bags to our room?"

The clerk nodded. "Of course, here are your room keys."

They headed to the coffee shop and Charlie spotted Hank at a table in the far corner. Hank stood as they arrived and hugged Susan. He then shook Charlie's hand. "I appreciate you two comin' down here. I'm sure you have some questions."

Charlie said, "Susan and I are hungry, let's git on the road. We can chat in the car."

After filling the Cadillac with gas, the trio headed toward Elmore City.

Hank rode in the front seat so he and Charlie could talk. It would also make it easier for him to guide Charlie to the oil field after lunch.

Charlie said, "Our well is west of Elmore City, but how far from town?"

Hank shifted so Susan could hear him too. "It's almost five miles. The well site is closer to the small town of Foster. I'd guess the well is about twenty miles or so from Pauls Valley."

Susan leaned forward. "So, the Leland Hotel is the closest to where we are drilling, right?"

"Not really, Lindsay is a little closer, but the places to stay are not as nice."

At the Badger Den Café in Elmore City, they each ordered the chicken fried steak plate and sweet tea.

As Charlie paid the bill at the cash register, he said, "That was the best chicken fry I've had in a long time. My buddy, Hank, says everythin' on your menu here is just as good. I need to come back and try it all."

The cashier, who was also their waitress said, "The owner is the cook and my husband. He'll be glad to hear this. C'mon back sometime and order our pecan pie. Hope to see you soon."

***

As they pulled up to the well site, Susan gasped at the destruction she saw. The derrick wasn't anywhere in sight, and it looked like a lumber yard had been dumped in the field. Everything was coated with oil and the stench filled the air. "Hank, surely several of your men must have been hurt. I'm amazed more weren't killed."

Hank said, "Four or five were hurt but with only some cuts, bumps, and bruises. No one required a doctor. I see the crew is takin' what's left of the wooden derrick apart. You can see that much of what used to be the top of the derrick is spread around on the ground."

A tall, broad-shouldered man walked toward the car as Charlie brought it to a stop.

Hank said, "Charlie, that's my new Toolpusher. I brought him down from Osage County yesterday."

Susan leaned forward. "Hank, what's a Toolpusher and a Worm? Those seem like crazy titles to me."

Hank laughed. "I guess they are crazy names. A Toolpusher is the supervisor. And the Worm is the new guy. He's usually got little or no experience."

They got out of the car and walked toward the big man.

"Charlie, this is Tom Sweeney. He's been with me from my days with Marland back on the 101 Ranch."

Susan said, "I'm surprised Charlie didn't know him then."

Tom said, "I was down in Payne County workin' a well site in Morrison, ma'am."

Charlie offered his hand. "I'm Charlie Kelly. Glad to meet you."

Tom wiped his hand on his pants. "It's my pleasure, Mr. Kelly. I've been hearin' about ya for a while. Sorry to have such a bad thing happen to get us together." Tom shook his head. "I'm not used to lookin' up at anyone. You're a big man, Mr. Kelly."

Hank turned to head to the derrick. "Tom, fill the Kellys in on where we are today in getting' this well producing."

Tom said, "I don't recommend you folks git much closer because the dirt is still saturated with oil. Ma'am, you'll be a mess, and I doubt you can ever git your shoes and pants clean. We have the pump in place and will complete hooking everything up to bring it online by tomorrow. The gusher took out the derrick and one storage shed. But everything else as far as piping, storage tanks, and the tool sheds are fine. Because of the damage, we can't take the derrick apart our normal way, and it's taking us longer."

Hank turned back to the group, scratched his neck, and

tilted his head. "So, we have a great well, but it is taking a few extra days to git it pumpin'. That's what I hear ya sayin'"

"Yes, sir."

Charlie looked around the area and back to Tom. "Hank, I'd say Tom's saved Kelly Oil some big money by gittin' this place cleaned up and operatin' as fast as he has. You agree?"

"I sure do. He's someone I've always counted on. And he's always come through for me. And now he's come through for Kelly Oil."

Susan stepped in the middle of the men. "I look at this and can see that the oil business, although a true money maker, is also dangerous. I don't need to see anymore and based on what I see and what I've heard today, Tom, I hope we have more men like you to help us grow Kelly Oil."

Tom smiled. "Thank you, Mrs. Kelly. You folks will always git my best every day."

Charlie said, "Susan is right. We owe ya, Tom. I wish she could have seen the crew and Seth Spaulding working to bring this well in... maybe someday."

Hank put his hand on Charlie's shoulder. "We better let Tom alone. He's got a big job still ahead of him. Do ya want to go meet Seth's family?"

Susan glanced at Charlie. "Hank, where are they?"

"I saw them last night at a place they were renting in Foster. Mrs. Spaulding is from Hollis and her folks still live there. Her father picked her and the kids up this morning to take them home with him. She told me last night about how much she appreciated us covering the burial expenses."

Charlie said, "We need to go back to Tulsa in the morning. So that means we won't be able to see Seth's family. When we git to the hotel tonight, let's call Uncle Curt and discuss everything."

Susan nodded. "Good."

Hank said, "Fine with me."

***

They arrived back at the Leland Hotel in Pauls Valley before sunset. They called Uncle Curt first thing. He agreed with the plan the trio had discussed, and he would send the check and forms by courier tomorrow. Hank would deliver to the widow.

After the phone call was complete, Hank said, "I've a date in Stratford this evening. It was great spending some time with you and be careful as ya head back to Tulsa in the morning."

As Hank walked away, Charlie looked at Susan. "Didja see

the patio with a fireplace on the west side of the hotel?"

"No, I didn't, Sweetheart. Do ya think we can have food brought to us there this evening? It's been warm today, but after the sun goes down the fireplace might be perfect."

"I bet we can arrange that. Let's see if we can end our day there."

Chapter 21

Bank Expansion

March 1920

CHARLIE STOOD AT THE foot of the bed in the Leland Hotel in Pauls Valley. "Sweetheart, we've gotta hit the road. I called Harry last night while you were changing before dinner and our meetin' with him and Bill Skelly at the Hotel Tulsa will be this afternoon. Did I mention it to ya?"

"Uh, no, you didn't! And if we're late, you're in trouble."

She jumped out of bed and went straight to the shower. Charlie went to the phone.

Charlie called the restaurant maître d' in Tulsa, and said, "Pierre, we're meetin' Harry and Bill this afternoon. If they arrive first, please seat them at our table."

He joined Susan in the shower, and they rushed to get ready.

***

That afternoon as Susan and Charlie walked across the hotel lobby, Bill Skelly walked through the hotel's main entrance. He waved and pointed behind them as he said, "Afternoon, and Harry is coming out of the elevator behind you."

Susan smiled and said, "Great timing, we were afraid we would be late. I didn't think we would make it from Pauls Valley."

The group was led to Charlie and Susan's usual table and took their orders. As coffee was delivered, Harry asked, "What's the latest on the vandals and the Chicago Mob?"

Charlie said, "Nothing new. Our security company president, Bailey Muldoon, has hired some specialists, and we're meetin' with them tonight. Bailey has been doin' some investigatin', and he and his crew are supposed to have some recommendations for us tonight."

Skelly said, "I've got a friend in the aviation business in Chicago. He says a group of gangsters continue to terrorize Chicago. Innocent people have been killed because they were in the wrong place when those hoodlums drive by and shoot Tommy guns at their enemies."

Susan shook her head. "How awful. Can't the police do anything about them?"

Skelly said, "These gangsters all have police on their payroll and know when to expect the raids when the police don't just turn a blind eye on their activities."

Harry said, "It sounds like they have more weapons than anything the police have, should they be inclined to do anything. Charlie, we have our work cut out for us, don't we?"

Charlie nodded, "We just need to put fear in their leaders. They use it, and now we must give them somethin' to fear. I hope our guys have some good ideas tonight. Now let's talk about banking and aviation, okay?"

Susan asked, "Harry, we want to grow Exchange National. Add some new branches, have you got any ideas beyond Greenwood where we should focus first?"

Harry said, "An obvious location would be Oklahoma City. It's the largest city in the state as well as the capital. I've been considering it for my oil interest as well as banking for a good while."

Charlie asked, "Why didn't ya move on the idea?"

"Money. I didn't want to pull cash out of the oil company, and my former banking partners only wanted to serve the oil business here in Tulsa."

Susan frowned as she shook her head. "They're being very short-sighted if you ask me. Our banking system wouldn't exist if we ran our operation using a similar policy. You can't be a successful leader in the banking business if you limit your clientele to one industry. You may not serve all industries, but you should never limit yourself to one."

Harry replied, "You're right, of course, but I couldn't go it alone. Do you have any ideas?"

Charlie answered, "Yes, we do. I want to explore three places. Oklahoma City is a good recommendation, but I want to add Cushing. I see it growin', and since it's got a growin' oil business it won't require much effort by your existing staff. The final place is right here in Tulsa. I want to add at least one or two more branches beyond Greenwood."

Harry's eyes grew big, and he leaned back in his chair.

Charlie asked, "What's wrong?"

"Don't we want to make sure Greenwood is successful, first?"

"After our meeting last month, I'm confident the businessmen will grow a very profitable bank in Greenwood. I was impressed with their imagination and their guts from the first time we met them. Johnathan was as well."

Harry asked, "You agree with this, Susan? You come from a family of bankers, and I'm curious what you think."

Without hesitation, Susan said, "We're in the banking business. We loan money to people who are smart at making money. I don't care whether they are Cherokee, Chinese, Mexican, Negroes, or Irish if they know how to make money and are responsible when paying back a loan, we'll continue to loan them the money."

Bill said, "Makes sense to me. There are some thriving businesses over in Greenwood."

Harry thought a minute and said, "Well, you're right. I'll start looking at where we could locate a branch in Oklahoma City, Cushing, and at least one more in Tulsa. I'm sure that'll be just the start of further expansion in Oklahoma."

Charlie leaned back. "Harry, we'll end up with more than three in Tulsa, Oklahoma City, and at least one in some other places as well."

Skelly asked, "Charlie, have you thought any more about aviation and joining me in supporting this fledgling industry?"

Charlie said, "I haven't thought about it much, but not because of lack of interest. I've had a lot on my plate with expansions in oil, banking, and retail interests. I promise when things settle down, especially with this Chicago bunch, I'll join ya, and we'll talk about nothing else."

The maître d' came to the table and said, "Pardon me, Mr. Kelly, but you have a call at the front desk."

Charlie turned to Susan with a concerned expression.

She said, "I hope everything is alright."

"Me too,"

He went to the lobby, and the desk clerk pointed to the wall phone.

"Hello, this Charles Kelly, who am I talkin' with?"

"Charlie, it's Boss. I wanted to tell ya we have an agreement to buy the 5,000 acres we discussed. They finally agreed to $125,000. I know ya would have gone higher, but I thought it was a fair amount, and they agreed to it an hour ago. I used the paperwork ya gave me to get it in writin', and I gave them a check for $10,000 as earnest money."

"Boss, that's great. Hank is sure we'll hit oil up in the north pasture near the old house. One oil well will make our money back. Good job, Boss. You should have his number, call Curt Schlegell in Kansas City and tell him all the details, and he'll work at gettin' the closin' date established. I'll let ya go. I need to git back to a meetin'. Again, great job. Goodbye."

Charlie went back to the table, with a smile on his face, and he shared the gist of the phone call. They wrapped up the meeting. As they were leaving, Bill Skelly said, "Charlie, don't forget to call when you're free. And I would love to see your ranch sometime. I'm sure it's nice."

Susan said, "We'll have you and Gertrude down to our Madison house soon, and we would love to have you down to the ranch. It is beautiful down there."

Harry said, "Call me tomorrow and let me know how the meeting tonight with your security folks goes, okay?"

"I will, Harry, you guys have a good day."

After everyone left, Susan said, "Cleta and Attie should be here anytime. They're bringing all their stuff and some of our clothes. Cleta said they would have one of the hands drive them up in a truck. Do you want to take them over to the house today or wait till morning?"

"I say, wait till tomorrow. Let's give Cleta and Attie a night off. We can have dinner here and give them money for a movie while we meet with Bailey. We can all go over there together in the mornin' after breakfast. Emilia should be expecting us around 9:00."

***

Charlie and Susan got the ranch crew settled into their hotel rooms and then took Cleta and Attie out to show them Tulsa. They had a nice dinner and then dropped the two women off at the theater.

Both Charlie and Susan wanted to change before meeting with Bailey and his team.

"I'm lookin' forward to spendin' the evenin' with the guys," Charlie said. "All of them are around thirty years old and compared to most have life experiences well beyond people in their sixties. Bailey is the oldest, and he's only thirty-four. The youngest is Josh, and he's twenty-eight."

Susan stopped on her way to the bedroom and looked at Charlie. "Then all of them are older than us. I'm twenty-six, and you're twenty-two. I would say you're the person who has lived a full life." She stood there a moment with her hands on her hips, focused on his eyes, and said, "They may not have captured cattle rustlers, beat a kidnapper to a pulp, or been shot by gangsters by the time they were twenty-two."

Charlie grinned, "Damn, you're gorgeous when ya git fired-up. Save some of it for the guys tonight. Do you have anythin' you want discussed on the agenda tonight?"

"I want to walk out of the room tonight, knowing these men are dedicated to you and me for reasons beyond a good pay-check. I don't know right now what needs to be said or what they need to see from us to create loyalty. But I think going against a bunch like the Chicago Outfit will require more than a paycheck. I'm not sure how you can put it on an agenda."

Charlie nodded his agreement. "I've been in meetins' where you can see men start to lean back in their chairs and go to sleep. I don't expect it from this group. We do need them focused on you and me and creatin' loyalty to us and our goals. I don't think it will be as hard for ya to git their attention. You'll do it with your good looks, but I'll need to capture their attention some other way."

Susan said, "I'm not worried about getting them to listen or look at me for the same reasons you do. I know I can ensure it happens." She smiled with confidence. "I'll be stunned if they don't stare at me some. But I want their buy-in to eliminate the threat posed by the Chicago bunch. This team needs to share our goals and want to wipe out that threat."

Charlie snapped the top button on his pants and tightened his belt. "I agree, so let's git movin'."

Chapter 22

The New Team

March 1920

CHARLIE AND SUSAN ARRIVED downstairs and went to the bar, which was still open despite them not being able to sell any alcohol. Bailey and his team were already there. "Bailey, good to see y'all. I hope you had a good dinner. Sorry we couldn't join you, but we had our staff from the ranch up here and we wanted to show them a good time."

Bailey said, "It was, and thanks for picking up the tab."

As they all took seats at a large corner booth Susan noticed all the men's eyes were on her. She knew she was showing some cleavage. She planned to use her looks to her advantage tonight, as she often did in business meetings. She needed to see if any of them could be easily distracted by a woman using her feminine wiles.

Susan looked at Bailey. "Although we've already met some of them, can you have these gentlemen give Charlie and me their names and something about them."

Bailey said, "Of course, Miss Kelly."

She looked around the group. "For tonight, gentlemen, it's Susan. Let's start."

Bailey smiled and nodded across the table. "Good. Men, include your most recent employer and what you did in the war. Josh, why don't you start us off."

"Of course, I'm Josh Harrington, I was a detective working for the BOI out of their Chicago office. I had been with them in Philadelphia until about a year ago. During the war, my specialties were weapons and medical support. I speak German, French, and Spanish."

The man sitting next to Josh said, "Good evening, I'm Wyatt

Hake. I also was a detective for the Bureau in Chicago. Before that, I was in New York. During the war, my specialty was intelligence. I speak German, Italian, and Greek."

The next man they had met at their earlier meeting. "We met the other day. I'm Karl Wagner. Recently I was Chief of Security with the Roosevelt family in New York. During the war, I was second in command to Bailey. I have trained in engineering, intelligence, and weapons. I speak German, French, Farsi, and Spanish."

The next man they had also met at the previous meeting. "It's a pleasure to see you again. I'm William "Red" Coyler. I was Chief of Security for William Vanderbilt III in Newport, Rhode Island. During the war, my specialty was weapons and explosives. I speak German, French, Italian, and Spanish."

"You're Briggs," Charlie said. "We met at breakfast the other day." He nodded. "Yes, I'm Briggs Collins, I was Chief of Security for the Rockefeller family in New York. John Jr. was my focus. During the war, my specialty was engineering. I speak German, Italian, and Spanish."

Bailey stood and pointed his left hand at each man and said, "I was their commander during the war. We were a unit created to execute special operations which the typical Army unit was not designed for or trained to do. I know you know my background but to make sure nobody here can't say I don't pull my weight," the group laughed, "previous to your hiring me, I was a Regional Manager for Pinkerton. Before that, I was with the U. S. Secret Service. I speak German, French, Italian, and Greek."

There was a period of questions that followed. Charlie could tell Susan was impressed with the men's professionalism. They certainly appreciated Susan's beauty but maintained an amazing focus on the questions asked of them.

Charlie said, "Thank you, gentlemen." He turned to look at Bailey.

Bailey, do ya have any new general information ya can share with us about this bunch from Chicago?"

"Yes, we do, Charlie. I discussed all three of the recent attacks with everyone. We have learned from Josh and Wyatt that the same kind of damage and messaging has often been used by the Outfit in other locations where they have started operations. They were part of a team dedicated to the Chicago Outfit by OBI. They can speak with personal knowledge about them, so Wyatt, the floor's yours."

Wyatt said, "Thanks, Bailey. I want to say before I start, I'm thrilled to be here. A while back I heard from Bailey about you,

Mr. Kelly. How you're willing to get involved and put your neck on the line. That alone made me want to be a part of this company. Ma'am... I mean, Susan, I also hear you're as brave as any woman Bailey had ever seen in how you handled the kidnapping."

Wyatt lit a cigarette and said, "Johnny Torrio, as of a few months ago, runs the Outfit. That's not official as Colosimo is still officially the head of the group. But he's been tied up in a divorce and Torrio has been taking on more duties."

"There are rumors on the street that Colosimo may be on the way out," added Josh. "But there's no proof of that."

"Torrio is sure acting like he's in charge," Wyatt said. "He's brought in a guy from New York named Alphonse Capone. Capone runs one of their brothels called the Four Deuces. He brings a nasty reputation with him. And Torrio is no angel."

"They also now have Joe and Pete DiGiovanni heading up their Kansas City crew," Josh said. "I'm sure they're the ones who sent the guys who are in custody here in Tulsa."

"These do sound like some dangerous men," Susan said.

Charlie said, "I don't care how dangerous they may think they are, I still aim to put a stop to this." He looked at Wyatt. "You know a lot about them. Can we meet with Torrio?"

"Well, Josh and I know where Torrio lives. We know his habits, and we know the guys he has as his bodyguards. The BOI has some informants who work within and around the Outfit. And we would not want to jeopardize those assets."

Charlie nodded. "My question is, how long would it take to prepare to visit Johnny Torrio's bedroom say at 3:00 some morning?"

Wyatt's eyes went a bit wide. "Bailey said you mentioned that. I thought it was a joke, but I guess not. It sounds like you're serious."

Susan shifted in her chair and faced Wyatt. "He couldn't be more serious, and I'm behind him on this."

Wyatt took a pull on the cigarette and then cleared his throat. "Well, first and foremost, this will require we do this on our own. No law enforcement agency would attempt this, and they would never authorize it by a civilian group." He looked over at Bailey and said, "Sir, do you remember the mission where we went in at night into the bedroom of that Austrian general?"

"A general?" asked Susan.

Karl said, "The general was in an Italian villa near Vittorio Veneto. The battle was the final offensive by the Italians about a week before the end of the war. They soundly defeated the Austro-Hungarian forces at the battle."

Red asked, "Do you think we could use any of that experience for this mission?"

Bailey rubbed his chin and smiled. "An excellent question and a good idea. We need to go to Chicago and look at everything, but my guess is we could do it and not have to fire a shot, the same way we did it in Italy."

Charlie became excited. He placed his elbows on the table as he leaned forward. "Bailey, develop a plan to execute me goin' with the team into Johnny Asshole's bedroom for a face-to-face visit. Come up with this plan as soon as you can. I don't want to drag this out. We've already had one person hurt over in Cushing. We had an employee killed in Kansas City last year by this bunch. Go to Chicago if you must, but I want to get this issue settled within the next thirty days. I need to know if it's possible."

Bailey looked at his guys and smiled, and in unison, they said, "Yes, sir!"

Susan said with emotion in her voice and tears showing in her eyes. "I'm so proud and happy you guys are part of our Kramer Group family."

Bailey looked at Susan and then back to his men and nodded. In unison again, they shouted, "Hoorah."

It startled Susan. But she smiled and said, "I love you guys and your enthusiasm. Charlie, I think we have some real winners here."

Charlie put his arm around Susan's shoulders. "There's no doubt in my mind. I can't wait to hear their plan."

They spent another hour getting to know the team better, including where they had grown up, gone to school, and how they had all met in the army. By the end of the evening Charlie and Susan had their answer as to the loyalty of Bailey's new team.

During their elevator ride as they returned to their suite, Susan said, "I was very impressed with every one of the guys. What about you?"

Charlie said, "I was too." He smiled at her. "But my question is this. Did they pass your test on their ability to focus while you were talkin'?"

"Honey, they didn't try to hide their love for the view, but they were able to maintain their focus and were very articulate. I was impressed, and I don't doubt they will do whatever it takes to get this Johnny Torrio and his bunch out of our lives."

Charlie put his arm across her shoulder. "Good, it's just a matter of time. Well, Beautiful, tomorrow we move into our home."

Chapter 23

The Move

March 1920

SUSAN PUT HER BRUSH down on the vanity, checked her hair in the mirror one more time, and walked from the bathroom into the bedroom of their hotel suite.

"Charlie, you better get up. We need to be at our new house by 9:00. I can call Milt and the girls and ask them to be down to breakfast in forty-five minutes."

Charlie yawned. "Oh... okay. I guess I needed a few extra winks this morning. We spent a long time talking with the men last night."

Susan walked over to the side of their bed. "Well, tonight you'll be able to sleep in our bed on Madison Avenue."

Charlie pumped his fist. "Won't it be great?"

She nodded. "I'll make the call; you go ahead and get ready. I wish I could join you in the shower, but there's no time."

***

They had entered the lobby heading to the restaurant when a registration desk clerk came running to them. "Mr. Kelly, you have what sounds like an important phone call."

Charlie and Susan hurried over to the wall phone.

They put their heads together and Charlie held the receiver so they could hear. "Hello, this is Charles Kelly."

"Charlie, this is George Miller, I got this number from Boss." He struggled to stifle a cry, gained control then said, "I've some awful news." His voice broke as he said, "My brother Zack is dead. He fell from his horse and struck his head on a corral rail."

Susan squeezed Charlie's arm. "Oh, Sweetheart."

Charlie's chin quivered. He hesitated long enough to control his emotions. "George, I'm so... so sorry." He struggled to continue. "Uh... how can we help you and your family?"

George said, "Can you come to the service next Wednesday?"

Charlie looked at Susan who was nodding. "Of course, is there anything else?"

"Well, the service is the main thing. Although, I was planning to call you in about a month on another matter. Would you and Susan be able to stay an extra day or so?"

Susan said, "George, it's Susan. Yes, of course we can, and will."

Charlie said, "We'll stay... I'll ask again. Is there anything else we can do?"

"No, but come on Tuesday, and we'll have a room ready for you here in the White House. I'll see you then. Okay?"

"We'll be there Tuesday afternoon, and again, we're so sorry."

***

They went to their table. The others had arrived and were looking at their menus.

Cleta saw their faces. "What's wrong? You both look awful."

Susan took her seat. "We just received a call from George Miller from the 101 Ranch. His brother Zack is dead." She looked at Charlie. "He can't believe it happened. George said Zack fell from his horse, and his head struck a fence rail. The funeral service will be next Wednesday. We told George we would come."

Attie leaned in. "Of course. What a tragedy for the Miller family. It was an accident, then?"

Charlie took a sip of coffee. "He implied it, and I'm sure it's true. Zack was such a brilliant horseman. I'm sure there must have been somethin' he couldn't or didn't see and it spooked his horse. George wants us there on Tuesday evenin'. He also asked for us to stay for an extra day or so. He has somethin' he needs to discuss with Susan and me."

Susan added, "We will stay however long we need to. But we do have a lot on our plate already. I hope he doesn't need your help with something requiring a long commitment of your time."

"I agree." He looked around the table. "Well, hello folks, how are ya? Oh, here comes the waiter, have ya picked somethin' out?"

Cleta smiled as she tried to lighten the mood. "Hello, Charlie." She looked around the table. "I think we're ready."

They ordered and ate, and while Cleta and Attie tried to keep the mood light and filled with excitement about moving in, the news of Zack's death had dampened Charlie's excitement a bit.

***

Emilia stood on the front porch waiting for them as they pulled into the driveway. From the car, Susan motioned for her to meet them around back. Charlie and Milt drove to the garage area and parked. As they got out of their vehicles, Cleta and Attie were awestruck by the home's beauty and the neighborhood around it.

Attie said, "This is a mansion. I can't believe we'll be living here."

Cleta nodded and spun around gazing at everything. "How can anyone afford this? Miss Susan, you and Charlie must be doin' even better than we thought."

Susan laughed. "Charlie and I are happy you like the place. We are thrilled to share it with you."

Emilia smiled as she came from the back door to meet them. "Welcome to your new home."

Susan beamed. "Thank you. Emilia." She indicated with her outstretched arm. "This is Cleta and Attie, they are our cook and housekeeper. They're also going to be living here in the servant's quarters."

Emilia turned to Cleta and Attie, "Excellent, I hope you like what we've done with your area. You'll share a living room and kitchen. You'll find that each of you has your own bedroom and private full bath."

Attie said, "I'm sure we'll love it. We'll start unloading, Miss Susan, if you'll show us where to go."

Susan said, "Emilia, why don't we start with their area?'

"Of course, Susan, let's go." She led them to their private entrance off the driveway.

Charlie and Milt followed them after a quick trip to the loaded truck.

Emilia entered first, turned and said, "Ladies, here is your new home."

Cleta gasped, "Merciful heavens, this is wonderful. The color scheme is nice. I love the beige walls and white ceiling. Those must be ten-foot ceilings in this living room and kitchen. And the furniture is so beautiful and fits the home."

Emilia said, "The ceilings are the same in the bedrooms, and the furniture comes from the same store and manufacturer used throughout the property. Look in your bedroom."

Attie walked toward the nearest one as she said, "Are they different?"

Susan answered, "They are the same size."

Attie said, "I love this blue one, if it's okay with you, Cleta?"

She stood at the door of the other bedroom. "Yes, I like this one better anyway."

Susan said, "Whew! What a relief. Well, Milt, why don't you work with the ladies and get them moved in. Charlie and I will tour the rest of the house. Come find us when you need to unload my clothes."

Emilia guided Susan down the long hall to the main residence and the front entrance. She turned and said, "I had planned to start here, but it was wonderful of you to see your employees were taken care of first. Their quarters in the separate wing will offer them privacy, and it will give you two the privacy you need as well."

***

Charlie joined them at the end of the hallway. "I just realized there are no windows to the backyard or patio area from their wing. Their windows are to the side yard. It is a beautiful yard for them to enjoy, and we get our privacy on the patio. Perfect."

Emilia said, "Now, let's tour the rest of your new home." She started in the living room and went from there to the office area and back through the living room to the dining area and through the large eat-in kitchen. Charlie and Susan had seen it all several times already but didn't mind the guided tour. From the kitchen, they transitioned into the huge den and into the massive master suite. The adjoining bath was elegant and larger than the secondary bedrooms upstairs. Their bedroom had beautiful glass French doors opening to the patio and pool area. After showing the couple around upstairs, Emilia said, "I hope you have enjoyed this tour. As I pointed out, the colors used were mostly neutrals, and the ceilings were light bluish-gray. I hope what you've seen follows the plan we discussed; does this meet your expectations?"

Susan sighed and said, "Emilia, this is everything I hoped for. I am pleased. I know every time Charlie and I'll have to leave, we'll hate it. This'll be our Tulsa sanctuary."

Charlie laughed and scratched the back of his neck. "I think her sigh was my cue to write you a check. Emilia, I agree this is beautiful and classy. Bill and Gertrude Skelly are buildin' the large estate home at the corner of Madison and 21st. They're our friends, and I wouldn't be surprised if they give ya a call when we show them this."

Emilia placed her hand on her chest. "It would be wonderful." She accepted her check, and after a few more minutes of conversation, she left.

Chapter 24

Loose Ends

March 1920

AS SUSAN WORKED WITH Milt to get their clothes put away, Charlie went to his new office to make several calls. His first call was to the Double Bar K Ranch.

The phone rang twice before it was answered. "Hello, this is Boss Bellamy."

"Boss, Charlie here. I'm callin' from our new house in Tulsa. I was goin' to call ya anyway to give ya our new phone number. It's Tulsa – 0113. But I guess George must have already called you about Zack's death and the funeral. You're plannin' to go up there for it, aren't ya?"

"You're right he did. I thought I would if ya don't mind?"

"I want ya to. I suspect ya were around when Zack was just a kid."

"Yeah, he might've been ten to twelve years old when I hired on with his father. I don't remember the 101 Ranch without Zack. It'll be tough for me on Wednesday."

"Me too, Boss. Susan and I'll be goin' up on Tuesday. Ya could do the same if ya like. Or even Monday if you want."

"I'll think about it. I could be there by noon on either day if I leave early."

Charlie and Boss went over a few more things about the ranches and the new properties then they hung up. Charlie went to the kitchen and poured himself another cup of coffee before his next call to the Leland Hotel.

"Please connect me to Hank Thomas's room."

"Hello, this is Hank."

"Hey, this is Charlie."

"Charlie, as you can tell, I'm back here in my room. I was

plannin' to call you. I don't have all the figures yet on our new well near Foster you and Susan saw, but we found oil so soon and not very deep that I have the crew already one full day into drillin' the second one about a half mile west of the first one. I'm sure it will be a good one, too."

"Love hearing it, Buddy. I called to give you our phone number at our new home."

He gave Hank the number.

Hank said, "Okay, I've got it. I'll get you the figures on the well as soon as I can."

"That's fine, Hank. Susan and I are goin' to be up at the Miller's 101 Ranch on Tuesday for several days. Zack Miller died, and we'll be attendin' the funeral on Wednesday."

"I'm so sorry to hear that. I met and was around Zack a little but never had a conversation with him. He seemed like a nice guy. I assume it was an accident of some kind 'cause he was a young man."

"It was. I don't have any details. George said he fell from his horse and hit his head. Hey, I need to make another call, so I'll let ya go for now."

Charlie next called Curt at his office in Kansas City. "Curt, Charlie here. Susan and I need to ask a favor."

"Sure. What do you need?"

"We want to have a day-long session with you regardin' everythin' goin' on right now. And we would love ya to see our new home here in Tulsa. Can ya come down here?"

"Sure, Charlie, your timing is perfect. I have a stack of contracts and paperwork for you two to sign. It's a little before 11:00, I can catch the 3:00 train out of here and be there by bedtime. Could someone meet me at the station at 9:30?"

"We'll be there. Susan will be thrilled."

Charlie stood for a moment still holding the phone, thinking of the Millers. Then he put the phone down and walked into their bedroom, where he found Susan putting away clothes.

Charlie walked over and put his arms around Susan from behind. "Sweetheart, guess what?"

"I can't guess, tell me."

"You're no fun. Uncle Curt will be arrivin' on the train here in Tulsa tonight. He'll be here through the weekend."

Susan squealed, turned, and jumped into his arms. "Oh, my heavens. That's wonderful."

"I told him we had some things we wanted to discuss. He said he had a stack of contracts and paperwork he needed us to sign, so he's comin' by train today."

Susan said, "Earlier I called and set up an account at Sheridan's food market, and Cleta gave them an order to fill both kitchens. They said they could deliver later today. Also, I thought I would let you know Cleta and Attie went into your closet at the ranch before they left and took about half of your clothes out, and now you have them here. I think you should thank them for being so thoughtful. We now have the clothes we were traveling with and half of what we had at the ranch."

"That's a good idea, Susan. I'll go right now." He went and found Cleta and Attie and thanked them with a hug. The grocery delivery had arrived a few minutes before. So, he helped them get the food put away in the proper kitchens.

***

At sunset, Charlie and Susan enjoyed a swim and a glass of wine from their private reserve. They would be picking Curt up in a few hours, so they took it easy on the wine and watched the time.

Chapter 25

Uncle Curt Arrives

March 1920

CLETA HAD THE COFFEE made and had started her breakfast preparation when Charlie and Susan walked into the kitchen area for their first breakfast on Madison Avenue. The table in the large welcoming breakfast nook sat across from the kitchen and provided a view through big windows overlooking the side yard's lush landscaping which included a dozen tall pines, a six-foot-high rock waterfall, a thirty-foot-long stream emptying into a beautiful small four-foot-deep pond.

Susan almost sang, "Good morning, Cleta, isn't this a wonderful day?"

"It sure is Miss Susan. We'll always remember Saturday, March 27, 1920, as our first full day living in this beautiful place. I love your ranch, but this is elegant, and I'm in heaven in this kitchen."

Charlie took a sip of coffee and put his cup back on its saucer. "Is there anythin' we need to get for you beyond what Emilia acquired? She and Susan created a list of kitchenware, towels, and so forth. They were hopin' they thought of everythin'."

"I missed my iron skillet from the ranch this morning. But I can get one here, and I'll season it just right, and it'll have a home here. It's all I see right now, Charlie. You guys picked up our visitor at the train station last night, didn't you?"

Susan answered, "We sure did. I'm sure Uncle Curt will be down soon. It was a hard day for him with his long train ride."

Charlie looked up and saw Curt coming toward them from the back stairs. "How'd ya sleep, Curt?"

"Like a baby. The bed was great. I wish I could take it home with me. Am I late for breakfast?"

Susan said, "No, we just got here a few minutes ago ourselves. Uncle Curt, this is Cleta our cook, tell her what you would like, and she'll fix it for you."

"Cleta, very nice to meet you, I'll have a three-egg ham and cheese omelet with fried potatoes and toast. And where's the coffee?"

Cleta responded, "I'll get you a cup and bring it to the table for you, and I'll have everyone's food ready in ten minutes."

Curt joined Charlie and Susan at the table. As he sat, he looked around. "Kids, this is a beautiful house. It's new, isn't it?"

Charlie responded, "A family started this design and construction project about a year ago. The house was almost finished when they had an emergency requiring them to move to New York City. We happened into the developer's office a few hours after he learned about the family's situation. We toured the house and didn't hesitate to make a cash offer, as you know."

Susan added, "We were able to make a few minor changes as the constructors finished up. We hired a decorator to paint and furnish the place for us. She had the house until two days ago. It has turned out wonderful, and we're glad we bought it."

Curt nodded. "It was night, but I saw several very large and established homes as we drove to this house last night. You said this area is called Maple Ridge, correct?"

Susan said, "Yes, and we can see it will become Tulsa's version of Ward Estates in Kansas City."

Curt took a sip of coffee. "My first impression from last night tells me you're right. It strikes me as a neighborhood that will still be elegant a hundred years from now. I'm happy you purchased this too."

Charlie said, "Curt, ya said ya had some paperwork for us to sign, right? So, how about after we finish here, we have a signin' party?"

Curt replied, "That sounds like a good idea. Let's get our business tasks out of the way. I'll go over everything as you sign things. No real questions, I'll just ask what I need to, so I can be assured everything is correct and prepared the way you wanted. I think you wanted some time to discuss some new ideas, right?"

Susan jumped in. "There are several things we want to make sure you understand. We have some ideas we want to share, and they will require your help to execute. That conversation could take hours to complete."

Charlie nodded. "We need to discuss office space here in Tulsa, and we would like to take ya to a building we now own as a result of acquirin' the Exchange National Bank."

Cleta brought their food, and the conversation dwindled to almost nothing as they ate.

***

After breakfast and a tour of the house and grounds for Curt, the three of them sat back down at the table with fresh coffee cups and Curt's stack of paperwork. Included in the pile were documents to complete all the business transactions to acquire land, mineral rights, equipment, the startup of the security company, and everything else they had not been signed over the last few months. Curt had signed many binding agreements using his attorney's power to avoid a hold on any action requiring immediate attention.

After signing the last of the paperwork, Charlie shook his right hand and said, "I wore my right paw out. Let's not let our paperwork git this backed up anymore."

Curt laughed and took the stack of paperwork. "We've had more activity requiring contracts and acquisition paperwork in the past several months than we had under Walter in his last decade. It's not a bad thing either way, but you two have kept me mighty busy."

Susan said, "Can we go out onto our patio? It's a nice warm day and we can sit at a table out there. It's in the shade, and if there's a breeze, it'll be perfect."

They went out and found the atmosphere was exactly as Susan had described.

Charlie started the conversation with, "Curt, we want to look at Tulsa's office space. Kelly Oil should have its offices here, and we're at a point where we may need to start hiring the necessary business skills to support the company's growth. We've been able to use the Kramer Corporate support staff, but our hope is to need more than the Kansas City folks can handle before long."

Curt said, "I'm glad you're thinking about this now and not waiting until something important can't get done because there is no one available to handle it. You mentioned the Exchange National Bank building. I've processed the paperwork you and Harry Sinclair signed a while back. We now own the property. According to the paperwork, it's a very large building. I would love to see it."

Charlie said, "We can go down there and tour the building in a little while and have lunch at Bishop's while we're downtown."

Curt's head snapped up. "Did you say, Bishop's? As in Bishop's Waffle House in Kansas City?"

Susan said, "I believe the same folks own both. And I hear there's one in downtown Oklahoma City. Our friends told us about it when we were staying at the Hotel Tulsa." She adjusted herself in her chair, cleared her throat, and asked, "Uncle Curt, we have been thinking a lot about how we've added or are adding so many different areas to the Kramer Group. So, should we consider some form of reorganization and maybe even a name change? We want your opinion on the pluses and minuses of both of those possibilities?"

Curt leaned back in his chair, holding his coffee cup below his chin, before he answered the question. He looked from Susan to Charlie, then back to Susan. "I've been thinking about those questions myself. You now have not one banking system but four. Not one railroad, but soon there'll be two because Owen will be closing the Rock Island deal soon. We have two retail companies and a growing oil company. You've purchased several ranches, and you're expanding the construction company as well as adding a security company. I could go on. When your father died, we had a bank and some branches, a railroad, a small chain of department stores, and a construction company. Susan, from those four areas, Walter became the richest man west of the Mississippi River. I'll have to say you two have added to the value of what you inherited and by no small amount. We've been very fortunate that every acquisition thus far has paid off, and I see you two working as a team with amazing precision and focus."

Charlie asked, "Don't ya think we need to recreate the Group structure and define the lines of responsibility and accountability?"

Curt shook his head. "Charlie, you continue to surprise me with your maturity and basic savvy. Yes, I think we should discuss this question and decide this weekend. Is a change what you want?"

Charlie answered. "Maybe, and we want you to understand we didn't want to make any decision without your counsel. We agree we do want to answer that question this weekend."

Susan placed her hand on Curt's wrist. "Let's take a ride downtown and tour the bank building, and by then, it should be lunchtime."

Curt smiled, "Sounds good."

Charlie stood and started toward the garage. "Good idea, I'll pull the Cadillac around to the front and pick ya up there."

***

It took over three hours to see all twelve stories of the Exchange National Bank building. During their tour of the twelfth floor, they agreed it could be remodeled and become an excellent location for corporate offices. The previous owners expanded and renovated the building only thirty months ago. The possibilities were exciting to the trio.

Curt said as they stepped out of the elevator on the ground floor, "This is an impressive building and one we were lucky to get as part of the acquisition. As I said upstairs, I can see the entire Kramer Corporate offices located here."

Susan responded, "I could too. But you wouldn't want to move to Tulsa, would you?"

Curt hesitated, then rubbed the back of his neck. "I don't know. I hadn't given it any thought. But I'm not prepared to say no to anything."

Charlie said, "I'm hungry. Let's walk over to Bishop's, and then we can head back to the house. We have a lot to discuss."

Charlie didn't take the shortest route back to the house. He wanted to give Curt an overview of Tulsa's downtown area and another look at the beautiful large homes between downtown and the surrounding areas near Maple Ridge.

Chapter 26

Dinner and a Discussion

March 1920

CHARLIE, SUSAN, AND CURT returned to the Kelly's house late in the afternoon. Cleta prepared dinner while the trio discussed Tulsa, the city's growth over the last decade, and why Charlie and Susan enjoyed living there.

After a pork roast meal with all the trimmings, Susan said, "Let's settle into the living room. Bring your glasses of wine and let's get comfortable. We have a lot more to discuss and decisions to make about the issues both good and bad facing us."

Charlie started a fire in the large fireplace before he took his seat. "Let's start by discussin' the trouble we're havin' with the Chicago Unit and how we have Bailey and his team addressin' it. Curt, as you know, we've had three locations damaged, and each time a threatenin' message was left. They wanted us to know who was takin' credit for the attacks."

Curt took a sip of wine and placed his glass on an end table. "And Bailey's pretty sure all the attacks are connected, right?"

Susan nodded. "Yes, he does."

"What about all these men he's hired? I've seen a lot of personnel paperwork come through in a short time."

Charlie and Susan knew Uncle Curt was expressing the same concern they had had before meeting all of Bailey's team. Susan said, "Bailey has hired some very experienced and very talented men. He has a personal history with each member of his team. He trusts them, and we do too."

"Well, that's good." Curt took a drink from his wine glass. "What does Bailey think should be done about the Chicago people?"

Susan said, "They are creating a plan to address the situation head-on."

Curt said, "Describe head-on."

Charlie leaned toward Curt. "I plan to go to Chicago and meet this bunch's leader face-to-face."

Curt rose erect so fast he almost came out of his chair and looked toward Charlie. He then turned and faced Susan. "My sweet niece, I don't think that's a good idea. It sounds dangerous."

Sitting next to her uncle, Charlie reached over and placed a hand on Curt's arm. "Nothing's decided yet. We'll see Bailey's plan before we take any action."

Susan shivered. "I'm scared about the idea too. But I'll wait for our experts to create a plan before I say anymore on the subject."

Curt leaned back and reached for his wine glass. "Well, okay. I'll trust you to make a good decision. If I'm understanding things right, Bailey and his team will create a security master plan for the entire Kramer Group. Is it your plan?"

Charlie said, "Yes, it's the reason I wanted to hire him. He'll set up a company to protect our assets, and he'll also create a capability to provide other companies and individuals protection."

Curt nodded. "Yes, it sounds like a solid idea. At some point, providing security to and paid by others might be profitable enough to cover some or all the costs for securing the assets of the Kramer Group."

Susan's eyes sparkled. "Yes, that was Charlie's plan from the start. Now let's talk about how we structure everything to support the growth we're experiencing."

Curt shifted in his chair. "First, let me ask this. Have you sat down and developed an organizational chart to address what you think you need to change?"

Susan bit her lower lip. "No, we haven't. We have talked about it, but we haven't created one."

Curt smiled. "Well, let's create one now as we talk through things this evening."

Charlie stood. "I saw an extra bundle of packing paper in the garage, I'll go git some large pieces, and we can use them to draw an organization on it."

They came up with an organization with eight corporate divisions which included headquarters/home office, railroads, construction, retail, banking, security, ranching, and oil. Each of these had activities below them and a president as their top official.

Curt pointed at the chart. "I can see this working, but I think you might want to have a Chief Financial Officer equal to where you have me. I see where I would not work for, nor would I be a peer to your division presidents, and neither would your CFO. And you need a CFO. Susan, as strange as it sounds, your father never wanted one. He thought he, with a little help from Gordon, could do it himself."

Susan said, "I agree we have the need, but I'm not sure how we find one. And I like having the headquarters as a division with its president. Again, I don't know how we find who we get to run it."

Charlie tilted his head toward Curt. "Do you think we need to change our name?"

Curt rubbed the back of his neck and cleared his throat. "Only if you want to. The Kramer Group can function fine as an eight-division organization as it has as a four or five-division company. What would you call it?"

Susan said, "I was thinking The Kramer-Kelly Group, similar to what my name is now."

Charlie shrugged. "I guess I'm okay with it. But so many people already know The Kramer Group. As far as I'm concerned, Kelly Oil and Kelly Ranching can be divisions under The Kramer Group."

Susan leaned back. "Being honest, I know when you say The Kramer Group, people in the business world know the name and the power and prestige my father developed. I guess what I want is for us to create our own legacy."

Curt said, "I don't think this is a question needing an answer tonight. Was there anything else we needed to talk about?"

Susan turned to her uncle. "Yes, I know as we toured the bank building today, we saw how we could use it as a location for some of our offices. What are your views on establishing an office here in Tulsa? Should it be a satellite of the Kansas City office, or should it be the other way around?"

Curt again pointed to the chart they had created. "Look at the organization and where the business is located in those divisions. There are six in Missouri and Oklahoma. I see two only in Oklahoma. I see two already expanding into Texas. It looks like, to me, a central location for the next several years is Tulsa. The building we saw today would be an excellent location for the corporate headquarters. Your presidents should be willing to move here, but a couple of them might want to have some time to prepare for the move."

Charlie said, "What a commonsense approach to making the decision. I don't think we need to make this decision tonight either, but maybe we can discuss it again in the morning, over breakfast."

Curt said, "I know you guys are just getting started, but I'm ready to head to bed with my murder mystery and fall asleep after my usual seven pages."

They laughed and said goodnight. Charlie and Susan decided to head to the patio. Cleta and Attie were already back in their quarters, and Curt would be asleep before long, so it seemed to be the right time for their nightly swim and to share a bottle of Cabernet.

Charlie said, "I'll go git the wine. Do ya want any cheese or crackers?"

Susan replied as she headed to the bedroom, "No. Oh, maybe just the crackers. I'll bring your robe out if you want."

"I doubt I'll use it."

He found the wine and corkscrew and opened the bottle. He brought the bottle, some glasses, and the box of crackers, to the patio. He poured the wine and opened the crackers for Susan. He took his clothes off and started toward their bedroom door.

Susan met him as she came out of the bedroom onto the patio and said, "I see we're swimming first?"

"Not necessarily. I prefer to see you wearin' nothin' or as little as possible. And you seem to like it when I wear nothing at all. So, I got ready for ya."

Susan reached and took ahold of his manhood. She dropped her robe and said, "God, I love you." She began kissing him and worked her way over most of his body. She looked up from her position on her knees and said, "Let's make this an extra special night."

It was early Spring with temperatures above normal. With their heated pool they were comfortable as they swam for a while then went to their loungers. They began working on the bottle of wine as they talked. Some of the conversation was about the topics they had discussed with Curt. But then Charlie brought up the death of Zack Miller and how it would impact the 101.

Charlie put his wine glass on the table. "Susan, Zack was among the best at evaluating cattle, horses, pigs, just about any animal you might find on a farm or ranch. I think George is going to want to discuss with me how he should move forward. I don't know this for sure, but why else would he ask us to stay an extra day or so?"

Susan said, "I don't know either, but he valued your ideas when you worked for him. He may want your opinion on something coming up this year."

"True, but I have a feelin' it's not goin' to be a happy subject. Boss and I have talked several times about the ranch, and we think it has suffered financially over the last several years because Joe restarted the Wild West Show after the War."

"How could you help him with it? If that's the problem he'll want to talk about, do we have a solution for him?"

"I gave him my thoughts back when I worked for him. If not for the oil income, he would have had to close the ranch and apply for bankruptcy back in '18."

"Charlie, I had no idea. George must be a brilliant businessman to have been able to keep the ranch going this long."

"He is the best at trackin' money I've ever seen or even heard of. He sees things so clearly and has a knack for when to invest more or sell off assets. He's amazin'."

Susan turned and looked at Charlie. "You have a concerned look on your face. Is it just concern for the Millers?"

Charlie leaned back and looked up at the stars. "No, not really. I have times, even whole days where I'm missin' my life as a real cowboy. Don't think for a minute I'm not lovin' our life runnin' the Kramer Group. I'm excited about what we have planned and all the possibilities we may come across in the future. But I'm a cowboy and I'll always be a cowboy. I miss the ranch work sometimes. Understand?"

Susan sat up, turned with her feet touching the patio, facing Charlie. "Sweetheart, it was your dream to be a cowboy at the 101 Ranch when we met. That dream meant you left me for a long year to go after it. I can't imagine that dream will ever die, and I don't want it to. We're in a busy and dangerous time right now, but we'll always make sure to keep us both grounded by owning ranches and staying in the cowboy world as much as possible. Okay?"

Charlie smiled. "Okay."

Susan grinned. "I'm ready to quit talking and start snuggling. How about you?"

"Yep, I'll come over to join ya on your lounger."

"No, let me come join you."

She climbed over and straddled him across his lap. She whispered, "It has been a struggle for me to keep my hands off you for the past hour. I enjoyed our conversation, but sometimes I just..."

Chapter 27

Key Decision

March 1920

CHARLIE AND SUSAN SAT at the breakfast table talking as they watched robins enjoying the waterfall and the lawn out across their manicured yard.

Susan poured her second cup of coffee as Uncle Curt came down the stairs carrying his overnight bag. "Morning, Uncle Curt. May I pour you a cup?"

Curt nodded. "You guys start early around here. And yes, please."

Susan filled a cup and set it in front of an open chair. "I'd like to say something like—early bird gets the worm—but when you marry a cowboy, you learn to get up with the roosters. Even if you don't have roosters in Tulsa."

Charlie laughed as he put his coffee cup on its saucer. "Yeah, she's adapted well to my clock. Didja sleep well last night, Curt?"

"I've got the same answer as yesterday. It's a wonderful bed. I wish it could go home with me."

Susan teased, "If you move here, we'll give it to you."

Curt turned to Susan with a serious look on his face and said, "Don't promise something you won't do, now Darling."

Charlie's head jerked back. "Whoa now. What'd ya mean, Curt?"

Curt sat down and took a sip of coffee. "I've slept on it. My advice is to remodel the bank and move The Kramer Group home offices to Tulsa. Leave what is required to support your assets in the Kansas City area, the Midwest, and move everything else here."

Charlie leaned back and picked up his coffee cup. Before he put it to his mouth, he looked at Curt. "It was my first inclination too. But history and everything was there in Kansas City. I wanted to know what you thought before sayin' anythin'."

Susan leaned toward her uncle. "So, would you move to Tulsa if we did move everything here."

Curt didn't hesitate. "I would. Tulsa seems like a nice city, and there is money here. And I think the money will bring all the arts and culture a person would want or need. You know how much they are part of my life. Besides, you and Charlie are all the family I have, and I want to see you more than I would if I continue to live in Kansas City."

Charlie looked at Susan and said, "Let's do it. We need to get Rice down here and have him and Emilia work together to design and construct what we need."

Susan smiled. "Settle down, Charlie. We do need to get Rice down here. I'm sure we can get Emilia involved too. Let's invite Bailey to be part of this. We can make those calls before we leave for Ponca City and the 101."

Curt looked at his watch. "It's a little after 7:00, can we eat so I can get to the train station by 8:30. My train leaves at 9:00."

Susan turned to the kitchen and said, "Cleta, we're ready."

Cleta walked over to the table. As she approached, she said, "I assume you two want your usual, so Mr. Curt, what'll you have?"

Curt said, "Two eggs over easy, bacon, and toast. I'm already enjoying your coffee."

Cleta had their food ready in ten minutes, and they were in the Cadillac pulling up to the station at 8:15.

At the train station, Curt hugged both of his kids. "Thanks for the ride to the station and your hospitality. I'm glad we were able to spend this time together. It's March, let's see if we can get me, and the home office moved here by summer, okay?"

Charlie nodded. "A good goal, maybe a bit aggressive, but it's what we'll shoot for."

Susan hugged her uncle again. "I can't wait for you to be here in Tulsa with us. Call me when you get home."

Chapter 28

Bailey's Update

March 1920

BACK AT THEIR HOUSE, the phone rang. Charlie answered. "Hello, Charles Kelly."

"Charlie, this is Bailey. I'm sorry to call you at home but I have a few questions for you and some ideas to run past you. I want to schedule some time to sit down with you tomorrow."

"We won't be here. We've had a friend die, and we will be travelin' to attend the funeral. Can you come to the house today?"

"I can leave now if you're available?"

"Yes, come on over, you have the address, and know how to git here, don'tcha?"

"I do. I'll be there in thirty minutes."

Charlie looked for Susan and found her on the patio reading.

She looked up. "Did I hear the phone ring a few minutes ago?"

"Yes, it was Bailey. He's on his way over here now. He needs to discuss some things. He asked me to meet tomorrow. We'll be at the 101 for the next several days, so I invited him to come here now. You're in my favorite lingerie, and I'm sure Bailey will love it too."

Susan grinned. "I'll go put something else on. Thanks for the warning."

"Well, okay, if you feel it's somethin' you need to do." Charlie laughed and shook his head as she walked into their bedroom.

***

Charlie and Bailey used the table in the shade on the patio. Cleta brought them glasses of sweet tea and cookies. "Can I get you two anything else?"

Charlie looked at Bailey, who shook his head. "This will do, for now, thanks."

She nodded and left the pitcher of tea with them.

As Cleta walked away, Bailey looked at Charlie. "Let me say again how much I appreciate your time."

Charlie looked pleased. "It's a busy time, and we need to take advantage of any breaks in the action when we can. But I do want and expect you and everyone to have some downtime. I mean time away from the job. But we also must address the hot issues in a timely manner." Charlie stopped and stifled a laugh as he said, "Listen to me, I'm starting to sound so formal, when did I lose my cowboy, and when and where did I find this Wall Street guy."

They both found the humor in what Charlie said.

Bailey had a crooked grin as he lifted his head to make eye contact. "We both need to find some downtime, but we must make several decisions about how we'll address the Chicago Outfit. My guys have confirmed the Kansas City folk's involvement, and they're taking orders from Torrio. We have confirmed Torrio's home address. Wyatt had been working on a stakeout of Torrio and Capone during his last two months in Chicago. The BOI wants to shut down the Outfit and arrest the leaders as part of it. But Torrio and Capone are careful to isolate themselves from the action. Wyatt said Torrio is a creature of habit, so he knows what his schedule should be on any given day."

Susan walked out onto the patio and joined the men. She wore a white body-hugging, full-length, ground brushing, gown from her favorite loungewear ensemble. She wore nothing under the outfit, and it displayed every curve. The neckline plunged deep enough to make it interesting.

Susan stopped about ten feet from the table. "Good afternoon, Bailey. It looks like Cleta has already served you two. I'll leave you alone, but I didn't want to be rude and not come say, hello." She turned to walk away, and Charlie said, "You can stay if you like. We were about to start discussing options to deal with the Chicago bunch."

Susan turned and gave them an innocent look, "Well, sure, I would love to." She took the seat between Charlie and Bailey. She didn't hesitate to make clear what her feelings were regarding the subject. She focused on Bailey "I'm concerned if we don't act soon, it will be a sign to them of weakness in us. What do you think?"

Bailey recoiled as a seriousness came over his face. He scratched his chin and thought for a second. "Miss Susan, you continue to surprise me. Yes, it would. We should respond as soon as possible. I had just mentioned to Charlie we had confirmed the use of men out of Kansas City in damaging the bank. They were used in the other two incidents as well. My team could be ready to hit the Kansas City crew later this week."

Charlie leaned in. "What do you mean by hitting them?"

"We would be armed but only use our weapons to respond to their actions. We'll covertly break into one of their strongholds and leave a message intended to scare them shitless." He looked at Susan. "Pardon my language."

Susan looked amused. "I've heard and used worse, Bailey. I don't use those words often, so when I do, people get the message." She smiled. "Please continue."

"We already know the businesses and other locations used by the outfit in Kansas City. Joe and Pete DiGiovanni head up the operation there. We also have the DiGiovanni's home addresses."

Charlie challenged Bailey. "How did you get this information this easily?"

Bailey was gracious. "I expected you might ask. As I said, Wyatt and Josh were working in the gangster world for the BOI, and they have friends embedded in that world around the country. They brought copies of their notes with them as they left their last assignment."

Charlie's eyes lit up. "This is Monday, would it be possible to hit the Kansas City crew in a few days? Maybe, Wednesday night and you have some information available for me on Friday?"

Without hesitation, Bailey nodded. "Yes, we can. My team has already created the scenario for a raid there. We were hoping you could be convinced to do it."

Susan turned to face Bailey as she interjected, "Do you mean you thought you'd need to talk Charlie into doing something? Then, you don't know my husband."

Charlie grinned. "Thanks, Sweetheart." He turned to Bailey. "I'll let you and your team do this on your own. Send a powerful message to these assholes. We won't tolerate another incident with damage, injury, or death. Afterward, if somethin' does happen, we'll plan a visit to Chicago. The visit I want then will include me face-to-face with this Torrio shithead. Got it?"

Bailey beamed. "Got it. I have all the information I need for now. I guess you'll want to see me Friday?"

"Yes, for an update on this effort, and I want you to be part of a meetin' on a renovation of the Exchange National Bank buildin'. We're movin' the Kramer corporate offices here to Tulsa. They'll be located inside that buildin'. You'll provide guidance regardin' all security matters for our new headquarters."

Bailey stood and nodded. "It will be my honor" He looked at Charlie and then lingered his look at Susan. "I'll get out of here and start working on the final plan to execute our mission for Wednesday night."

Susan said, "Bailey, be careful, and you have our complete confidence."

Charlie said, "Come to the house Friday. See ya then."

***

It was early evening, and Charlie sat at his desk, putting notes together regarding what he saw coming up over the next few weeks and months when Susan walked in and said, "Cleta needs to know if she needs to prepare dinner for us. I'm happy to give her the night off. Attie has finished packing our things for the trip, and she's already back in their residence. What do you need?"

Charlie said, "Tell her she's done for the day. I'm good with sandwiches, and I can make my own. I'll be done here in a few minutes, and I'll come to the kitchen."

Susan turned to leave then stopped and said, "Great, I'll tell her. There's leftover roast, I'll make each of us a sandwich, and later we can have it and our bottle of wine on the patio. I'll see you when you're done."

"Sounds like a great plan, Sweetheart."

He returned his focus to his notes. He had listed: (1) Chicago Outfit (2) bank remodel (3) realignment of Kramer Group (4) Cushing project (5) Shawnee project (6) new oil wells (7) Rock Island (8) banking expansion (9) construction company expansion (10) oil company expansion (11) moving corporate headquarters to Tulsa.

He looked at the list and said to himself, *Gee, It's a shame I don't have somethin' to keep me busy. I think I'm done with this. I need to be done, at least for now.*

***

Charlie saw Susan wearing her robe standing at the counter as he walked into the kitchen. "Hello, beautiful. I'll be back in a second." He patted her behind as he passed her and continued to their bedroom, where he removed his clothes and put on his robe. He returned to the kitchen in time to help carry the two trays of food and beverage to the patio.

Susan took her tray from him, placed it on the side table

nearest her lounger, and dropped her robe. “I’m swimming a few laps first.” She walked over and dove into the pool.

Charlie placed his tray on the side table nearest his lounger and opened the bottle of Cabernet. He poured them each a glass and took his first sip. He looked over at Susan swimming and decided the pool was where he needed to be.

Chapter 29

Back to the Miller's 101

March 1920

AS USUAL, CHARLIE WAS awake before sunrise, even without a rooster. He was in the shower when he heard Susan rustling around in the bedroom.

Charlie hollered, "Susan, Sweetheart, want to come join me?"

The shower door opened, and she stepped in.

Susan stroked his manhood. "You know your shower time just got lengthened."

Charlie looked down and tilted his head. "Looks like somethin' else did too."

After they quit laughing, Charlie said, "I'd like to get on the road by 9:00. I want to stop near Burbank and check our wells. And maybe we can have lunch in Ponca City. I have a place I want to show you. I've not eaten there in a long time."

Susan kissed him. "You're such a clown sometimes. Okay, I'll be ready. I love road trips. It's a time when it's just you and me."

Because Attie had packed for them, all they had to do was shower, dress, and eat.

Charlie dressed, went to the garage, moved the Cadillac around near the front door, and loaded the suitcases. When he arrived in the kitchen area, he looked at the clock and saw it was 8:35.

Cleta asked, "Mr. Charlie, do you want your regular?"

"You betcha, Cleta. I'll pour my coffee and join Susan."

Charlie saw her sitting facing the windows looking out at the side yard. She was wearing a yellow blouse or shirt he didn't recognize.

As Charlie neared the table, he asked, "Something new?"

When he got to where he could see Susan from the front, he knew she had a yellow blouse made like her white and pink form-fitting blouses which had become so popular with him and other men. "Wow, Susan. It's like the pink and the white one, right?"

"Those were so popular; I decided I needed more made in other colors. They are all pale colors like the others. I now have one in blue, green, off-white, and red. I thought you might be happy about it. They were delivered yesterday a few minutes after Bailey arrived. Attie packed several for the trip. I'll have a new one for you every day."

"All I can say is I love it. I hate myself for askin' this, but you do have somethin' appropriate for the funeral. I didn't even check to see what I have."

"Yes, I worked with Attie to make sure we have what we need for the funeral service. I'll be glad when the service is over. I hated my father's service. It was the first one since my mother's. The sadness is hard, and you can never say the right thing."

Cleta arrived with the food and refilled the coffee cups. They were on their way a minute or two after 9:00.

***

East of Burbank, Charlie turned north up a dirt road to drive to the oil leases Kelly Oil owned. He knew there should be signs along the west side of the road about two miles north.

Susan waved her arm. "There it is, I see a Kelly Oil sign coming up. It's so great to see a Property of Kelly Oil Company sign."

Charlie got out and opened the gate and drove the Cadillac down a path through some trees and into a clearing. Two pumps were operating about a quarter of a mile apart and a large holding tank sat halfway between them.

As Charlie got out of the car and began walking toward a pump, Susan took off her blouse and laid it on the car's fender. She began unsnapping her pants. "I'm turned on, and you need to make love to me right now. We're at the first site where we struck oil, big guy. Let's mark our spot."

Charlie shook his head and smiled. "I've been ready for this ever since the gas station and you flirtin' with the attendants. This is a quiet private place, and it will give us a great memory." There was no hesitation in Charlie, and he dropped his pants in no time.

***

It was a little past 1:00 when they pulled onto Grand Avenue in Ponca City.

A few minutes later, Charlie said, "I wanted to take ya to Hal's Café here on Grand. It's about another block down here. The food was always good when the gang came to town, and Hal's a hoot."

"I see it, Honey. It's a cute place and I'm hungry for more than just you right now."

Charlie laughed as they parked out front. They were able to get a table against the front window. It didn't offer much privacy, but they could see their Cadillac.

Charlie pulled the menus from the condiment rack on the table and offered one to Susan. "I recommend their chicken fried steak lunch special and their sweet tea."

Susan handed the menu back to Charlie. "I'll order it then."

The waiter came to their table and said, "Can I get you guys somethin' ta drink?

He looked at Susan and froze. He dropped his pencil on the floor.

Charlie said, "Hal, we'll take two sweet teas and two of your chicken fried steak specials."

Hal picked up his pencil and looked at Charlie. He squinted and scratched his neck. "I remember you're from the 101 bunch, right? I can't call yer name, though."

"Hal, it's Charlie Kelly."

"That's right, yer the guy what captured them, rustlers." He looked again at Susan and said, "There was this big write-up in the newspaper. You'd a been proud, Missy." His eyes lingered below her chin too long.

Charlie grinned and said, "Hal, ya got the order, right?"

"Oh, let's see. It was sweet tea and chicken fry for ya both, wasn't it?"

In her best cowboy voice, Susan said, "Yep, that'll do us."

Hal smiled, nodded, and headed for the kitchen.

Susan laughed and said, "Charlie, he is a hoot. And I'm sure he's much smarter than he sounds. Should I have used more than these two buttons? I only have four anyway."

"You're good. I'm sure Hal hasn't seen a woman in his entire fifty-some years with your assets."

Hal brought the tea and said, "Your food will be here in a few minutes. Good ta see ya, Charlie. Ya must not be livin' out at the 101 anymore, are ya?"

"No, Susan, and I live in Tulsa. Susan, this is Hal, the owner here. Hal, this is Susan, my wife."

Hal responded with, "Miss Susan, it's my pure pleasure to meet ya. Charlie here is a shur-nuff hero around these parts for savin' Thad Spencer and gittin' those rustlers."

She looked at Charlie, smiled, and back at Hal. "I'm proud of him for many reasons, but I truly appreciate your kind words."

They enjoyed their meal and then drove around Ponca City for a few minutes. Then they drove toward the 101.

As they were getting close to the ranch, Charlie said, "This may be hard for me, Susan. These folks treated me like family. It's gonna be hard on me to see them hurtin'."

Susan reached over and patted his leg. "Be yourself, Sweetheart. You know they love you too."

Charlie turned the car right, entered the front gate, and drove to the same parking spot they used back when this place was home. They climbed the stairs to the front door and entered the White House.

Charlie didn't recognize the young lady at the desk, so he said, "Hello, we're Charlie and Susan Kelly. George and May should be expectin' us."

The young lady said, "Yes, Mr. Kelly, Mr. Miller is in his office." She pointed toward the hallway. "His office is the last one on the right."

He didn't feel the need to say he once had the office next door to her boss. "Thank ya. We'll go on down there."

They walked down the familiar hallway past Charlie's old office and knocked on the open door.

George looked up and smiled. "Charlie! Come in. And Susan, you look as beautiful as ever." George stood and came around his desk and embraced Charlie with immense passion. It was as if he had been holding it inside forever.

Charlie said, "George, how can we help ya? We're here to give whatever support your family needs."

George looked over at Susan, then back to Charlie, as tears began to show in his eyes. "Charlie, I do have some important issues I need to discuss with you, but they need to wait until after the service. You and your sweet Susan are helping me by just being here. Now go unpack and rest up from your drive. I'm so happy you're here. Please join the family at 6:00 at the café for dinner."

Charlie and Susan each hugged George, then went out to the Cadillac, gathered their suitcases, and went to their old suite on the second floor.

After reading a while, Susan laid the copy of the Saturday Evening Post she had found on the nightstand. She stood and walked over to where Charlie sat reading his sports page in the Tulsa World newspaper. "Charlie, can we take a walk down to the Salt Fork? I want to see our special place along the river."

"Of course, let's go. We should have time to do that and be back for dinner."

As they walked through the gate and headed toward the river, Susan looked up into Charlie's eyes, and said, "Won't this always seem a little bit like home?"

Charlie let out a big sigh, looked over at his sweetheart, and said, "My God Susan, way more than just a little bit."

Chapter 30

The Funeral

March 1920

CHARLIE DIDN'T SLEEP MUCH on their first night back on the 101. His mind was racing between the loss of Zack Miller, the comment George made about wanting to talk about some important issues, and the comment he had made to Susan about how this ranch as a place still felt like home. He was awake when the rooster let out his morning reveille.

Charlie tried to climb out of bed without disturbing Susan. But the floor creaked with his first step toward the bathroom. It prompted, "Good morning, Charlie. How's my man this morning?"

He turned and looked back. "I'm, fine, but a little tired and sleepy. I'll be good after a cup or two of the café's coffee."

"Didn't you sleep well?"

"No. I couldn't settle down. I kept thinkin' about Zack, what George said about havin' issues, and how much this place means to me. But once I git some coffee in me, I'll be just fine."

Susan lifted the covers off her naked body. "I'm so sorry you had a rough night, but I can understand why those things matter to you. You go ahead and get started in the bathroom. I'll lay out my clothes and join you in a minute. We do need to get over to the café, because I'm starving."

***

Charlie and Susan held hands as they walked toward the café. The sun rose over their right shoulders letting them see the Open sign go up in the window as they approached the front door.

Charlie said, "Looks like we're the first ones here. It'll be nice. We can eat and chat while it's still quiet."

When they walked through the front door, they heard, "Is that, Charlie Kelly?"

Charlie looked over and saw Pete Logan, his old friend from his days as a cowboy here, standing at the cash register.

Charlie hollered, "Well, I'll be damned, Pete, how are ya." He walked over and hugged Pete's neck.

"I'm doin' real good, Charlie. I guess you're here for the funeral today, aren't cha? Mornin' Miss Susan. You're lookin' beautiful as ever."

Charlie squeezed Pete's shoulder. "Yep. It's a shame it took a death to git us to come over here from Tulsa."

Pete said, "I thought ya had a ranch in Pott County. You're in Tulsa?"

"We have three ranches now. But we're livin' in Tulsa as our main place right now."

Pete shook his head and said, "Damn it, ole pal, you must be rollin' in money."

Susan laughed. "Pete, we're doing great in many more ways than just money. But as Charlie sometimes says, we'll make it through the winter."

Pete grinned. "Yeah, I've heard him say it a bunch o' times. I've gotta take this sack of thermoses full o' coffee out to the barn. Several of us are gonna be workin' till noon. I'll see ya at the service."

Charlie patted his shoulder. "No rest for.... Ya know the rest. See ya later."

The couple found their usual table and got comfortable. The waiter came over with two full coffee mugs. "I recognize y'all. Do you need menus?"

Susan said, "No, we'll each have two eggs, over easy, bacon and toast."

The waiter looked at Charlie and back to Susan and smiled. "Thanks, your food should be out in a few minutes." He turned and went to the kitchen.

After he had drunk half his first cup, Charlie was awake enough to see Susan had worn the light green blouse from the set she had described to him yesterday.

Charlie commented, "Susan, you look beautiful. Your new blouse is amazin'. I'm glad you had them made. Its fit is so flatterin'. I'm lookin' forward to seein' ya in them all. I'm not sure what we can do until the service at 2:00, do ya have any ideas?"

"Why don't we go walk around to see all the buildings and what might have changed. George said there were issues. We might see something to provide us a hint of what he means."

"Great idea, and I'll enjoy seein' everythin' anyway."

They spent the entire morning walking around the headquarters area, bordered by the Salt Fork to the south, orchards to the east, and gardens to the north and west. There were over thirty buildings housing everything from animal barns to stores and a bank.

They were heading back from the arena when Charlie said, "I'm hungry, how about some lunch? Are ya ready to go back to the café?"

Susan laughed. "You're always hungry. But I am this time too. It's after twelve, so we better eat now and then go get dressed for the service."

***

Dressed in a black suit and a black, demure dress, the couple walked down from their suite and into the White House lobby at 1:45 to find the Miller family preparing to go outside. George walked over to Charlie and said, "You two walk out with us and sit in the chairs behind May and me. You'll see Boss and Tom on the same row of chairs too."

"If it's what ya want, of course we will."

Joe came over when he saw George talking to Charlie and said, "Charlie, I was off the ranch down in Guthrie yesterday on business, or I would have welcomed you then. Thanks for being here. It means a lot to us you have come."

"Joe, I hate why I'm here, but I wouldn't want to be anywhere else. You folks are family." Charlie saw George's eyes fill with tears as he squeezed Charlie on his right shoulder.

They all walked out as a group and took their seats. Charlie saw Boss and Tom, as they solemnly nodded to him.

Charlie leaned forward and whispered in George's ear, "There must be several thousand people here. I see the Ponca Chief and his court seated over across the casket bier."

George whispered, "Based on our father's funeral, we expected a large crowd. I think you'll recognize most of the pallbearers. Most were in your crew. It's no surprise they grew into top hands Zack depended on."

The service was short but dignified. It included the Ponca Chief, and there was a representative from the Governor. At the end of the ceremony, the pallbearers came forward to take Zack to the horse-drawn hearse."

George turned and said, "See, Charley, there's Thad, Pete,

Burt, Jodie, Matt, and Ephraim. Your crew plus Pete."

Charley whispered, "What an honor for them."

George replied, "And for you, my friend."

They buried Zack in the ranch cemetery next to his mother.

At the graveside, Joe and George said a few words of adoration for their brother. And a few close friends said their final goodbyes.

Back at the White House, the family, the pallbearers, Boss, Tom, Charlie, and Susan shared a meal in the formal dining room.

Joe stood and said, "On behalf of the Miller family, we want to welcome our guests. If you are here, it's because this family considers you as someone particularly special. We Millers were born into this family. It so happens we are close and love being a Miller. Those of you who think you are here as one of those guests I mentioned, well, think again. By our choice, we decided you are family too. You have become so important to us and the 101. We welcome you to be part of this family dinner." Joe raised his wine glass and said, "Salute and welcome."

Even among the cowboys, it was hard to find a dry eye in the room.

Charlie leaned over to Susan and said, "He was remarkable. Joe has always been a great speaker, but that had to be tough even for him."

Susan whispered, "This is an honor I'll never forget. I knew how much you meant to George when I saw how he reacted in his office yesterday. But now we know how much the entire family thinks of you."

The rest of the evening was warm, colorful, and filled with folks sharing their best memories of good times with Zack.

Chapter 31

What George Wanted to Talk About

March 1920

THE NEXT MORNING, SUSAN shook Charlie awake. "Hey, big guy, the rooster welcomed the sun an hour ago."

"Wha... wha... what time is it?"

"It's 7:00, and you're supposed to be in George's office at 9:00. You better get up and going."

They arrived at the café at 7:45 and Charlie told the waiter as they walked to their table, "We'll have our usual, today."

Susan asked, "Did you make up for the previous night by sleeping so late?"

"Maybe. I'm sure It helped. But I'm still tired. I need coffee to help me clear the fog."

"Charlie, you must be worried about what George wants to talk to you about for you to feel like this. By the way, I'm going to visit May this morning while you're with George. She invited me to come to their suite at the same time you guys are talking."

Charlie put his cup down, having drunk the last of the coffee. He shook his head and said, "I must have been in a deep fog, because I'm just now seein' what you're wearing. You look marvelous in your light blue blouse. I'm all for you havin' at least one for every color in the rainbow."

Susan leaned forward, giving Charlie an even better view. "I hope so because after the way you reacted on our drive here, I called my seamstress, and she's making me more of these. I'll need to wear other things once in a while, but these can be our favorites."

Charlie leaned back and smiled.

Susan reached over and squeezed Charlie's hand. "You didn't respond to my comment about what's concerning you. But it's fine."

They finished their meal and walked back to the White House.

On the front porch, Charlie pulled Susan to him and kissed her, and said, "I love ya. You and May have a pleasant mornin' together. When George and I finish, I'll go back to our suite. Whoever arrives first waits for the other. Okay?"

"Okay, Sweetheart."

Charlie walked to George's office. As he passed the office he once used, he noticed two young men close to his age shared it. He knocked at George's office door.

"Come in, Charlie, Let's sit at the table. Can I get you some coffee?'

"Sure, George, another cup sounds good. I think I'm still about a quart low."

George grinned as he went to the door and called up the hall. "Margaret, can you bring Charlie and me some coffee? A full carafe and two cups, please?"

After they both had enjoyed their first sip, George said, "I need to share some information with you, and it must be kept just between you and me and of course Susan. Only my brother Joe and I know this. You can tell Susan because I know you two discuss everything and since you own The Kramer Group you both contribute to its day-to-day guidance. Oh, I guess I'm rambling. Let me get to the matter at hand."

Charlie interrupted George. "I won't even tell Susan if you ask me to keep it to myself."

George said, "No, you can share this with her. I'm sure she'll need to be part of this anyway. I apologize, Charlie, I'm still rambling. That's not like me. I need to just settle down and let's talk." He gathered himself, sighed, and looked at Charlie. "The 101 is struggling financially. Joe and I are at odds about what we need to do to fix things. Losing Zack is a real blow to the ranch and not just in his ability to run the ranching operation. Joe valued his judgment on some subjects, and I don't have those experiences. But my biggest concern is, we've lost money for several years in a row. You must remember we were not doing well at the time when you married Susan. We haven't had a profitable month since. We owe a big note to the Exchange National Bank in Tulsa which is coming due at the end of the year. I've nowhere while back to get enough money to pay for what will be owed. Our oil business is still making good money, but not enough this year to cover the note."

Charlie rubbed the back of his neck then leaned forward,

picked his coffee mug, and paused. He then looked George in the eye. "Have you talked to anyone at the bank?"

"Yes, and the loan department manager said our note is so large it would take Mr. Sinclair or maybe the new owner of the bank to approve any extension or modification. I haven't reached this Sinclair, and I don't know who this new owner is."

Charlie smiled and said, "I do." He leaned back in his chair. "He can be reasonable, but I'm sure he would want to counsel with his partner before committin' to anythin'."

George said, "You do? Well, who is this guy?"

"My dear friend, it's me. A while back we as the Kramer Group purchased the bank from Harry Sinclair and his three partners. They needed an influx of capital, and we wanted to get a foothold in bankin' here in Oklahoma. I hear The Exchange National Bank has a history of limitin' loans to only companies involved in oil, how were you gettin' money out of them?"

George couldn't look at Charlie. "It was because we are in the oil business. When we got the money, I had to spend it wherever the 101 ranch industries needed it."

Charlie shifted in his chair and again looked George in the eye. "Before I left after Susan and I married, one of our last conversations was about the fact it was lookin' bad for the 101. Joe had restarted the travelin' show, and he was tryin' to make movies like this ranch was Hollywood. Those things were big financial drains on the rest of the 101. Oil was the only business makin' enough to offset those losses. George, you're a magician, a genius, the best I've ever heard of at makin' a business stay afloat in hard times, but I said then, and I may say now, you need to shut down the travelin' show and the movies and focus on what is makin' money. You say the oil business is still doin' well. I know that's gotta be true because I'm in the oil business with you. Your ranchin' and farmin' businesses are second to none and should be makin' money." He took a breath, leaned forward, and said, "Okay my friend, what do you need from me?"

George smiled as he reached over and picked up something from his desk. "I have a folder here with all the financial information you'll need to analyze and figure out if you can help us. Take it. You and your beautiful and brilliant wife go over it and tell me what you can offer, if anything, to help me fix this mess. If I can't fix it within the next few months, we'll lose this ranch to bankruptcy."

Charlie slumped in his chair for a moment. He was saddened at learning this. He took a deep breath and rose from his chair. He reached out his hand. "Give me the folder, and I'll go upstairs and get Susan. We'll find a private place somewhere, and after some study and discussion, we'll come back tomorrow mornin' with what we can offer you and Joe. Seem reasonable?"

George smiled as he stood and handed Charlie the folder. "Tomorrow morning is more than reasonable."

Charlie turned to go then paused and asked, "And George, who's in my old office?"

"Charlie, it took two to replace you. It's Joe's two young sons Joe Jr and George W. They're sharp as a tack. One handles the books on the ranch and farm. The other one handles the oil business working with your fellow. I'll see you tomorrow at 9:00 here in the office, okay?"

"Yep. And have Joe here too; see ya then." Charlie left George's office and headed to the suite.

***

Susan was in the suite when he arrived. She hadn't been there for long.

Susan greeted Charlie with a hug and kiss. "May and I had a wonderful time talking and getting to know each other better. I told her I needed to be here when you finished because you might want to go somewhere exploring here at the ranch."

"I'm glad ya did. We do need to go somewhere, but to review some things and talk." He held up the folder. "I have some information we need to discuss, and we can't let others here at the ranch overhear us. Let's drive into Ponca City, and we can have lunch at the Arcade Hotel's restaurant. I'll give you what I know on the way there,"

Susan turned and reached for her things. "Is this subject a serious issue?"

Charlie nodded, "Very serious. I hope we can come up with an answer for George and Joe they can be satisfied with."

Chapter 32

A Plan

March 1920

IT WAS A LITTLE past noon when Charlie and Susan sat down at a table in the far corner of the Arcade Hotel's Ponca Room restaurant.

The waiter dried his hands on his apron as he hurried to their table. "What can I get you to drink?"

As had become their routine, Susan responded with their order. She looked up at the handsome young man. "We'll have sweet tea. And we don't need menus if you have club sandwiches. We prefer bacon over ham, and if you can, toast the bread please."

The young man fell victim to Susan's physical charms. She needed to give him their order again. She asked him to repeat it to her, and on his second try, he got everything correct.

Charlie grinned at Susan. "Poor guy, between your curves and beautiful face, he didn't stand a chance."

Susan returned his grin. "I can't help it, and you don't want me to try anyway."

She placed her napkin on her lap. "Now, let's get to the issue at hand for the Millers. You described on the drive into town how the ranch is in financial trouble. Before we open the folder and go over the information, I want to make sure I understand your concerns. Did you say you believe the problem is the traveling Wild West Show and Joe is trying to get into the movie business?"

Charlie shook his head as he crossed his arms over his chest. "That's about it. We do need to go over everythin' in detail George has provided. But when I brought up what I saw was happenin' back about the time we married, and how it was obvious to me this crisis was comin', George didn't say anythin' but handed me this folder and said, 'tell me what you can offer to help me fix this mess.'"

Their food showed up, and they ate and began to read. After finishing their sandwiches, they shifted to finishing their reading, taking notes, and talking.

After a few hours and several glasses of sweet tea, it was mid-afternoon. Susan put her pencil down and looked at Charlie. "Sweetheart, what are you seeing?"

Charlie stretched his back. "They do have a big problem, and it's obvious to me what it is. They've tightened up operations in a few areas, but the main thing is they need to get out of the entertainment business."

Susan looked at the paperwork in front of her. "You're right. And I bet George knows it. What I see is the ranch, as an enterprise, lost over $300,000 last year. It's only had one year in the last five it made a profit, and it was a very small one. I can see over $1,000,000 in assets as I've looked at things and it's more than their liabilities. But everything is heading toward a very bad outcome without new money and some different financial policies. Again, I bet George sees this and what I want us to do is find a way to back everything down a notch or two and allow Joe to have somethin' he can contribute to a solution. I think we need to influence him to focus on agriculture again. You have convinced me he is a world-class expert in agriculture. You've also said he's among the best in animal husbandry as well. But based on what you've said, growing fruit and produce, he's the best there is."

Charlie stood. He walked around the room for a minute, came back to the table, and picked up his tea glass. "I'm seein' the same thing, Sweetheart. We can help fix this. And I'm sure George knows we can."

They read and talked for several more hours. George had provided them with legal pads and pencils, and Charlie had worked and reworked numbers, and nothing made sense except what they saw early on. A distinguished-looking middle-aged man approached their table and said, "Has anyone checked on you folks in a while?"

Susan stopped what she was doing and turned in her chair. "It's been a while, but we're going over a business's books looking for ways we can help. Therefore, we're grateful for the uninterrupted silence. Although, I could use some more sweet tea."

The gentleman placed his hand over his heart. "Of course.

My name is Lew Wentz, and I own the Arcade. I'll get your waiter over here for you."

He turned to leave, and Charlie said, "Pardon me. Did ya say, Lew Wentz?"

"Yes, do I know you?"

"No, but I believe we may have some friends in common. Bill Skelly, J. Paul Getty, Harry Sinclair, and of course, E.W. Marland. And I believe you have some oil interests yourself."

"Why, yes, I do, and I consider all those men close friends. And you are?"

Susan turned again to face Wentz. "We're Charles and Susan Kelly. We own the Kramer Group, and one of our new companies is the Kelly Oil Company. We're also the new owners of the Exchange National Bank in Tulsa."

Lew's eyes grew large with excitement as he said, "So, you are the young lions I have heard about. Charles, you were out at the 101 Ranch for a while. Susan, I had the pleasure of meeting your father several years ago on a trip to Kansas City. It's my genuine pleasure to make your acquaintance. Are you visiting because of the funeral?"

Charlie said, "Yes, we are. Zack's death was a shock to us all."

Lew said, "I need to let you get back to your task. I'll have your waiter bring you more tea. Maybe we can discuss a little business someday."

Charlie said, "It would be our pleasure. We have some wells pumpin' over around Burbank."

Susan added, "They should give us an excuse to come visit."

Lew smiled. "And I'm in Tulsa often. Next time I'll look you up. Are you in the book?"

Susan looked pleased. "Yes, we are, and Harry and Bill have our phone numbers as well."

After some more discussion and another glass of sweet tea, they decided to drive back to the ranch. They had a plan and hoped George and Joe would support it.

***

Susan and Charlie ate a light dinner at the café and then decided to walk out to the banks of the Salt Fork one more time because they would leave for Tulsa after meeting with George and Joe in the morning.

As she sat down on the riverbank's grassy area, Susan said, "I love this place. I sure hope the boys let us help keep it alive."

Charlie put his arm around her and hugged her to him. "I

agree. The plan we'll offer will create a way for this ranch to exist for many more generations."

Susan looked amused as she said, "I just wish it had a swimming pool, Charlie. The Salt Fork isn't a creek. It flows too fast through here for comfortable swimming. But it doesn't mean we can't do everything else we did on the bank of the Rock Creek." She began unbuttoning her blouse, and Charlie began to match her efforts. They made their evening on the Salt Fork a romantic one.

***

Charlie and Susan were asleep early, so they were both up with the rooster and dressed for their trip back to Tulsa. They packed the car and were on their way to the ranch café by 7:30.

As they entered, the waiter seemed delighted to see them and said, "You want your regular?"

Susan purred, "We sure do, Honey."

Charlie had made some notes to follow as he would later describe the plan they would recommend. He got the pad out and turned it around so Susan could see it. It listed each element of the project.

Susan sipped her coffee as she read the list carefully. She placed her cup on the saucer and looked up from the page. "Sweetheart, these are all the things we discussed, and you're cutting the right areas. I know we worked this together, but you must be the messenger. Are you covering these in this order?"

"Maybe, I'll start with the idea they are in a tough situation, and they must make some changes, or they will lose it all."

Susan countered, "You must find a way, to be frank, and sincere without beating them over their heads. I don't envy your job."

***

The Kellys arrived at 9:00. George and Joe sat at the conference table in George's office waiting with coffee mugs in front of them.

As he saw them in the office doorway, George said, "Come in, can I get you coffee or something?"

As Susan took her seat she said, "I'll have another cup. How about you, Charlie?"

"Sounds good to me."

George said, "I know Charlie takes his black. What about you, Susan?"

"Me too. As my Honey says, good coffee don't need no help."

They all laughed at her humor and settled into the meeting.

Joe said, "Well, let's get right to it. Charlie, you or Susan give us what you think we need to do?"

Susan raised her hand. "Let me say this; Charlie will share our plan for the 101 Ranch. And please understand it is a plan I endorse and most of it is Charlie's work." She raised her arm in Charlie's direction. "Sweetheart, the floor is yours."

Charlie nodded. In as tender a tone as he could muster, he started. "First, Susan and I consider you askin' us for our input on this subject to be the most special opportunity since our marriage. Joe, you, and George are goin' to have to make some tough decisions startin' today. The issues you're facin' aren't goin' to wait for a miracle. But Susan and I are positive this is fixable." He shifted in his chair as he looked from George to Joe. "It'll require you to accept a major change here at the ranch. You can't keep doin' the same things the same way and expect to get a different outcome. I figure everythin' I've just said, you already know, but I needed it said to put us on the same page. Here's what Susan and I feel must happen.

"You need a fresh start with new money and a restructuring of how you operate. There are activities you have been puttin' way too much of your money and time into that aren't breakin' even. Anyone who would come to your aid will not help you if they don't see major changes to your operation."

Joe asked, "Do you know anyone interested in coming on board with us? We have a loan already with a bank in Tulsa. The Exchange National Bank."

George said, "I should have told you, Joe. I learned yesterday that Charlie and Susan own the bank now."

Joe gasped as he fell back in his chair. "The whole bank. Lock stock and barrel?"

Charlie replied, "Yes, Joe, we own several dozen banks, Lock, stock, and barrel. Susan and I can come in here and put together an executable plan to pull the 101 out of the financial situation you find yourself."

Joe asked, "How much do you know about our situation?"

George turned to face Joe. "They have the complete picture, Joe. I provided them with everything I had, and I assume they have gone over all of it."

Joe glared. "I'm not real happy about that, George."

George looked at Joe. "I told you no one has been willing to give us a dime. And even our current bankers wouldn't talk to me without a complete listing of every asset we have and everything we owe. I gave Charley and Susan the same information everyone else would have required."

Joe stayed grumpy. "Well, okay..."

Charlie raised a hand to interrupt them. "We need to discuss what will be required for The Kramer Group to get involved here."

Joe grouched, "Who's this Kramer Group?"

George cleared his throat. "I apologize for Joe. He is great at some things, but he doesn't know beans about the business world you two live in daily. Joe, The Kramer Group, is one of the largest corporations in the United States. We're talking about a company with billions of dollars in assets and very little debt. And you're sitting across from the two owners of The Kramer Group."

Joe shook his head. "This snot-nosed young cowboy sittin' there is a rich man?"

Susan was about to take another sip of coffee. She laughed so hard at Joe's comment she almost spilled coffee on the table full of paperwork. "Joe, my full name is Susan Kramer Kelly. Charlie learned right before we married that I was very wealthy. He forgave me for keeping it from him then and now following Charlie's lead, we have added close to a billion dollars in assets to the Kramer Group. Charlie is brilliant at seeing problems and fixing them. What he has planned for you will give the world the 101 Ranch for generations to come. I am an economist. I know the business world well. If you don't change, you will be bankrupt in months, and you and the world will lose a treasure that handled right, as I said, will be here a hundred years from now."

George said, "Charlie, can you give us the bottom-line?"

Charlie replied, "Okay. First, The Kramer Group buys the ranch. I mean everythin'. Includin' the name, the brand, everythin'. We assume the debt. Joe, we would want you to stay and run the agriculture side of the ranch. We would pay you an executive's salary and you would get a bonus of two percent of the agriculture area's net profit every year at Christmas. George, I want to offer you a position within The Kramer Group. We are goin' through a reorganization ourselves, and we are desperate for a brilliant mind to fill the role of Chief Financial Officer. I want you in that role."

George and Joe looked at each other then back to Charlie and Susan, but kept quiet.

"Now as to the way, we must reorganize the ranch. We'll git out of the movie business. The travelin' show will also be gone. We'll replace them with a local show using the arena on weekends from Memorial Day to Labor Day. We'll have rodeos on the openin' and closin' days each season. Joe, those will be your babies, too. But, I want your primary focus to be farmin', and I'll help create a cooperative program between Oklahoma A&M and the 101 as soon as possible. I would love to see your research and theirs workin' together. I'll have Boss, who's workin' my cattle operations now, work with Thad to make everythin' involvin' the cattle operation more efficient. We'll sell off all the exotic animals and reinvest the proceeds into primary farm animals. I'll move some of the horse trainin' we do at some of our other locations to the arena.

"The entire oil business will continue under Kelly Oil. Joe Jr. and George W. will continue to do the books, and they will, at least for the next year, need some guidance until you say they don't, George. After I have all this in place, we'll run this way for two years. Then we'll re-evaluate all of it. We'll be lookin' for profit. If we aren't making a profit, we'll figure out why. I plan to keep all the businesses going like the café, the general store, meat packing, the dairy, and so forth. They are coverin' expenses or, in some cases makin' money."

Charlie paused and looked at both Miller men. "I'm certain with The Kramer Group buyin' you out at fair market value and then retirin' the debt Joe, you and George will have a nice nest egg to build a wonderful retirement. Plus, I plan to pay you as the executives you'll be. Your salaries should also provide a wonderful life for you without touchin' your nest eggs. The best thing about this plan is that this place I love remains in operation. Now since I understand the financial situation, I couldn't live with myself if I didn't do everythin' I could to keep this place alive. My passion for this place is the emotional part of the solution. The rest will be focusin' on what we do well which the public is happy to buy from us. Joe, you're a genius at farming, the world will pay you to run a big farm and feed many people. George, you're brilliant with finances. You kept this place afloat for years beyond what most people could have. You'll now help run the finances of one of the largest companies in the world. And the world will be payin' you to do it. Well, gentlemen, those are the basics of it. What do you say we do a deal?"

Joe squirmed in his chair for a moment then said, "I was gonna fight ya tooth and nail. You're practically rippin' my heart out of the 101 as the show and the movies are what I enjoyed. But Charlie, you're a mighty smart young man. And I believe you can take our daddy's legacy a whole lot farther than we could. George, whattaya think, brother?"

"Charlie, your plan is what we need to do. Joe is right. If the Colonel was sitting here facing these issues, he would sell and then be proud to help run the new operation with the focus needed to reach the current and future generations. Let's do the deal."

Over the next few hours, Charlie and Susan answered detailed questions, and a strategy for transfer of ownership was agreed on.

When it was obvious all the questions had been answered, Charlie, with misty eyes, gathered himself and said, "Great, I... uh... consider this a sacred trust. Susan and I will have Curt Schlegell, our corporate attorney, git with your attorney, Bill England, and create the paperwork for us. George, thanks for reachin' out to me and Susan."

Everyone shook hands and Charlie and Susan left George's office. As they went down the stairs of the White House, Charlie was almost in tears. "Sweetheart, pinch me. This must be a dream. Many nights I laid in my bunk over in the north bunkhouse and dreamed maybe one day I could own this ranch. Now I'm livin' a true Cowboy's Dream."

Chapter 33

A Pawhuska Conversation

April 1920

CHARLIE AND SUSAN WERE in their Cadillac a few miles north of the 101 main gate coming into view of Ponca City and were hungry because the meeting with George and Joe had lasted almost three hours.

Charlie said, "I can't wait until Pawhuska to git somethin' to eat. Let's go back to the Arcade Hotel and have lunch."

Susan said, "I'm starved too. The meeting was long. It was impactful, and you were amazing in there, Sweetheart."

Charlie looked over at Susan, as pleased as he could remember, and said, "We make a good team. You added comments at the perfect time with the right information."

Susan acknowledged his thought with, "Thanks, but I was following your lead. That must have been the toughest negotiation you've faced. Those men are like uncles to you."

"It was. I couldn't afford to fail."

Charlie turned onto Grand Avenue and drove the few blocks and parked in front of the hotel.

They sat at a table where they could look out onto the corner of Grand and First Street through a beautiful picture window. Susan said, "This would have been nice yesterday, but we needed to have quiet and no distractions for our work."

The same young waiter who had helped them before came and got their order. Charlie smiled as he said, "Can you bring us two egg salad sandwiches and two sweet teas, please." This time he got the order right the first time.

"Right away, sir." He glanced over at Susan, saw the same view but framed by a light blue blouse this time, and grinned big as he left the table.

Lew Wentz came to their table and said, "I saw you come in and thought I would say hello. I got a call from George about ten minutes ago. He said you were the new owners of the 101 as soon as the paperwork is ready. Preparing an offer must have been what you were doing here yesterday. You were working up the offer, weren't you?"

Susan responded, "Yes, we were. I'm surprised George shared the information so soon. We have agreed to purchase the ranch and all its assets."

Lew said, "George and I have been close friends for years. He has been discussing the issues he faced with me for months. He is so excited. He can't wait to start his new role with you at the Kramer offices. It'll be the first time he'll live anywhere off the ranch."

Charlie said, "We're happy he came to us. I love the ranch, and we'll do whatever it takes to git it back, makin' money and makin' people happy."

Lew said, "I know you will. I have some significant oil holdings here in Kay and Osage counties along with some up in Kansas. I may want to divest myself of them soon. I'm looking at buying into citrus orchards and maybe a baseball team in Florida. George gave me your contact information; will it be alright to give you a call sometime later this year?"

"Please do, Lew. We'll stop by here when we're in the area."

***

An hour or two later they were pulling into Pawhuska and Charlie looked over at Susan. "Let's drive up on Agency Hill. We haven't been there in a while. Then maybe stop and have a glass of sweet tea before heading on to Tulsa."

Susan tilted her head and smiled. "I saw the café we ate at last time. Do you remember the Union Cafe?"

"I sure do. Hank and I ate there a time or two also. We usually saw several oilmen there and they always seemed to be busy."

At the café, Susan reached over and tapped the tabletop near Charlie. "Don't turn around, but there's a man who continues to stare at me. Charlie, men often give me second looks, some stare for a moment, but this guy makes my skin crawl."

"What does he look like? I saw two men at a table when we came in. I know who they are because Hank pointed them out to me when we were at an auction."

"The one who is making me shudder is wearing a blue suit

with a brown vest under the coat. He wears glasses and the man at the table with him is much bigger, barrel-chested, and appears to be younger."

Charlie nodded. "The man in the suit is named Hale. I think Hank said he's Bill Hale. Hank doesn't trust him, period. He lives down in Fairfax and owns a pool hall. But he's always around when Osage oil rights are being sold. The guy with him is his nephew. I think his name is Ernest Burkhart. I guess he works for Hale. Hank calls him a thug who does Hale's dirty work. The way Hank talks about them, they must be much like Willard and his goon were. The reason he may be glaring at you is he may remember me and Hank gittin' the Burbank property. Hank noticed he didn't seem happy when we got it. Although he quit bidding early. Now it also could be he's guilty of staring at the most beautiful woman he's ever seen."

"No Charlie, it's not a look of admiration or even lust. It's nothing but an evil look and I'll be happy when we're back in the car."

"Well, I'm finished here. I guess you want to leave?"

"Yes, please. the guy scares me more than Willard ever did."

Charlie stood and picked up the ticket to pay as Susan got up and grabbed a hold of his free arm. They went straight to the cash register and paid. They had to walk past Hale's table to get to the front door.

Charlie looked at Hale and smiled. "Fine day out don't ya think?"

Hale growled, "What's it to you?"

Charlie just had to laugh.

They were down the road and driving through Skiatook at 4:15. Susan was already mentally out on their patio with her glass of Cabernet. She asked, "About how much farther, Sweetheart?"

Charlie was amused. "Can't wait to git home, huh? We'll be home before 5:00. I'll unload the car, and you can find Attie and Cleta and give them the evening off. With them in their quarters, we'll have our pool and patio for a swim, some wine, cheese, crackers, and some lovin'. Sound good?"

"Oh, my goodness yes, Charlie. I love our new home, and the very private patio is the best. It's our little piece of heaven."

Chapter 34

Telling Boss the News

April 1920

CHARLIE WAS AT HIS desk working on his ideas for the 101 while Susan sat in the living room reading as they awaited the arrival of Bailey, Rice, and Emilia for the meeting on the remodel of the Exchange National Bank building.

Susan put her book down and walked into Charlie's office. "This has been a wonderful few weeks despite losing a good friend. Our opportunity to save the 101 Ranch is what I mean. I know how important it was to you."

Charlie reached over and picked up a cup sitting on the corner of his desk He took a sip of coffee, sighed, and said, "Yes it has been somethin' for sure. Over this past month we've met with Curt and agreed upon a plan to improve our overall corporate operation, said a respectful goodbye to a great man, saved an iconic ranch, and then today we address a threat from some hoodlums after plannin' a new headquarters. Susan, that's a good year, and it all happens in a month."

Susan sat in a chair next to his desk and took a sip of his coffee. "You just described our life for a while now. We keep saying yes to opportunities, and your brain comes up with new ideas all the time. I'm not complaining, life with you is exciting and so far, financially profitable."

Charlie put his pencil down and looked at her. "I hope it all continues, but you know we are bound to have a few misses come along with all these hits. On another subject, I can't believe I haven't called Boss. Now the paperwork isn't final, but I need to let him know about buyin' the 101. It's after 7:00 and he'll be up and on his third cup of coffee by now. He knows George wanted us to stay and discuss some things. We agreed with Joe and

George to keep it quiet until the lawyers were done."

Susan said, "Uncle Curt called last night to tell us everything on the sale was going to be easy to complete. I was surprised you didn't call him last night. Boss'll be shocked, won't he?"

"Yep, and he'll know his responsibilities will increase as well."

Susan said, "Tell him we'll compensate him well and try to lessen his load elsewhere."

"I'm thinkin' the lighter load will be as important to him as the money. We might add a nice convenience to his house or buy him a new truck, which will make him as happy as a raise in pay. I can hear him now. Charlie, I ain't got time now to spend whatcha pay me."

Susan laughed. "You're right, but he'll appreciate how we trust him with our entire cattle business, which now includes the 101."

"He will, and I think he'll be excited. He has told me he loves workin' for us and with Dan, Tom, Bill, and Hank. But he must miss the 101. It was home for him for thirty years. I need to make the call." Susan went back to the living room and got back to her book.

After the second ring, Charlie heard, "Hello. This is Boss."

"This is Charlie. We didn't hear different, so I guess you and Tom got back safe and sound the other day?"

"Yep, and we've got a good start on workin' the new property up the road into our operation. The added land is sure gonna be nice. Hank showed me the part up north he has his eye on, and it won't be an issue with our cattle operation."

"Boss, I need ta tell ya, somethin'. Ya sound mighty excited. But I've got some more good news."

"Oh, sure, you're the one called. Whatcha got for me?"

"Susan and I are the new owners of the 101."

"Wha.. wha... you gotta be shittin' me. Sorry, Charlie, but I thought ya said ya own the 101."

"We do. I told ya George wanted Susan and me to stay over because he wanted to talk. Susan and I met with him, and he shared how bad the finances were and asked if we had any advice. He gave Susan and me all the ranch's financial information, and we found a quiet place to study it. We went back the next mornin' and shared our ideas with George and Joe. We said the best solution for them was to sell us the ranch, and we would restructure the operation into what should be a profitable situation that'll last for many generations. Joe will stay in charge of the farming operation; George will come to work for us at

Kramer, and I'll fill you in on the details later. But the bottom line is they agreed to sell us the ranch. Susan and I want the cattle operation to come to you with whatever support you need. I was thinkin' Thad might remain as the lead up there, and he would work for you. He took guidance from Zack before. Whattaya think?"

"It could work, I'd need to go up there from time to time, but Thad has become a solid cowboy, and he knows the operation. We've become an Angus outfit here, and I like it. We could do the same up there."

Charlie said, "I thought ya might, so here's what I'm thinkin'. We would be willin' to give ya a raise in salary, and of course, now your annual bonus will be based on the 101 cattle profit too. But instead of a raise in salary, how about we give ya a new truck of your choice. You'll have it to make the drive up to the 101 easier on ya. We can make one of the suites in the White House your room for when ya go up there, and ya eat at the café for free."

"First, Charlie, ya know me well. I make enough in salary, although the bonus gettin' bigger will make my retirement nest egg grow faster. I'll appreciate those new benefits a lot. I'll enjoy seein' the 101 from time to time, and it sounds like ya saved it from goin' under for good. What are the big changes needed to make it profitable every year?"

"The big thing is the travelin' show is gone and the movie business too. You, Dan, Tom, Thad, and Hank will discuss how we will blend the cattle business, the horse business, and the oil business up there into what we are doin' here. Does that make sense?"

"It sure does. How did ya get Joe to give up show business?"

"He'll still get some of the show business stuff at the ranch in the summer, and that mollified him on losing the rest of it. The rest of the time he'll focus on the farmin', which he also loves, though maybe not as much as the movie stuff. Plus, we made him a millionaire as soon as all the paperwork flowed."

"Okay, I know Joe's happy."

"Boss, I have some people comin' to the house soon, so, I need to go, but ya got the main parts. Share this with Tom and Dan. Susan and I'll come to see ya soon."

"Okay, goodbye, Charlie."

Chapter 35

Planning the Move

April 1920

RICE SHOWED UP JUST before nine and Attie brought him to the kitchen area. He joined Charlie and Susan at the table overlooking their colorful yard.

Charlie and Susan stood and she said, "Good morning, Rice. Hope you had a pleasant trip. How are things in Kansas City?"

Rice smiled and took a seat across from Charlie. "Good morning to you both. Things are good, including the train ride. I'm excited to update you on some developments and today's meeting sounds interesting."

Susan placed her hand on Charlie's arm, "We want to hear everything. But let's not start now because the others will be arriving… oh, well, here they come now."

Attie ushered Emilia and Bailey into the room. Cleta came from the kitchen and said, "Can I bring you folks something to drink? I have some freshly made chocolate chip cookies ready as well."

Everyone wanted coffee, and Cleta placed a platter of cookies in the middle of the table.

Charlie looked around the table. "Welcome everyone to our new home. Susan, do you have anythin' you'd like to say to start us off?"

Susan scanned their faces. "We appreciate you being here. I know Rice and Bailey work for us, and we have them heavily tasked already, but they are here without a whimper, and I want to thank you. And Emilia, we're enjoying what you created here and want to hear your ideas on a big project we need to execute."

Charlie said, "Let me be clear as I describe our reason for being here, that we're open to ideas and questions. I want us to stay at this until we have a solid plan." The others all nodded as they settled in with their coffee.

"Susan and I love Tulsa. Our company headquarters is in Kansas City, and the location had made sense up until recently. But much of the company's recent growth, across all divisions, comes from Oklahoma, and may soon include Texas. Lookin' ahead our growth will continue in those states and further west for the next decade. Therefore, we have decided to move our corporate offices to Tulsa and locate them in the renovated Exchange National Bank buildin'. We want the twelfth floor to be dedicated to offices for Susan, me, Curt Schlegell, our attorney, our new Chief Financial Officer George L Miller, and the executive conference room."

Rice had a look of concern on his face. "I have some general questions, but," he turned to look at Susan, "when are you going to run this by the board? I think this is a decision that all of the board members should be a part of, especially if you are going to disrupt their lives in Kansas City."

Susan said, "I understand your concern. I have already asked Curt to add this as an agenda item for the next board meeting. But we strongly believe this is the best move for The Kramer Group at this time. We will listen to everyone's suggestions and concerns, but we also want to get ahead of this now assuming the board agrees with our decision."

Rice nodded. "Okay. I can live with that." He opened a notebook and pulled out a pen. "How many stories does the building have? You mentioned the twelfth floor, is it the top floor?"

Charlie replied, "Yes. The bank is on the ground floor, and offices supporting the bank occupy the second and third floors. Floors four through eleven will be available for use by the companies within Kramer by moving the offices located in the Commerce Bank of Kansas City's main tower. We'll have more square footage available here in Tulsa, but we'll need more because we are addin' offices for Kelly Oil, the security company, and the Abrams Stores."

Rice said, "I'll need to reach out to George Winkler, who was the architect used in 1917 to design the building. Once I get the drawings I'll confer with him to ensure we don't miss a load-bearing wall or cause some other major problem."

Charlie said, "That's the kind of thinkin' we need. Anythin' else?"

Emilia said, "I guess I'll be coming into this project last. While Mr. Coburn and Mr. Muldoon are doing their work, I could go to Kansas City and look at what is there and make sure I know your current staff's environment. I'll also want to look at the bank here. I may recommend you move the furnishings with the staff or use what's already at the bank if it makes good sense. When something works well, why spend money and replace it."

"I agree with your thinkin'," Charlie said. "We'll send ya to Kansas City. If ya want, we'll get ya a photographer to allow ya to have pictures to use when ya come back."

Bailey said, "I will have AT&T come out and do a complete checkout of what we have. I assume the bank is already using the best available security system and is already tied to the police and fire departments. If not, I recommend it. Once we have the new layout of the building, we'll update the security to meet our new requirements."

The five of them began an hour-long conversation regarding the project. Charlie, anticipating questions about the current offices, had asked Curt to send down the drawings of the space used in Kansas City so they could see how the various business functions were laid out.

Charlie ended the meeting as he said, "Rice, I'm askin' you to be the project manager for this remodel and move."

"If the board approves it," Rice added, making his point again.

"I'm confident they will," Charlie said. "I would like you to take the next week and meet with the leaders with office space in Kansas City and get a clear understandin' of what will be required here. Get with Chester Abrams and discuss what he'll need for his company, and I'll have a meetin' with the key folks within Kelly Oil and they will provide you with the information. Let's meet back here in two weeks."

"That might spook the rest of the board members if we present this move as a fait accompli before they have a chance to hear the reasons and vote on it."

Susan said, "That's a good point. Charlie, we can work with Kelly Oil and Bailey's group for now, but we have to present this to the board in a delicate way. Rice is correct that this might ruffle their feathers, especially if they don't get a say in it."

Charlie rubbed his chin and nodded. "Okay, I guess I am just so excited about this and I know it is the right move for The Kramer Group. But I'll wait until we have a chance to present it to the board."

The group stood and made their good-byes. Charlie turned to Bailey and said, "We need to have our meetin', but I need a break,"

Bailey said, "Okay, but we must talk today."

"You sound serious."
Bailey frowned, "I am."

Chapter 36

Mob Issues

April 1920

CHARLIE PATTED BAILEY ON the shoulder as he arrived back at the table. "Bailey, I apologize but I needed to call Kansas City and talk to our attorney. I also asked Cleta to prepare some sweet tea for us. Let's go use the shady table out on the patio."

Bailey stood. "Sure, Charlie. Lead the way."

Bailey took his seat across from Charlie and pulled a folder from his briefcase He took an envelope out, pulled a sheet from it then handed it to Charlie. "This will show you everything we know about the people who have been terrorizing you here in Oklahoma."

Charlie took the sheet, read it, and he shook his head. "Well, now I at least know more than just their names. Joe and Pete DiGiovanni sound like some real bad hombres."

Bailey leaned in, "You could say that. These two are some bad individuals. They're out of Palermo, Sicily, with criminal lives already well established. In Kansas City, they own a wholesale grocery business, and it appears they may also own a couple of restaurants and a construction company. But their real money comes from extortion, and the word on the street is that they are aiming to control the bootlegging industry in and around Kansas City. Since January, the underworld liquor industry has exploded. Whoever controls it has access to enormous wealth and power. The DiGiovanni's have the backing of the Black Hand and the Chicago Outfit."

Charlie set the letter down and looked Bailey in the eye. "This doesn't tell me what happened on Wednesday night."

Bailey cleared his throat. "At 3:00 Thursday morning, my

guys began planting signs at the businesses known to be owned and operated by the DiGiovanni Family. They also placed signs on the front porches of their homes. Wyatt and Josh staked out their homes to see their reaction when they saw the signs. They both became furious."

Charlie looked delighted as he asked, "What did the signs say?"

Bailey looked prideful. "The ones left at the businesses said, 'We could have destroyed this business tonight, but we didn't. Stay out of Tulsa and away from the Kramer Group.' The ones left in front of their homes said, 'You'd be dead if we wanted it. Stay out of Tulsa and away from the Kramer Group.'"

Charlie took a sip of tea, cocked his head, and thought for a moment. "Ya say the brothers were furious. But do ya think they were fearful?"

Bailey leaned back and crossed his arms. "Hard to know. Anger would come first, but fear comes with realizing what the signs said is true. We may not get a response for days, weeks, or more. They had to be shocked we could gain knowledge and access to the businesses. We surprised and subdued their night watchmen, and they had no one at their homes. It may change now. We'll keep watch for a while."

Charlie wrung his hands. "We can't let our guard down. This will tweak their tails, and like a ragin' bull they're likely to lash out in an unexpected way" Charlie got out of his chair and walked around for a minute or so. He stopped and looked at Bailey. "I know ya need to be workin' on gettin' the security company up and runnin'. And now we've also asked ya to help design the security for the new offices here in Tulsa but keep somebody workin' a plan to go right into the hornet's nest in Chicago if needed."

Bailey put his paperwork back in the envelope. He stood. "I'll have Wyatt and Josh come up with a plan to hit both Kansas City and Chicago. We may get a response from Joe and Pete requiring a more direct and painful reply at them. And I already had those two creating the Chicago plan."

Charlie wrapped the meeting up by offering his hand. "Bailey, thanks for the report. Tell your men I'm impressed. I hope not, but we may end up in a war-like situation, and I don't want them to worry. I'll have their back. If it gits bad, we'll have whatever resources we need to defend ourselves and go on the offensive. We won't lose to this bunch. I read in the newspapers all the stories about this Chicago bunch and how they are runnin' the city and maybe the state. I hear they have so much money they buy police and politicians like there are penny candy. Well, I'm not someone they can buy or scare. Look at me, Bailey. I'm gittin' all worked up. Have a nice weekend, fella."

"Thanks, and you and Miss Susan enjoy the weekend as well."

Chapter 37

Texas, California, and the Stars

April 1920

LATER THAT EVENING THE young couple ended another busy day their preferred way. On their patio with dinner and a bottle of their favorite wine. Tonight, they would swim, enjoy the Cabernet, and it would also be a time of reflection and planning.

Charlie marveled again at how Susan's skin seemed to glisten in the soft evening twilight as she walked from the pool. "Susan, this is a sight I'll still be cravin' fifty years from now."

"Sweetheart, you keep thinking those thoughts, and I promise I'll do the best I can to give this to you. You're such a romantic, and I love it."

Charlie took a sip of wine. "I'm guessin' ya want to know what Bailey and I talked about, right?"

As she sat down on her lounger and picked up her wine glass, she glanced at Charlie. "Wow, talk about changing the subject. But, yes, I wanted to eventually hear about it."

"Well damn it, I think I must have messed up there, huh? Sorry, sometimes my mind jumps around like a toad in a pond."

"I guess I can let it go this time big guy. But when you say something romantic, I'm ready to start making love, not discuss mobsters."

"I git it, Sweetheart. I can be an idiot sometimes."

She laughed. "Yes, you can, but I still love you."

They did snuggle a while, then Susan said, "Go ahead, tell me what Bailey said."

Charlie told her about the signs placed around Kansas City, and how they had messages directed at the DiGiovanni family. He shared the hopes he and Bailey had regarding the Mob and their response.

Susan picked up the bottle of Cabernet and topped off her glass. "Do you think they will stop their harassment and leave us alone?"

Charlie rubbed his chin and considered how he wanted to answer her. "I don't know. I want them to see we can be daring and capable of being a threat. It might convince them to back off. But I do have doubts.

Susan took another sip, leaned her head back, and sighed. She couldn't hide her concern as her voice trembled. "Does it mean we could end up in a war with them, similar to what we talked about with Zane and Jim? You know, where they drive by and start shooting. I hear they have even blown-up buildings; it's a war, Charlie!"

He rose and turned to her. He then reached over and took her hand. "Susan, that's the last thing I want, but if it does become somethin' like a war, Bailey and I agree, we'll respond straight at Torrio, the boss. We'll end it as fast as we can. Let's leave this subject and discuss where we are in other areas..."

They heard the phone ringing through the open door to the living room. Charlie stood. "I'll go see who's callin'."

He put on his robe as he went inside. "Hello, this is Charles Kelly."

"Charlie, this is Hank. I'm in Oklahoma City planning to catch the train to Los Angeles in about a half-hour. But I thought we should talk before I go."

Charlie said, "I agree. And I thought you would be heading to California next month. Why now? Don't you have a lot to git done here?"

"We've drilled all the wells we should in Garvin County for now. And Burbank is pumpin' a lot of oil for us, but I need to tell you about an incident."

"I wanna hear what ya expect we'll see our Burbank wells producin'. But, what's this about an incident?"

"First, the four wells up there are doin' over 5,000 barrels a day."

Charlie said, "At that rate we're makin' between fifteen and twenty million a year in income. Do ya have any idea how long we'll get similar production from those wells?"

"I'd say we can pump them at that rate for at least a year at the current depth. Then we should be able to drill deeper and continue the same production, but of course there are no guarantees. You know, we've gotta lay some pipe from that oilfield to Sinclair's refinery in Ponca City. And I'm sure there's more oil up in Osage County, we just need to find it.

"Now about the incident. We've got one of our roughnecks in the hospital in Ponca City because of a fight over in Whizbang."

Charlie said, "That's that boomtown about ten miles from where we've been drillin', right? I've heard that's a rough place."

"That it is. I've told our leadman up there to keep his folks out of there from now on."

"Hank, is there anything I can do about Whizbang?"

"Short of barring any employee from going there, no. And if you tried that you'd upset a lot of the men and they'd quit. No, you know how roughnecks are. They need to let off steam and Whizbang allows them to do that. But I think we need to consider some strict rules around showing up to work drunk, late, or gettin' in trouble with the law."

"I suppose we could dock their pay more for infractions and fire folks who can't learn a lesson."

"That's what I'm thinking. My toolpusher up there will take care of it. He's a no-nonsense guy and I trust him. I guess we do need to ask about it from time to time, but it should be fine."

Charlie sat down on the sofa. "I'll leave it up to you. You said there were two things. What's the second one?"

"Right. I got a call about some oil exploration options in North Texas from some old friends of mine. Sid Richardson and Clint Murchison are two oilmen I've known for several years. I don't think ya know that I spent some time down in the Texas oil fields a few years before we met, and I've stayed in touch with these guys since. I told them recently we had formed Kelly Oil, and we're doin' well. They also formed a partnership at about the same time we did. Last month, I called them and gave them my number at the hotel. They called last night and said they have options to acquire oil and gas leases in what's called the North and East Texas oil fields. Drillers have found oil already around Burkburnett and Mexia. My friends are lookin' for fundin' and are willin' to go in as equal partners if we give them the cash they need."

Charlie said, "I'm interested; we already know there's a lot of oil in Texas. But what do you know about these guys? There are swindlers out there sellin' worthless oil stocks."

Hank said, "I hear ya, but I think these guys are legit, Charlie. They need only $100,000 to secure the leases they've identified. I could go to Texas before headin' to California and check everythin' out. But as you know Getty and I have stayed in touch, and things are happenin' fast out in California. The Huntington Beach area is hot, and he asked me to come out and have a look. And he's also interested in Long Beach. I told him if I do and give him advice, it'll cost him half interest in any wells he drills based on my advice."

Charlie stood and walked around the room. "You didn't promise Getty we would go halves on the cost of drillin' did ya?"

"Oh, hell no, it all falls on him. My expertise in decidin' where to drill is all I give him, and Kelly Oil gets half the proceeds. I'll find us some land and get leases for Kelly Oil in Long Beach. Getty is not the only person out there, I know. I hear Long Beach is the next hot spot. Any questions, Charlie?"

"Not about California, I'm glad you're gittin' out there."

"Hey, the train is pullin' into the station, Charlie, what do I do about Texas?"

"Contact your Texas friends and tell them we're in. Change your train ticket to go and meet them in Dallas. After you've checked everything out and signed contracts then catch the next train to California out of Dallas."

"Okay. I'll let Getty know about my change of plans. I'll be in touch, Charlie."

"Thanks for callin', Hank. Good luck and give me a call when ya git settled in California."

As he approached his lounger, Susan said, "Who called?"

Charlie sat and looked at Susan. With delight in his voice, "It was Hank. He's headin' to Dallas before goin' to Los Angeles. You know already that he and Getty have been talkin', and things are hot out there, and Paul wants Hank out there to consult with him on some drillin' sites. Hank just shared information about an opportunity to buy into some oil exploration in Texas with some fellas he says he trust. So, I told him to go to Dallas and close a deal with them first then head west."

"I thought we had things we needed Hank doing here, and he would go out to California in another month or two. Right?"

"Plans can change." Charlie shared what he and Hank discussed.

Susan refilled her glass. "Okay, he's going to Texas and then on to California later. That does make sense after I hear the rest of it. So, we're getting involved in Texas oil. That's good."

"We are. It'll cost us $100,000 but our new partners will do all the work. We get half the income off the wells."

"Okay, that sounds reasonable."

Charlie took the bottle of Cabernet and filled his glass.

She gave him a pouting look. "I'm sorry, I should have filled yours too."

He grinned. "Don't worry about it." He took a sip of wine.

"I'm goin' to swim a few laps. It's been a warm day in more ways than one." He walked to the pool.

Susan laughed as she clapped her hands. "I'll sit here and enjoy watching your naked body. You seem to like watching mine, and so this is my turn. Oh, my goodness, Charlie, you're making me hot. I think I better join you."

After twenty minutes of play, they came back to their loungers and restarted their discussion.

Charlie said, "I think we covered the Chicago Outfit enough earlier, and let's hope we won't be experiencin' any more issues with them. Our bank remodel project had its first meetin' today. Would ya agree we might see it completed by June sometime?"

Susan finished chewing a cracker. "Yes, as long as the board agrees to it. Rice was right to remind us about that. We may own the company, but we still have a board to report to on many things. You need to keep that in mind when you get a great idea. But I got the feeling that Rice liked the idea of the move. I spoke to him a bit while you were talking with Bailey. He didn't have any real objections other than us moving forward without telling the board what we were doing and giving them a chance to participate."

"Yeah, that's somethin' I need to remember. I'm so used to making decisions just for myself or for one man like George. It's a bit different for me to get used to thinkin' this way."

Susan patted his arm. "It's okay. Rice was sounding enthusiastic about the move when he and I got done talking, so I think he'll vote with us on approving the move. Rice also said he didn't see major construction as part of this project. We'll move a few walls and make some cosmetic changes, but nothing should take a great deal of time and effort. The physical move will take no more than a week."

Charlie said, "That's good, I just don't like having to trust a bunch of people to agree to somethin' I know in my heart is the right thing to do."Susan said, "You get used to it." She changed the subject. "When was the last time you talked with Bunk about the refinery and pipeline project?"

"I don't know. It had to be back when we had the vandalism. I need to call him. I guess if he were havin' problems, I'd have heard from him. I care a great deal about that project, so I should call him. It's another one we should wrap up by the end of the summer. Operationally it is rerouting the pipe distribution, but there will be some changing of office and support function space too."

Susan said, "Bunk is someone who will be a tremendous asset when we get all of the refining assets in place. And we need to decide if Cushing is the only refining location we'll have."

"I think the obvious answer is no. Harry Sinclair and I haven't talked about it, and Hank should be part of that conversation. I could see more than one location here in Oklahoma. There's large oil production in California and Texas already, so even if we don't do a lot of drillin', we could be the primary company in the refinin' part of the process at those locations. The same could be said about the oil field cementin' business too. We want to service the entire oil industry with our cementin', refinin', and pipeline assets."

Charlie finished his glass of wine and poured another.

Susan reached over and took the bottle. "Leave some for me, big guy."

Charlie grinned. "I didn't mean to not share."

"I'm teasing you. I better get us another bottle. This one's empty. I'll be right back."

She returned with a new bottle already opened and filled each of their glasses before she sat down.

Charlie said, "Thanks and to continue our conversation, on the business side, I also need to call Abrams and git updated on the Shawnee project. Last I knew they were plannin' to open the store by summer so they could be part of the back-to-school shoppin' and later be ready for the Christmas season. Since he hasn't called us, I assume the political problem was worked out to our likin'. I need to call Chester."

Susan had a happy lilt to her voice as she said, "This is fun, Charlie. We have so many wonderful things happening. We've made some good decisions over the past year, and we'll be putting a lot of people to work. It will be interesting to look at how many people we've added to our payroll this year at the next board meeting. Also, what do you hear about the Rock Island acquisition? We own the railroad now, and Owen is working hard to add to the passenger and oil tanker cars inventory. He mentioned to Curt he would like to discuss an agreement with the AT&SF folks to carry passengers to California. I'm curious about where it leads. He is planning to be ready to tell us everything by the next meeting."

Charlie nodded. "I haven't talked to him, but if it's true, he should be able to have a lot figured out by then."

Susan shifted on her lounger. "I remember my father saying, Owen has forgotten more about railroads than I'll ever know. I'm glad we have him. What have we heard from Gordon about our banking expansions? Besides here in Oklahoma. Maybe he'll have something solid to talk about down in Texas too. Gordon mentioned the Dallas-Fort Worth area banks are growing because of the stockyards more than anythin' else. I thought you might want to go down there sometime soon."

"I would, and the stockyards in the Oklahoma City area are doin' well. Another reason to git a bank or two into that area."

Charlie took a drink and then laughed. "You know, we haven't even mentioned anythin' about adding 110,000 acres to our cattle ranchin' operation with all its other businesses. The 101, along with our ranches in Earlsboro and Perkins, will become another valuable part of the Kramer Group."

After another hour of conversation and swimming Susan leaned back and stared at the stars. "Sweetheart, I know I've had more than I usually drink, but could you pour me another glass of wine? I want to stay here and think for a while about what we've accomplished since we got married. Most people our age would still be trying to figure out what job they want or should I get married. They aren't deciding whether to spend more than three million dollars to buy a place like the 101 Ranch. I'll grant to anyone who questions us we are different. My father left us a large fortune. But I'm proud to say we've made it even bigger, and what we've just discussed will grow it some more."

Charlie poured the last of the second bottle into her empty glass. He then reached over and took Susan's hand and said, "We're lucky we found each other. We want to make a difference in the world, and we aim everythin' we do at givin' others a chance to profit financially and personally as we are."

Susan squeezed his hand and said, "I love you, Charlie Kelly."

Chapter 38

The Weddings

May 1920

WHAT HAD BECOME THE daily routine in the life of Charlie and Susan Kelly the last few weeks had been tranquil. For Charlie, it was almost boring. He was sitting at his desk in their Tulsa home sipping coffee and daydreaming about being in the saddle on the back of his horse Tony working cattle at the 101 when the phone rang. "Hello, this Charles Kelly."

"This is Bunk Severs. I hope this is a good time to call."

"Yes it's fine, Bunk. What's on your mind?"

"You may not have heard, but last night a huge twister hit Peggs, Oklahoma."

"Holy Cow, Bunk. Where is Peggs, I've heard the name but don't recall being through there?"

"It's a small town, maybe thirty miles east of Tulsa. I'm from Peggs so I can understand why most people don't know where it is. My parents and a lot of family still live there. I had a cousin call me less than an hour ago. He says the town was destroyed and there are many people missing. He hasn't been able to reach my folks. I need to go there and see what I can find out."

"Of course, Bunk. Are you still in Cushing?"

"I am. Things are going fine here. My number two man, Delbert McDaniel, can cover for me for a while. I don't know how long I'll need to be in Peggs, but I can give you an update in a day or so."

"Take whatever time you need. I know Delbert and he's a good hand. Please keep Susan and I informed about your family. I sure hope your folks are okay."

"Thanks, and I'll call you when I know more."

Susan walked into Charlie's office. "Who was on the phone?"

"It was Bunk. You know how we had a lot of wind and rain durin' the night. A big tornado hit a small town east of here as part of the storm. A place called Peggs. It's Bunk's hometown and he has family there includin' his parents. He's headin' there today and will let us know what he and his family are facin' as soon as he knows."

"I'm sorry to hear it. When the phone rang, I had just ended a phone call with Tess and her mother. You know it's less than two weeks until Tess and Dan's wedding."

Charlie looked up from his paperwork and scratched at the back of his neck. "I hadn't thought about it for a while, but you're right. Do they need anythin' from us?"

"I offered for us to come over to Perkins next week on Wednesday and be there to help with any last-minute details. Claudia told me we could stay with them like before and even if Tess wouldn't have asked, they could use the support."

"Well then, we go to Perkins next week. But we can stay in Cushing at the hotel if needed. Dan will need the room we stayed in and of course, the rest of my family will need to stay somewhere. My goodness, Susan, we've done a terrible job of bein' a best man and matron of honor. I'll git ahold of the family and arrange for everyone to have rooms at the Hotel Cushing."

***

The next day Bunk called and reported his parents were alive although their property was damaged and not livable. Charlie said, "It's good your folks are fine. Will they be able to rebuild? What kind of help can we be?"

"We haven't discussed all of it yet. Thanks for the offer. The sheriff and firemen have already found over fifty people dead. No one in my family is among them, but I do have a nephew and his family missing. I know I need to be here for several more days if it's okay."

"Like I said yesterday, stay as long as you're needed. Once everythin' settles down let's talk about how we can support your family and their friends recoverin' from all this. Susan and I will be attendin' some weddins' over the next week or so. You may find me harder to reach."

"Oh, I had forgotten about Jess and Dan getting married about this time. Sorry for pulling you away from your obligations there."

"It's fine. You focus on family, and I will too. But keep me informed."

"I will, Charlie. Goodbye."

***

The final few days before the wedding were more of a celebration than work and on Friday evening at the barn where the ceremony would happen, everyone gathered for the rehearsal and the dinner.

As dessert was eaten Charlie stood and looked at Susan then turned to the honored couple. "Can I have everyone's attention? Susan and I would like to share what we're givin' Dan and Tess for their wedding gift. From what we've heard Boss and I have kept Dan so busy he and Tess haven't had time to plan their honeymoon."

Susan stepped up and stood next to Charlie. She took a breath. "I heard maybe they might go over to Oklahoma City and stay at the Skirvin for a night or two. We've not stayed there, and I hear it's a very nice place. But we want to give you something a little more special, if that's okay? We want to send you to Jekyll Island, Georgia for a week. Charlie and I spent time there on our honeymoon and it was wonderful. We own a cottage there with staff to support you. Would you accept a trip there from us?"

Dan and Tess looked at each other. Tess burst out with, "Oh my goodness. Yes, we would love to accept it."

Dan scratched his neck. "Well, I guess I can be gone long enough to go..."

Boss laughed as he pounded Dan's back. "Yeah, young man. As valuable as you are, we'll manage to let you have a fine honeymoon. Go make some memories."

Charlie turned to Jess and Diana Sue. "Now before we go back to dessert, Susan please share the rest of the story."

Susan nodded and looked at Diana Sue then Jess. "We'll be giving you two the same gift. Our hope is you'll enjoy your week on the island as well."

Diana Sue gasped. "It's the place where all the very rich people go isn't it? You own a house there?"

Charlie said, "Yes, we do. We hope you'll enjoy everythin' while you're there. And to both couples. Train fare and all expenses will be covered. Go enjoy yourselves then come back refreshed and excited to start your lives together. We love ya."

***

Later, Hank Cottrell was out at the barn feeding the horses in their stalls. Charlie was in the kitchen and saw flames coming from the barn and Hank struggling to get the horses to safety.

Charlie screamed, "FIRE!" He ran out the back door and toward the barn. As he approached the corral he yelled. "Hank, where are you?"

Nothing.

The part of the barn where the horse stalls were located collapsed. Flames rose to thirty feet in the air and the intense heat kept Charlie from getting closer. He heard the awful sounds of Hank and the horse he was trying to save. "Hank! Oh my God, Hank."

Everyone else came running. Bill took Charlie by the arm. With a cry in his voice, Bill said, "Stay back, son. It's too late to help him now."

Charlie looked at Bill. "I'm so sorry."

Bill said, "It looks like we've lost the barn. But it can be replaced."

Charlie shook his head with tears running down his cheeks. "But not Hank."

Bill sniffled. "No, not Hank."

After a few days had passed the small group held a service to help them through the pain of losing such a dear friend.

***

Following the tragedy, it was decided to postpone Dan and Tess's wedding. Two weeks later there would be a double wedding for Dan, Tess, Jess, and Diana Sue at the First Baptist Church in Cushing. Charlie and Susan stood up for Dan and Tess. Jess was still working with Chester Abrams who stood with him as best man. Diana Sue, a teacher at Cushing High School, was attended by a friend, Brenda Waldron. Jess and Diana Sue would leave on their honeymoon from Tulsa on Sunday. Dan and Tess would wait to go to Jekyll Island in July.

Charlie and Susan returned to Tulsa after getting a tour of the refineries and pipeline installations by Bunk Sever, who had returned from Peggs.

As they pulled into their driveway in Tulsa, Susan said, "Isn't it wonderful how your brothers found their partners for life. Tess and Diana Sue are amazing women who seem to fit Dan and Jess perfectly."

Charlie stopped the Cadillac and turned the car off. He looked at Susan. "I couldn't agree more. They seem to be perfect for each other, but even my brothers didn't find a better match than I did when I found you."

"Charlie, you always say just the right thing. Let's unpack and find our patio to end this day the right way."

Chapter 39

The Quarterly Meeting

June 1920

IT WAS A HOT breezy late afternoon, and the sun was almost setting, when Charlie and Susan pulled into the long, tree-lined drive at 1007 Westover Road in Kansas City. It had also been a long day, but their blue Cadillac sedan and Susan's feminine wiles had made it as comfortable and entertaining as possible.

Beverly, their Kansas City cook, and Kathryn their housekeeper had waited with a dinner of prime rib sandwiches, potato salad and their favorite wine ready.

Kathryn ran to the car with arms out. "How was the drive? Are you tired and hungry?"

Beverly joined them as Susan hugged them both. "Yes, but it's so great to see you folks and be back here in Kansas City for a while."

Bernard joined the group as he rushed out the front door. "Welcome you two. Mr. Charlie, did the car do a good job for you? Is there anything I need to check on or do for you?"

Charlie patted Bernard's back and grinned. "It purred like a kitten all the way. You might give it a good bath, check all the fluids, and give it one of those prized Bernard inspections while we're here."

Bernard squeezed Charlie's bicep. "I sure will." He took the Cadillac and parked it in the garage after helping unload the suitcases.

The couple went to their bedroom and bath area to freshen up. Susan couldn't wait to shower and get rid of the road she felt she was wearing. Charlie joined her in the shower and the meal Beverly had prepared waited a little longer.

***

The tired and happy young couple took their dinner plates and a bottle of wine to the pool area to eat and relax.

Susan noticed they were settling into their loungers at about the same time they would have been enjoying their patio in Oklahoma. As the evening's twilight created a soft romantic mood, she looked at her lover. "Sweetheart we have another beautiful sanctuary to enjoy each other's company." She swallowed her first sip of wine.

"Susan, you are so right. We're fortunate to have these wonderful homes. And I'm still amazed we've added the 101 Ranch to our sanctuaries. On another subject, besides attendin' our quarterly meetin' what do you see as any real issue or task we need to tend to while we're here in Kansas City?"

Susan leaned back and thought for a moment, then looked over at him. "First, I agree with your comment about how owning the 101 Ranch will impact our lives. I believe it will put us, especially you, in a position to make a huge difference in the farming and ranching industry. And it will be another sanctuary for us. As to your question, once the board agrees to the move, we need to meet with our facility manager to discuss his views on what he and Emilia decided we need to move to our new offices in Tulsa. We should also talk with him about leasing out the space after the move is complete to bring in some more revenue." She took a sip of Cabernet. "We can meet with him after the board meeting."

Susan finished her sandwich, stood, stretched, and nodded toward the pool. "I'm going to cool off." She walked toward the pool house, hesitated, and looked back. "Are you coming?"

He grinned. "You betcha."

They both went to the pool house, took off their clothes, and went for a swim.

***

The Kellys rose early Wednesday morning. They went for another swim. After a shower and their morning meal, Bernard drove them to the office. As Susan got out of their Kansas City Cadillac sedan, she said, "Bernard, please come back this afternoon and pick us up. Charlie, Uncle Curt, and I will be going to Pete's Bar-B-Q tonight."

They took the elevator to the top floor and entered the boardroom. Susan stood at the end of the conference table and opened the meeting, "Thank you, everyone, for a great quarter. You've provided Charlie and me with excellent detailed financial reports, and we have continued confidence in you and your teams as we move forward. We look forward to your comments today. We'll cover the basics on the performance for all the divisions and then when we get to the new business Charlie and I will discuss our ideas for moving The Kramer Group forward in the new decade." She turned to Rice. "You're up."

He adjusted his glasses. "Strawberry Hill Construction enjoyed significant growth locally as the report showed. I'm excited to say our Tulsa branch will open next month. After a brief halt early on we have crews working punch list items in Shawnee and prepping to begin work in Ada for the Abrams Stores."

Charlie said, "Rice, how was the issue in Shawnee settled?"

"The City Council had a major problem on their hands. They wanted to extend the streetcar line on Main Street west to Aydelotte Street. They were short of funds to do get the roadwork prepared based on the bids they had from several construction companies. Strawberry Hill has the equipment and experience to do the work, so I agreed to do it for what they could afford so long as we could have their support to build the Abrams Store where we wanted."

Charlie slapped the table. "Brilliant work Rice. Way to solve a problem. How much did it cost us?"

"Not a dime. We made a little money. Very little, but we got the corner lot to build on we wanted."

Susan put her coffee cup down. "Rice, good job. Thanks, and now Anson, let's hear about our retail stores."

Anson had a big smile as he bragged, "First, our local stores are beating last year's numbers. I'm amazed because last year we broke records. But my problem is, I'm having trouble controlling my enthusiasm about the Abrams Store in Cushing, Oklahoma. Its revenue growth beats anything we've ever experienced. We couldn't have expected such an amazing launch for a new company. Charlie, your brother is doing a great job. And I know they have a few minor things on the punch list but the Shawnee, Oklahoma store will open soon, and following up on Rice's comment, his crew will be breaking ground on the Ada store in less than two weeks."

Susan asked, "With our solid numbers from Hartsfield, do you see expanding those stores anytime soon?"

Anson smiled and nodded his head. "I'm glad you asked. Yes, I do. And it'll start with a look at the Tulsa area, based on what you've told me of the city. I also want to have a team explore Oklahoma City and maybe even the Dallas area."

Susan looked delighted. "Exactly what I wanted to hear. Those are markets where Hartsfield should do well. Thank you, Anson, Gordon, you're next."

Gordon said. "Thank you, and I guess we sound like we copied off each other, but our gross receipts are the best we've ever had at our Commerce of Kansas City branches. I'm excited, but where I would like to focus is elsewhere. We have made great strides in converting Texas banks to our way of bookkeeping and behind the scenes processes. We determined we wanted to keep the relationships with the branches and their communities intact. It has paid tremendous dividends to us. Charlie, the oil industry in Texas is booming. We are benefiting from it. After my conversations with our Texas branch managers and with Harry Sinclair at the Exchange National Bank, we've a strategy to support success in Texas. We see tremendous growth coming in the Houston area. Any questions?"

Susan said, "No, I don't, do you, Charlie?"

"Yes. Are you getting' updates from Johnathan or Harry about the new Exchange National branch in Greenwood. If not, I would like to participate in your first meetin' with Harry and Jonathan on the subject, if I'm in town. Don't schedule the Greenwood meeting around me, though."

Gordon said, "I've not received anything new. You may know more than me. I know Johnathan is excited about it. I'll follow-up and let you know what I find out."

Susan nodded at Owen McGill. "Owen, how's the railroad business?"

"Pretty good," he said with a smile. "Our Kansas Missouri and Southern operations continue to expand into new markets. Our revenue isn't as up as much as Anson's stores, but they are higher than last year at this time. But our big news is the acquisition of the Rock Island railroad. That has greatly expanded our trackage and added additional assets to the books. Our plans are to use the Rock Island to expand our operations to the east while the KM&S continues to expand into Texas and to the west. I know that Charlie is trying to build pipelines to carry his oil, but I think that there is growth opportunity in train freight carrying oil and oil products from the oil fields to refineries and from the refineries to other companies that need those products."

"You're right about that," Charlie said. "There's more oil comin' out of the ground in Oklahoma than the pipelines can handle. There'll be opportunities for your trains to help out."

"That's all I have," Owen concluded.

Susan turned toward Bailey Muldoon who looked his usual calm and collected self despite this being his first board meeting. "Bailey, welcome to your first leadership meeting. You're up."

Bailey stood so everyone could see him. "I'm excited to be here, and I've met all of you as I went around sharing and discussing how we as a team will be addressing security within your part of the Kramer Group. We have discussed what your requirements could and should be in the future. After hearing from you, I've begun to create a staff of security professionals to build the necessary security capabilities the Kramer Group requires. As I've done it, I've also addressed some vandalism, terror, and threatening situations some of you've seen here in Kansas City and Oklahoma. The first personnel I hired were men from my military days who worked special assignments requiring a unique set of skills. As a Kramer team, we've worked to identify and respond to those responsible for those illegal and dangerous events. We continue to monitor the people to this day. Long term, you can be assured we'll create a safe and secure environment for your home office staff and all personnel throughout the company. Then, we'll build a set of similar capabilities to sell security services to other companies and individuals worldwide. That's what I have for you today."

Susan pointed to Charlie. "Mr. Kelly, please give the room an update on our oil company ventures."

Charlie smiled, and said. "Kelly Oil is growin' fast. We have wells already producin' enough oil to create well over a million dollars a year in revenue. We have wells in Osage and Garvin counties in Oklahoma pumpin' today. We have refineries and pipelines creatin' oil and gasoline products and movin' the products to transportation terminals. Hank Thomas is currently out in California working with J. Paul Getty on some partnerships between his company and Kelly Oil, as well as scouting possible locations for our own leases. He is confident that California will be a big opportunity for Kelly Oil in the coming years. I expect to have more details at the next meeting.

"Bunk Severs and the leadership he has shown in bringin' the refineries and pipelines operational has also been instrumental in getting Kelly Oil goin'." He paused then turned and looked at Rice.

"Rice, I want to praise you for the work you did with Bunk to get our Cushing site operational. I'm hoping that experience will benefit us as we look at expanding our refinin' operations into other places."

Charlie looked at Gordon and said, "Gordon, you're right

about Texas. Hank and I have heard the same stories about Texas oil. Before going to California, Hank went to Dallas and signed contracts with some successful oilmen. Kelly Oil is in Texas at this point, even if we haven't yet drilled our own wells. I'm glad you are looking to continue expanding our banking into Texas. We'll be there as soon after the first of the year as we can. Susan, back to you."

Susan said with a smile, "Oh no, you're not done yet, mister." There were chuckles from the others around the table. "You may as well give your report on the ranching operations since you have the floor."

Charlie said, "Well, I didn't want to be accused of monopolizing the meeting. We own and control almost 130,000 acres of farm and ranch land in Oklahoma. We own thousands of cattle, horses, and other animals typical of a farmin' and ranchin' operation. We're in the Angus cattle, dairy farmin', and horse trainin' businesses. We own the largest and most sophisticated produce and fruit farmin' operation in the state of Oklahoma and maybe the nation. How many of you folks have heard of the Miller's 101 Ranch?"

Most of the people in the room raised their hands.

Charlie asked, "Owen, ya raised your hand. What can ya tell me about the ranch?"

Owen said, "I'm no expert, but my grandfather used to tell me about how he worked for a short while, back in the '90s, at this huge ranch in northern Oklahoma called the 101. When he talked about it, he was almost reverent as he described it."

Charlie's face was filled with pride and delight when he said, "Folks, we own the 101 Ranch, lock, stock, and barrel. We also own three other ranches in Oklahoma, but our pride and joy is the 101 Ranch. Like you said Owen, the ranch is special to folks. When the opportunity came up this year to add it to our operations, I knew we had to do it, not only for the sake of nostalgia but because with the right focus, I know the 101 will be profitable."

Gordon leaned forward. "What's this I hear about hiring George Miller as the Chief Financial Officer for the Kramer Group?" He turned to Susan. "Your father never needed one."

"You're right, Gordon," Susan said. "But in just a short amount of time I have grown the Kramer Group beyond what father would have imagined possible. We are much larger than ever, and we need someone at the top with the financial know how to help us be successful."

Gordon nodded and seemed to accept her response. Anson

said, "I heard from folks down in Oklahoma that the 101 ranch was about to fail. Why would we want the man that was running a failed ranch to be our CFO?"

Charlie had to bite his tongue to not react to a threat to his friend and mentor. Instead, he said, "George L. Miller is a financial wizard, and the fact that the ranch was still operatin' and hadn't gone under a couple of years ago is a testament to that. I believe he has been keeping the ranch afloat through sheer force of will. He also taught me everything I know about not only runnin' a ranch but about finance in general. The problems at the 101 were not of his doin'."

Susan said, "Anson, Charlie and I reviewed the 101 finances before we made the offer. Charlie is right. George Miller is a genius at finance and we will be happy to have him as part of the Kramer Group."

That seemed to satisfy everyone so Charlie concluded. "When we meet again for the next board meetin', George will be with us and you'll be able to see for yourself. I'm done, any questions?"

There were none. Susan looked at the group. "Now that the routine updates are done it's time to move on to new business. As most of you have heard by now, Charlie and I want to move the corporate office for The Kramer Group to Tulsa."

There were nods all around the table, and a couple of questioning looks from Gordon and Anson.

Susan said, "What are your concerns, Gordon?"

"Rice gave me an update about this idea to move to Tulsa last month. I agree it makes geographic sense as more of our operations are centered around that state, but I am concerned how this will affect our staffs."

Anson said, "I second that. It's fine to want to have an office for Charlie's companies down in Tulsa, and even for Mr. Muldoon. But there's a lot of folks who have worked for many years for our companies in our offices here, in Kansas City. They have families here. Their children go to school here. Are you asking them to just move to Oklahoma?"

"There are business concerns as well," Owen said. "The Kramer Group has a lot of connections to other companies here in Kansas City and the surrounding areas. We order supplies and equipment from local businesses. Our employees eat at local restaurants and buy their groceries here. The Kramer Group is so big that our absence will be felt by many other people."

Susan put her palms on the table. "Those are legitimate concerns, and we have a reputation as being generous with our employees. That has helped us in the past keep and retain good workers. We don't want to jeopardize that."

Charlie added, "But at the same time, keeping the headquarters here, further away from the center of our operations, will have an impact on business too. Many of you already spend a good amount of time down in Oklahoma."

"We know that, Charlie," Gordon said, "And we don't disagree with that. However, you need to understand how the decisions we make here in this room affect everyone in the Kramer Group. This is not as simple as decreeing that something should be done and everyone does it."

Charlie was starting to form a response when Bailey said, "Gentlemen, I know I am new to this group, but I feel I have some insight here. With my time in the military and with the Pinkertons I traveled a lot. I had to move many times to new army posts or new offices in new cities for the detective agency. It can be hard on a person and a family." He gave Gordon a sympathetic look.

"But I think that a solution can be found because there are good reasons for this move. Not only for financial reasons, but reasons of security too as securing one headquarters is easier, and cheaper, than doing two." There were a few chuckles at that observation.

"My understanding is that the renovations to the bank building in Tulsa will take a few months to complete, is that correct Rice?"

"Yes. We've not started any work yet. Once we do the work is straight-forward, but it will still take until the end of August at least."

"I recommend we approach this in a few ways. We announce the decision to move the headquarters to Tulsa to our employees first, before this gets to the papers. That way they hear it directly from the horse's mouth, so to speak. We offer those employees who want to move a moving allowance, assistance in finding places to live, and other help as needed. If there are employees who don't want to move, we see if there are places for them in any scaled down presence here in Kansas City. Just because the headquarters is moving doesn't mean we are pulling out completely from here?" He paused and got nods from the others.

"For anybody who doesn't want to move and doesn't want a different position we can offer them a severance package and assistance in finding other work here in Kansas City. That way I believe that we will retain the goodwill of the employees."

Gordon nodded, "I believe that is a plan that we can get behind. Anson? Owen?"

"I agree," Anson said.

"I think that will work," agreed Owen.

Susan said, "Very well. Let's make this official. All in favor."

Everyone raised their hands.

"Motion carried. We will begin the process to move the Kramer Group headquarters to Tulsa."

She turned to Curt and said, "Uncle Curt, I believe we need to talk about the reorganization plans now."

Curt responded, "Susan, with the growth of the company in the past year, and the acquisition of several new businesses, we needed to look at our organizational structure to better operate and coordinate the businesses. Now that we have agreed to the move I'm happy to give everyone what I see at this point. We'll continue to have the capability to perform these functions within every Kramer company. This includes typical personnel functions, financial tracking, marketing, strategic planning, facility management, and public relations. The creation of policy and procedure will remain at the home office level. The home office staff will combine all inputs from the field and combine them with inputs from the functions at the corporate level to allow the CEO to easily see the big picture. In addition to the previously mentioned CFO, there is a need for a new President, or some executive level officer hired to lead this group level activity. Some group level staff will be embedded at the company level and will report to this new leader. But they will provide daily support to the company where they reside. Some of what I've described already exist, but we'll finish creating these functions as part of moving to Tulsa. Any questions?"

Susan said, "I don't think we should field any questions on the subject right now because we already know there are more questions than we have answers. But each of you will be depended on to help define what needs to be created, as we go forward."

Everyone nodded agreement.

Susan stood. "Very well. It's been a great day, and I'm thrilled with each of you and what we've accomplished this quarter. What you shared in your detailed financial reports and in person today provides me with a great deal of information to support our optimism as we continue here in 1920. I look forward to seeing you all in Tulsa and be safe and successful."

Chapter 40

New Neighbors

June 1920

IT WAS A MONDAY, and things were hectic but positive across the Kramer Group after the board meeting. The process of informing the personnel in Kansas City and getting the move organized was underway. And the problem with the gangsters out of Kansas City or Chicago seemed to have gone away.

Charlie sat at his desk in their home when the phone rang. "Hello, this is Charles Kelly."

"Charlie, it's Hank."

"Hey, Hank. How's California been?"

"Very good so far. At this point, I've helped Getty find two very productive well sites and acquired rights for Kelly Oil to several potential drillin' locations in the Huntington Beach and Long Beach Signal Hill areas. I'm wonderin' how this is figurin' into what you had planned for Kelly Oil, overall?"

Charlie thought for a moment. "We're ahead of schedule as far as acquisitions and havin' operatin' wells. And I'm excited about what you tell me about the prospects we have out there. I'm also hearin' a lot is goin' on in Texas. What do ya recommend we do next?"

"I talked yesterday with Clint and Sid. They have several wells drilled in east Texas. We'll start gettin' checks from them next month. As soon as possible, we need to decide if we want to be major players here in California and Texas. I can see us settin' up in both of those states the same way we've started creatin' Kelly Oil in Oklahoma. I also agree with you we should create several ways to make money from the oil business, startin' with exploration and continuin' through to retailin'. That should happen in California and Texas too."

"Hank, I think Susan and I should come out to California soon. It may take us a few months to git there with the move of the Kramer offices to Tulsa. Go ahead and hire some crews and start drillin' wherever you think best."

Hank said, "I'll get us some drillin' started out here then. I'll stay after our Texas friends, too."

Charlie said, "I'll cover things at the next board meetin' for Kelly Oil, so you can keep your focus on findin' more oil. But we'll come out there soon, okay?"

Hank replied, "Sounds good. I'll have at least one well goin' by the end of next month. When you come out here, allow yourself time to explore the area. There are citrus orchards everywhere and mountains to enjoy. The weather is great. It never gets blazing hot, and I hear it's never cold here unless you go to the mountains."

"Okay, call me when you're ready to drill, so I know what's happenin'."

"Yep, I'll call you."

***

Charlie woke up and found Susan not in bed. He walked to the French doors to the patio and saw Susan swimming. He called to her, "How long have ya been swimmin'?"

"Maybe fifteen minutes. We're hosting the Millers tonight, which means we may not be able to enjoy our nightly swim."

"Oh, right. They're comin' to spend some time lookin' for a house. We promised to show 'em around Tulsa, didn't we?"

"Yes, we did." Susan rolled to her back and started backstrokes. Charlie's eyes followed his favorite view. "Come join me, Charlie, it'll wake you up."

"I believe I will, Sweetheart." They swam and played around for a while, showered, and had their breakfast.

During the meal, Charlie said, "Have ya talked with May about when to expect them?"

"She called me yesterday. They're planning to be here by noon. I told them we would have lunch ready when they got here."

The Millers arrived a few minutes after noon, and Attie brought them into the living room. Charlie and Susan took them out to the patio table under the shade tree.

Cleta had the table set and was standing there waiting. "Good afternoon. You must be the Millers. I'm Cleta." She pointed at Charlie and Susan. "I'm their cook. What would you like to drink?"

May looked at Susan. "My goodness, would you have sweet tea?"

Susan smiled, "Of course. Cleta, please bring some for all of us. May… George, I've asked Cleta to prepare club sandwiches for everyone. Is that okay?"

George said, "Perfect, Susan. We love them."

Charlie pointed to the empty chairs. "Let's sit down and chat while Cleta gets our drinks."

After the meal, the Kellys took the Millers house shopping in the general area of Maple Ridge. It was late afternoon when they got back to the Kelly's home. The evening was beautiful, so the couples returned to the table on the patio.

After everyone had a glass of wine George said, "A toast to Susan and Charlie. Wonderful friends and great hosts."

Susan said, "We're happy you're here and we look forward to you being neighbors so we can see you often."

Charlie lifted his glass again. "Yes, we can't believe how fortunate it is for us to have people we love become neighbors. What did you think of the houses we looked at?"

George said, "We saw some beautiful houses with you today. The last one over on Hazel Blvd is my favorite, and it's only six blocks from your house. The price was $65,000 and seemed about right. Whatta you think?"

Susan said, "I think if you offer them $60,000 cash, they'll take it. It would be a good deal for you and them."

May said, "I'm not in favor of us putting so much cash into a house. We're in transition, and it's a lot of money."

Charlie said, "Very accurate thinkin', May. I know ya have it, but it doesn't mean ya spend it. How about this, you put $15,000 down and have the Exchange National Bank carry the balance against the house. I'll call the bank tomorrow, and George, you call the folks who own the house and make them a cash offer. We can close in two weeks, a month, or whatever the seller wants."

George said, "May, let's do it. It's a nice place, and we can easily afford the payments."

May smiled and said, "It was my favorite too. Oh, yes, call them."

***

Later in the evening, Charlie called his folks to check and see how they were doing.

"Hello, Dad. Sorry, I know I'm calling a little late. How are you and Mom doin'?"

"Good, Charlie. It's been a few weeks since we last talked, hasn't it? Are you younguns' doin' good?

"We're fine. Susan and I are goin' to Kansas City soon, so I thought I would check on ya before we head off."

"I'm glad ya called. Have ya heard about Dan and Tess?"

"No, what about 'em? Are they okay?"

"Oh yes, Son. They've bought a place near Harjo. It's about two miles from your ranch. They are two excited youngsters. I'll let them tell you more about the place."

"Good for them. Dad, Susan wants to talk to Mom. I'll give her the phone. See ya soon, I hope."

Susan got on the phone and talked with his mom for several minutes and got caught up on things around Maud and Earlsboro.

***

The Millers had been sitting out at the table on the patio while Charlie and Susan made the phone call to Maud. Charlie and Susan walked out to them, and Susan said, "We're going to have some more wine, would you guys like to join us?"

George looked at May and nodded, he turned to Susan and said, "We would love some more. If you don't mind me askin', how'd you buy wine with the Prohibition now in full effect?"

"Some of it we stockpiled before the law went into effect. But these bottles are all sacramental wine," Susan said with a laugh. "We make a financial donation to our church in Kansas City to cover the cost of their wine, and in exchange, they help us get some of the wine they are allowed to purchase for holy communion."

"Holy wine, eh?" said George. "Well, I guess the Lord does move in strange and mysterious ways."

Susan laughed, "That He does. I'll have Cleta bring us another bottle."

As Susan walked away, Charlie said, "Thanks for givin' us some time to call my folks. My dad runs the Sinclair Gas Station in Maud, and the weekends are long days for him. If we didn't call tonight, we wouldn't be able to talk for another week."

George said, "We're happy you could call them. I know you've given me another few weeks to get everything settled at the 101 and allow May and I to get moved and set up here in Tulsa. But I'm excited to be part of the Kramer Group."

Charlie said, "I'm excited to git ya started. While I'm thinkin' about it, do ya think I might be able to persuade your brother-in-law Bill to come work for us? He's an expert at farm and ranch law. I have big plans for the farm and ranch portion of Kramer, and he could be the lead legal for us."

"I'd love to see you get him. I don't know what it would take to get him and Alma out of Winfield, Kansas. The 101 was a big client for him, so he's gonna miss our income. Call him and see what he says."

Susan came back out to the table and said, "Cleta will be here in a moment with our wine, some cheese, and crackers. I know you're still full after the huge dinner, but I love cheese and crackers with my wine."

They enjoyed a pleasant unusually warm evening of conversation and wine on their patio.

Chapter 41

Pete's Bar-B-Q

July 1920

CHARLIE AND SUSAN RETURNED to Kansas City in early July to get things for the headquarters move started. They spent most of the day talking with the facility manager for the Commerce Bank building as well as meeting with staff. Many of them had agreed to move to Tulsa, which Charlie and Susan were glad to hear. And even though some didn't want to make the move, they were willing to continue to work until they were no longer needed.

Charlie had spent most of his day on the phone with Hank in California and Boss and George Miller in Oklahoma. In addition to the facility manager and employees, Susan met with Gordon and Owen to discuss banks and trains. Anson was down in Tulsa to meet with Jess who had come back from his honeymoon at Jekyll Island refreshed and ready to dive back into his work.

At 4:45 Susan looked up at the clock. She rose and walked to Charlie's office. "We need to be down at the curb in ten minutes. Bernard will be there to pick us up. Remember, we have reservations at Pete's Bar-B-Q for 5:20." She walked to Curt's office and gave him the same message. They arrived on time, and Bernard stood waiting on the sidewalk next to the car's rear door.

The drive to Pete's was short. As the restaurant came into view Susan said, "Bernard, park the Cadillac, and come inside and join us, please."

Bernard glanced back at his passengers. "Oh, I'd love to, Miss Susan."

The table reserved for them was near the rear of the restaurant, as far away from the front door's traffic as possible.

***

Charlie, who always sat with his back to the wall, said, "I sure love their Bar-B-Q here. It's spiced the way I like it."

Curt said, "This is classic Kansas City style. I've tried the styles in the Carolinas and Texas, but this is my favorite." He winked. "I'll admit it, though, I do like them all."

The four enjoyed a pleasant couple of hours and lots of different meats, corn-on-the-cob, and butter-filled baked potatoes.

Charlie looked around the table and could tell Bernard was having a wonderful time.

Susan teased Bernard. "Hey, big fellow, is that one or two dozen ribs for you tonight."

Bernard laughed so hard he dropped the rib he was eating onto his plate. "I think it'll take a wheelbarrow to get me outta here."

They all ate a little more. Curt leaned back in his chair and sighed. "I'm so full I can't breathe."

Bernard said, "I'll go get the car and pull it to the front door."

Charlie motioned to the waiter to bring him the bill. He paid it and added a generous tip.

As they approached the front door, Susan saw their Cadillac, and said, "Bernard has our ride home ready for us. It was nice to have him be part of our dinner; don't you think.?"

Curt squeezed her shoulder. "It was great. He's a funny guy. I'm ashamed to say; in all the years he supported your father, I'd met him but had never spent any time around him."

As he held the restaurant door open, Charlie said, "Having him be a part of the evening meal was great, Sweetheart."

Bernard opened the rear door of the car. As they walked the short distance from the restaurant to the car shots rang out. A metallic hailstorm sprayed the Cadillac. A truck with a faded Pendleton sign on the door slowly drove past, the barrel of a Tommy Gun sticking out of the window. Flames seemed to leap from the end of the weapon.

Susan screamed as Charlie shoved her inside the Cadillac. He then picked up Curt, who was lying on the ground, then pushed him into the back seat. Bernard, who had been trying to shield his employers, yelled in agony and fell to the ground as another barrage of shots rang out. Charlie felt the impact and sharp stabbing pain in his left shoulder caused by a bullet as it spun him around.

"Stay outta Kansas City!" came a shout from the truck as it sped away.

Charlie, on the sidewalk next to Bernard, looked up and saw the waiter standing in the doorway. He yelled, "Call for an ambulance and the police now!"

Charlie looked at the driver, "Bernard, talk to me, Bernard." He was lifeless.

From the car, Susan squealed, "Charlie is Bernard, okay?"

He shook his head. "I think he may be dead, Susan. He's not breathin'."

She screamed, "Oh my God!!! No, not Bernard, no..."

Curt clambered out of the car, "Charlie, is that Bernard's blood I see on your shoulder?"

Charlie winced, and said, "No, it's mine. They hit my left shoulder. Hurts like a son-of-a-bitch too."

Susan whimpered, "I didn't think you were hurt, the way you were looking after us and then Bernard. Sweetheart, how can I help?"

"You stay put. Curt, you seemed hurt, did a bullet hit ya?"

Curt replied, "No, I just dove to the ground and landed wrong on my bad knee. I'll be sore, but okay."

Sirens screamed in the distance, and the crowd from the restaurant began to come outside into the heat of the July night. A voice from back in the crowd hollered, "Please step aside. Let me through, I'm a doctor."

After he made it past the mass of people, the doctor said, "I'm Dr. Shepherd. I'm sorry, but I didn't hear the shots, and it took a while for me to get through the crowd. What can I do?"

Charlie said, "First confirm my suspicion, is my friend dead?"

The doctor turned and examined Bernard. After a moment he sighed and said, "Yes, I'm afraid so. I'm so sorry. I can see you're injured. Is anyone else hurt?"

From next to the car, Curt said, "I banged up my knee, but they shot Charlie in the shoulder."

At that moment an ambulance arrived. The medics joined the doctor in examining Charlie. Several police cars also arrived. There was more chaos for a while. The police interviewed a few folks in the crowd and then came to Susan, Charlie, and Curt.

A large man in a police uniform with gray hair peeking out from under his hat walked toward Charlie who was still on his back on the sidewalk. The policeman asked, "Did you see your assailant?"

Charlie responded, "Yes, I might not be able to pick the shooter or the driver out from a crowd, but the truck had a faded Pendleton sign on the door. It means we were being shot at by members of the DiGiovanni bunch. They took over here when Pendleton died. They work with the Chicago Outfit."

The policeman said, "You've offered a lot of assumptions, mister."

Charlie looked sternly at the policeman and stated, "No assumption, just fact. We have plenty of proof that the DiGiovanni brothers have taken over for Pendleton, and that they are tied to Johnny Torrio in Chicago. This is not the first time they've messed with us, though it is the first time they shot at anybody."

Susan spoke up, "Officer, I'm Susan Kramer-Kelly. We own the Kramer Group. Have you heard of us?"

The policeman gulped. "Yes ma'am. Why would gangsters be shooting at you folks?"

Again, from the back of the car, Curt raised his hand, palm out. "I'm Curt Schlegell, the Kramer Group attorney. As a corporation, we've outbid those mobsters on more than one occasion for business property or something they wanted. We're the only business in this part of the United States they consider a financial threat to them."

The policeman nodded. "I've all I need from you now." He looked down at Charlie. "We need to get you to the hospital, sir. We'll gather your formal statements there."

***

Charlie was getting his shoulder sewn up when he heard Susan, standing near his bed, call Bailey. "Bailey, this is Susan Kelly. Sorry to call this late, but I'm glad you were in town today. You need to know we're at University Hospital. Those asshole gangsters shot and killed our driver, and Charlie was shot in the shoulder. It was a drive-by shooting. Can you come to our house in the morning? Charlie's going to want to talk with you."

Bailey hesitated. "I'll be there. Do you need anything now? I can be at the hospital in less than thirty minutes."

Susan said, "Well, we're going to need a ride home tonight. Our Cadillac is full of holes and impounded by the police. So, I guess you can come on over to the hospital."

Bailey arrived at the hospital about the time the doctor finished with Charlie and Curt. He would take them to their homes after their release. As they walked out the hospital door to Bailey's Ford, he looked at Susan. "What did the doctor have to say about these two?"

"Charlie's wound was a deep crease in his deltoid muscle and will create a scar, but the bullet missed the shoulder joint.

Curt will recover from a bad sprain in his left knee."

Bailey nodded. "I guess they are lucky to be alive. As are you, Susan."

Her face distorted into a display of anger and conviction. "We've gotta get those bastards, Bailey. I'm outta patience with this whole situation. Now we've lost a dear friend, and my Charlie has been shot again. It's time to end this." She sighed then laid her head against Bailey's shoulder.

Bailey settled his nerves enough to say, "We'll let Charlie heal and then we'll get this settled." He stopped and looked at Susan with his anger still showing. "Don't you worry, we'll get this settled."

Chapter 42

Another Morning After

July 1920

SUSAN REMAINED STILL UNTIL she sensed Charlie was waking up. She then rolled over and kissed him to welcome him to another day with her by his side.

Charlie sighed and looked at Susan. "My very favorite way to start a day. I love ya, Beautiful."

She snuggled her naked body to his and said, "I love you too." Tears were forming in her eyes. "I almost lost you last night. I'm sure it was what those assholes intended. We've gotta do whatever it takes to end this."

Charlie shook his head. "So much for my passion and some amazing sex with my beautiful wife. Now we're talkin' about killin' people off." Charlie tried to get up and felt a sharp pain in his shoulder. "Man!" He laid back down. "That hurt." He settled his head back on his pillow. "And I guess you're right. We do need to end this thing. I know I'm tired of bein' shot. That's twice now. Bailey is comin' over in a couple of hours, right?"

With deep affection, Susan caressed his chest and abs. "Yes, Bailey is coming to our house, and I could tell last night if he could've, he would've gone on a rampage terrorizing and killing those gangsters. I hope when he gets here, he'll be settled down a little. But I'm okay with him and our team having some anger in them. You know Charlie, I guess not being back to normal is where we all need to be until this is ended."

Charlie grinned, "I'm ready to put them out of business. We'll see what we can figure out. Let's get goin'. I'm hungry. I guess gettin' shot didn't change my appetite."

***

They had finished their breakfast when Bailey joined them in the living room. Bailey took a chair across from Susan. "How much sleep did you get last night?"

Charlie said, "I got to sleep about midnight, and I woke up around seven. The doc gave me some morphine tablets at the hospital and said I could take aspirin if the pain continued."

Bailey said, "It's good if aspirin will work for you, use it. But I was asking Susan the question."

Charlie grimaced. "Of course, sorry Sweetheart."

She giggled. "Always gotta be the center of attention, don't you?"

Charlie grinned as he looked down and shook his head.

"I managed to get a few hours of sleep. I'll be fine."

Bailey looked at Charlie. "With that settled, and I heard Susan's thoughts last night, what do you want to do with the DiGiovanni crowd and those sons of bitches in Chicago? I think it's local shitheads harassing us, but they're doing it for Torrio I'm sure."

Charlie said, "I want to shoot 'em. But we need to keep ourselves out of jail. Let's put the Kansas City bunch out of business. And I still like showin' up in Torrio's bedroom in the middle of the night, holdin' weapons on him and his wife, if she's there. I want to pound the asshole into submission. I want to take him right to the edge. When he's sure he's gonna die, I leave him with the message I have the resources to kill him or put him out of business. But we'll leave him with this message. As long as he lets us alone, we'll let him alone. There's plenty of legitimate business to go around, but because they killed my friend Bernard last night, the DiGiovanni's will no longer have anythin' in Kansas City. While we're in Torrio's bedroom, I want ya to have men blowin' up every business the DiGiovanni family owns around Kansas City. We'll wipe them out."

Bailey took a sip of coffee, then sighed. "It's powerful and it's doable. I think I've settled down some since last night. Susan, please pardon my language from last night."

She laughed. "Bailey, I'd have killed the bastards myself last night if I could have. I can cuss like a sailor when needed and sometimes it's the best way to describe the person or the situation. Don't ever worry about what or how you say something around me."

Bailey nodded. "Okay, I get it. Now let me share what kind of ideas we have come up with. First, Wyatt and Josh have an executable plan to get you into Torrio's house in Chicago after midnight. We can be in and out well before daylight. Second, I know the DiGiovanni family are owners of a grocery wholesale business, two restaurants, and the concrete company Pendleton had before. I'm unaware of anything else."

Charlie said, "You described what I know of too. So, while we're scarin' the shit out of Torrio in his bedroom, we need to be blowin' up all of those businesses here in Kansas City."

Bailey leaned forward. "I want to be clear on this. We destroy the businesses, not just damage them, right?"

Susan didn't wait for Charlie to answer. "Right. You must destroy them. We want them out of business. I wouldn't care if you blew their houses up. They were shooting at Curt and me too. Bailey, the shooter was using one of those machine guns. Our Cadillac is riddled with bullet holes."

Charlie said, "I agree with Susan, I want the message to be hands-off anythin' owned by The Kramer Group. Death means we destroy. We want this ended now."

Bailey leaned back and looked at the ceiling for a moment. "I'll make it a point to never get on your bad sides. I can see even beautiful, sweet, and kind Susan would be ruthless." He chuckled. "Now, Charlie, we can do this. It's early July, when do you want to execute this night of terror?"

Charlie looked at Susan and went back to Bailey. "How about next Sunday or Monday night?"

Bailey said, "Your emotion is talking. You must heal up first. You know, you're paying me and my guys to do things like this Chicago thing. If you don't want to be part of it, me and my guys could go do it by Monday night. But, if you plan to go to Chicago and be in the bedroom, I want your shoulder to be completely healed."

Charlie tilted his head and thought. "Okay. But, Bailey, there are things a boss needs to do himself. I must be the one delivering this message. After being shot the last time, I was good in two or three weeks, so then let's target Friday, July 23rd, and we'll take the train up there. We're gonna need to have eyes on this local bunch and someone watching Torrio too."

Bailey said, "Agreed and we will, I'll send some guys to Chicago. While you stay home and heal. I'll also have a man watching your house twenty-four hours a day until we execute this plan."

Susan said, "Thanks for everything, Bailey. We'll keep our heads down. There's only one thing we must do over the next few days. We want to have a service for Bernard. He was an orphan, so we are his only family. We can do the service here at the house. Beverly, our housekeeper, found a will up in his room this morning, which said he leaves everything he owns to the YMCA. He wanted cremation, not burial in a casket. And he wants his ashes spread across the back part of this property. This was his home."

Bailey put his coffee cup back on its saucer. "I'll let my men know what you're planning. I want you to have your privacy, but we'll always be watching the perimeter of this place.."

Susan asked, "It sounds like you're planning to have two men here. You'll have them do a twelve-hour shift each day, right?"

"Yep."

"Have them swap out every day at 9:00 in the morning and evening? We'll feed them three meals a day. Two can be brought to them by Kathryn, but breakfast will be with Charlie and me. We'll talk and give each other feedback."

Charlie reached over and squeezed her hand. "Susan that's a good plan. I like it."

Bailey stood. "Then that's what we'll do. I'll have someone here by noon to start, and he'll be relieved at 9:00 tonight. We'll start the twenty-four-hour cycle. I'd like to come back tomorrow and give you feedback on the overall plan after discussing this with my team."

Charlie said, "Great idea. See you tomorrow for lunch."

"See you then."

Chapter 43

Goodbye to a Friend

July 1920

ON THE FOLLOWING SATURDAY, a private service was held in the backyard at the Westover home for Bernard. His only family and close friends were Charlie, Susan, Beverly, Kathryn, and Curt. They all attended his service.

That morning standing in front of her full-length mirror, Susan said, "Charlie, this is going to be hard on me today. Bernard has been like family, all my life. My father hired him before I was born. Sometimes he felt like a big brother and at other times like an uncle. But as I said, always like family."

From the wash basin in the bathroom, Charlie stopped shaving and said, "I didn't know he had been a part of your life for so long. I guess that bit of your background has never come up. I can see where he would have been like another uncle to you then."

"Yes, he was. He would always have a gift or create something special just for me on my birthday or at Christmas. Now, that part of my life is gone." She began to cry.

Charlie walked out of the bathroom with shaving cream still on his face and embraced her. "Sweetheart, you, your father, and even your uncle Curt treated Bernard like family. Bernard wouldn't have changed a thing, I'm sure. He was a happy man and what happened outside Pete's not you nor anyone else could have kept from happenin'. Well, other than those goons and who they work for."

Charlie and Susan finished getting ready and headed downstairs. Soon enough Curt arrived with Bishop Thomas Francis Lillis, who had conducted Walter's memorial and would do the same thing for Bernard. Kathryn and Beverly were already waiting having set out food. Everyone shared hugs and there was a lot of crying before they headed into the dining room. They ate a late brunch together and then walked out to where the final rites for Bernard would be performed.

Per Bernard's wishes, he had been cremated. After the Bishop read the eulogy, Susan poured his ashes among the plants in his favorite garden near the back wall of the yard.

Susan, with tears flowing down her cheeks, turned back to face the small group and was joined by Charlie. He stood beside her and draped her shoulders with his arms. She looked at everyone, gathered herself, and began to speak. "I loved this kind and sweet man like an uncle as I admitted to Charlie earlier this morning. I'll have a monument created and placed here to memorialize what he has meant to the Kramer family and to each of us. I believe Father would have done the same."

As the others walked back to the house Charlie paused and looked at the spot where Susan had spread Bernard's ashes. He whispered, "Bernard, I'll git the assholes who did this if it's the last thing I do."

Chapter 44

Some Good News for a Change

July 1920

MONDAY MORNING AS CHARLIE was taking his first sip of coffee, Kathryn came into the kitchen area. "Mr. Charlie, you've got a call from Mr. Peabody."

He sat in an overstuffed chair next to the telephone table. "Hello Anson, what's on your mind? Good news I hope."

"I just got off the phone with Chester, and the new Shawnee store opened Friday, as you know. The sales over the weekend were almost twenty percent above what the Cushing store did at its opening. He was so excited; I felt as if I needed to peel Chester off the ceiling. I'm planning to call Rice today and schedule with him to have his team head to Ada and begin exploring where we will locate the next store."

Charlie leaned back in his chair and smiled. "Anson, great news. We have a winner here, and we better start a plan to expand it into more counties in Oklahoma and maybe down into Texas. You mentioned it before at the meeting. I think it's the right idea. Keep us informed as you see figures for the first month."

He returned to the kitchen and hugged Beverly. "Oh, I needed some good news, and he had it for me." He sat down and picked his coffee cup back up.

A few minutes later, Susan came in and joined Charlie. She saw the big smile on Charlie's face. "Okay, what's got you so happy this morning?"

"Anson, and he had great news about the Abrams store in Shawnee."

Susan poured herself a cup of coffee. "Glad to hear it."

Beverly put their breakfast plates in front of them as she

asked, "Don't you have a doctor's appointment today, Mr. Charlie?"

"I do, Beverly. We'll finish our meal and be leavin' as soon as Curt arrives. He's due anytime, and my appointment is in a little over an hour."

Curt walked in as Charlie finished. He laughed, and said, "Talking bad about me, Charlie?"

Charlie held one hand up since the left was still bandaged and sore, shook his head, grinned, and smiled. "Of course not Curt. Let Susan and I finish here, and we can go."

Susan took a bite and turned to Curt. "We have plenty of time, do you want some coffee?"

Curt shook his head. "No, I had all I needed at home. How's your wound, Charlie?"

"My shoulder seems to be doing fine but is still sore. I can do some things like swim, but as you know, the doctor said I couldn't drive until he says it's okay. Thanks for comin' over and drivin' for us."

Susan frowned at Charlie. "I need to get better at driving. I'm still sorry for the damage I caused to the truck when you were trying to teach me."

"You'll get the hang of it, but we might need to buy more trucks first," Charlie said, then regretted it as Susan playfully swatted him on his good arm.

***

As Curt drove them to Charlie's appointment, he said, "What's the latest you hear from Bailey regarding any response to what got you shot and needing to see the doctor today?"

"Susan and I met with him, and we have a plan we'll execute soon. Maybe as early as sometime in the next few weeks. We know what we want to accomplish and now he and his team are doin' the final research to support the plan."

"Care to share what the plan is?"

Susan, who was in the front passenger seat, reached over and put her hand on Curt's shoulder. "Not yet. I think Charlie will agree there are still too many things we need to decide on. Right, Charlie?"

"Right, we need to hear more from Bailey."

Curt looked at Susan. "I worry you two could be targets again for these barbaric people."

Charlie leaned up from the back seat. "It's why I want to respond as soon as we can. The faster we gain control of this situation the better."

Curt sighed. "I agree. Please hurry and get this settled."

The doctor was ready for Charlie and completed a thorough examination of the wound and even added what might have been done at an annual physical. As Charlie put his shirt on, the doctor wrote some notes for Charlie's medical records.

Charlie looked at Susan and gave her a wink. Then he turned to the doctor, and asked, "Doc, I feel fine can I go back to my normal life?"

The doctor rubbed his chin before responding. "Your wound doesn't look infected and is healing well. But this is too soon to be back to normal. I want you to be careful not to reopen your wound. You must hold off any activities beyond what we've already allowed for another week. You're young and a fast healer, but you could still tear the wound open. In another week, you should be fine."

Chapter 45
Conspirators
July 1920

CHARLIE WAS STANDING IN his office, gazing out his window at the colorful flowers and greenery in the yard. He was enjoying his second cup of coffee and thinking about the letter from Dan he had just finished. In the letter, Dan said, "I'm amazed by the 101. The size and quality of everything. Charlie, we're goin' to be able to do so much with these resources..." There was a knock at the front door. A moment later, Kathryn entered his office and said, "Mr. Charlie, your lunch guest, Mr. Muldoon, has arrived."

Charlie stood and saw Bailey standing behind her. "Let's go into the breakfast area, and Kathryn, let Susan know Bailey's here."

Charlie and Bailey sat at the table overlooking the patio and conservatory area. Bailey looked at the large windows. "This is a beautiful place to start your day. I'm amazed by this view every time we sit here."

Beverly joined them. She welcomed Bailey to her kitchen and asked, "Can I get you some coffee, tea, or water?"

Charlie offered his cup to her and said, "Coffee for me." He looked at Bailey, who grinned and said, "Me too, thanks, Beverly."

Beverly had a big smile as she poured them each a cup and left the carafe within their reach.

A few minutes later, Susan walked into the room wearing the blue version of Charlie's favorite blouse, with her cup in hand. Charlie poured some coffee into her cup and said, "This should freshen it up for you."

Susan smiled and said, "Thanks, Sweetheart, you can sometimes be such a gentleman."

Bailey couldn't resist, "Do I want to know what he is the rest of the time?"

They laughed and enjoyed the friendly poke at the cowboy-turned-big businessman.

Charlie looked at Bailey. "I assume you had a chance to talk with the team about the plans we discussed yesterday?"

Bailey's eyes sparkled and he sat erect in his chair. "Yes, I did. And we agreed it was the right proportional response, and we could execute it as you described it. We'll have Wyatt and Josh with you and me in Chicago. Briggs, Red, and Karl will be here in Kansas City. We have already hired some highly skilled people, and they will assist them. And an interesting thing has happened I want to share it with you."

Susan and Charlie both sat up to hear the news.

"Remember our meeting after the bank incident? We had Richard from the OBI and Lindsey from the Tulsa Police Department there. They called me last night after seeing an article on the Tulsa World's front page about the shooting here. They asked what, if anything, we had planned as a response to the incident outside of Pete's. I said it was not something I could discuss with them without you approving it. They each individually asked to meet with us. They were going to drive through the night to come up here. I didn't tell them anything. But they know the three of us are meeting here."

Susan asked, "Is it smart to tell anyone what we have planned? We're going to destroy property, and people might be hurt as well. I think that's against the law, isn't it?"

Bailey said, "Being a vigilante is very much against the law. Those are the reasons I didn't want to lie and didn't want to say anything without your knowledge and approval."

Charlie said, "I won't ever expect you to lie. But I do expect you to protect us from as much harm as possible. I consider going to jail harm. Lettin' us answer those questions is best." Charlie turned toward the kitchen. "Beverly, can ya hear me?"

"What do you need, Mr. Charlie?"

"We're gonna have two more guests in a short while, better plan for them to be hungry."

Bailey said, "We can discuss as much detail as you want before, after, or during the time Richard and Lindsey are here."

Charlie scratched his wounded shoulder as he thought for a moment. "I want to wait until they get here and discuss why they're expectin' we're goin' to have some kind of response."

They took the opportunity while waiting for Richard and Lindsey to discuss the other areas that Bailey's department was working on. With the move, the security of the headquarters, and starting a security-for-hire company, in addition to the plans for Torrio and the gangsters, Bailey's days had been full. They were able to address a lot of the questions and listened to his suggestions for the direction he wanted to take the division.

A couple of hours later Kathryn stepped into the room. "We have two additional guests. They say you're expecting them." She stepped aside, and Richard and Lindsey came into the kitchen area.

Susan waved. "Welcome, gentlemen. Find yourself a seat around the table."

Beverly walked over and asked, "Would either of you like something to drink?"

Richard said, "Coffee is fine." Lindsey nodded his agreement.

Charlie pointed at the table. "Bring a fresh carafe for all of us."

Bailey started the conversation. "Richard and Lindsey, I was telling Charlie and Susan earlier about your phone calls last night." He pointed at Charlie. "He has some questions for you."

Charlie said, "He's right. I was a little surprised you each asked what our response would be to the incident here in Kansas City. Why do you think I have a personal response?"

Richard initially had a grin on his face, then got more serious before speaking. "I was there when Willard kidnapped Susan. You were angry, and the first thing on your mind was getting her back safe, but you also wanted a piece of the varmints who took her. The other night, you were shot, and according to the newspaper, you lost a loyal household employee, which I imagine was like losing a family member. I assume Susan could have been shot. I'm sure you want a piece of the people involved. I don't blame you one bit. I'm here to help you however I can."

Charlie replied, "Okay, I can accept that assessment." He turned to Lindsey. Who didn't wait for Charlie to ask him. "I saw something in you after the bank incident in Tulsa. It told me you were struggling to hold yourself back from responding to the vandalism, and this thing at the restaurant here in Kansas City goes way beyond vandalism. The gangsters are trying to get a foothold in Tulsa, and I have a friend on the Kansas City Police Department who says the gangsters here in Kansas City already feel they can do anything they want. I called Richard yesterday, and we talked all this out. We drove through the night and we're here to help you with whatever you're planning. If we can help you here in Kansas City, maybe they won't come to Oklahoma."

Susan's jaw dropped and her mouth gaped open. She gathered herself. "You two are amazing. Charlie, what do you think?"

Charlie looked at Bailey. "I'm glad you invited them to come. I can't believe you drove here from Oklahoma. This is your last chance to back out. I believe what we are doing might be considered conspiracy to commit a crime to some lawyers, so this is your chance to stay out of the fire."

Lindsay merely nodded his head. Richard leaned back in his chair and crossed his arms.

Charlie smiled. "We're plannin' to hit those assholes and hit them hard. They killed a friend, who, like Richard said was like family. Now we ain't aimin' to kill anyone, but we will put them out of business here in Kansas City. I'm plannin' to go to Chicago myself and meet face-to-face with the overall boss of this crime family. When I'm done with him, he'll understand and agree the Chicago Outfit and all its associates are done messin' with our Kramer family. Bailey, fill them in on our plan."

"We're waiting until July 23rd to execute a plan involvin' activities in Kansas City and Chicago. I'm not goin' to say more before I have an answer to these bluntly worded questions. You might have satisfied Charlie, but this is my operation, and I have the final say." He looked at Richard and Lindsey. "Are you here out of curiosity? Or, to get the information you can sell to the mob? Or because you're plannin' to come on board and participate as a team member?"

Richard's face turned very serious, and his voice indicated he was surprised he had to answer the question. "I'm here to be a member of your team. I'll take some vacation time and be here as much as needed."

Lindsay again didn't hesitate. "I'm planning to apply to come to work for you if the plan is to wipe out these bad guys. Too many of the leaders within the police departments are getting bought off, or they're living in fear. I want to be with an organization and a leader who will fight back."

"Good. I didn't mean to offend either of you, but I had to make sure. As Charlie said, what we are doing could be considered illegal by some. I needed to understand your motives better."

Charlie leaned toward Lindsey. "We don't ever go lookin' to start this kind of fight, but we sure as hell will finish it. Lindsey, we are not in the business of wipin' out all the gangsters, but if they come after us, I assure you they will lose."

Bailey went into detail as he shared the plan to be executed. He covered the details about dealing with each of the DiGiovanni businesses in Kansas City, as well as the plan to shock Torrio in his home. He went over how they would coordinate their work and the importance of keeping everything quiet to not give away their hand before they were ready. Through it all Richard and Lindsey were quiet as they listened to the details. After Bailey finished, Charlie said, "I do not intend to be an eye for an eye person. When they killed Bernard, they intended to kill me, Susan, and anyone who was there at Pete's. We do not intend to kill anyone, but I don't want them to be able to do business in Kansas City when the sun rises on July 24th. We must leave everythin' they own in a pile of rubble. And in Chicago, I want Torrio to know complete devastatin' fear. I will personally see to it."

Chapter 46

Cooling Off

July 1920

SUSAN CAME OUT ONTO the pool patio in the conservatory wearing a see-through negligee and carrying two wine glasses and two bottles of Cabernet. She saw Charlie swimming. "Well, Sweetheart, I see you've beaten me to the pool. How's your shoulder? I guess the doctor didn't say you couldn't swim." She held up the wine and glasses. "After this tough day, I considered bringing two bottles to start with."

Charlie swam to the edge of the pool. "The shoulder is fine. A little sore, but this may be helpin'. I had to get cooled off in more ways than one. I'm still angry about the other night."

Susan put the wine and glasses on the side tables as he climbed out of the pool. Susan enjoyed watching water drip off his manhood and the rest of his body as he walked toward her, "A mighty handsome sight, Mr. Kelly."

"And a mighty beautiful little thing you're wearin', but you know I'm just gonna take it off as soon as I can reach it."

Susan laughed and had it off before he got within six feet of her. "I don't know why I bothered to put it on."

"Me either. But it was pretty." He took her in his arms and kissed her welcoming lips, then down to her breasts. Her hands began exploring his body as their passion exploded.

They both needed to release the tensions created during the day. They both still felt the loss of Bernard.

Eventually, they broke their embrace and walked to the loungers. Susan poured each of them a glass of wine. From her lounger, Susan leaned over and ran a finger around Charlie's wound. "I know you say you feel fine but don't do too much. You don't want it to get infected or tear out these stitches. That might keep you from going to Chicago with the boys."

Charlie took a sip of wine. "I'm bein' careful. Nothin' is gonna stop me from goin' to Chicago."

Susan set down her glass and then straddled Charlie, who responded as she expected. "You know, I think I will like you even more with the scar." She gave him a passionate kiss.

"Maybe I should get some more scars then," Charlie said with a laugh.

Susan pinched him under his ribs. "Don't you dare. The scar is sexy, but I don't want to lose any more of the man I love."

They made love and then snuggled for a bit before going into the pool to cool off. Susan couldn't keep her hands off Charlie though and they embraced in the pool.

Susan said, "I am so glad that I have you to protect me."

"And I am glad I have you. We have our physical sanctuaries, Westover Road, Madison Avenue, The Bar K Ranch, and the 101 Ranch. But you are my mental sanctuary. You mean the world to me."

Chapter 47

Mission Brief

July 1920

A WEEK PASSED AND Bailey arrived at the Westover home of Charlie and Susan on Monday morning July 19th. He came to visit Charlie to find out how he was healing and to give him an update on the mission. It was a warm pleasant morning, so they sat out on the patio, and Susan joined them.

After some small talk and finishing their first cup of coffee, Bailey said, "Folks, I'm here for more than just checking on the status of Charlie's shoulder. I'm glad to hear it has healed up nice, so I can give you our final plan on the mission."

Charlie leaned in with his elbows on the table and smiled "Okay, let's hear it."

Bailey put his cup on its saucer and opened a folder of notes. "Wyatt and Josh left by automobile earlier this morning for Chicago. The Kramer Security Company bought them a new Buick Touring Sedan for them to use on this trip. They should get there by bedtime tonight, and tomorrow they'll begin surveillance of Torrio and his residence. They will pick us up at the train station on Friday evening. Our train should arrive in Chicago around 5:00. We'll have dinner and get a briefing from Wyatt and Josh on what they have seen over the past several days. We'll use the Buick to go to Torrio's house and then depart and drive straight back here on Saturday. We should be back here in Kansas City by dinner time. I'm not expecting the team to be at Torrio's home longer than twenty to thirty minutes. Josh was in the house before when he was undercover for the BOI. He'll guide us to the bedroom. All my men have the skill to trick the lock on residential doors, including deadbolts, which we know to expect. Any questions?"

"Well, uh... Never mind." Susan started to say something and stopped.

Charlie said, "What is it, Susan?"

"Well okay. Doesn't this Torrio have guards around his place?"

Bailey nodded. "Yes, but after midnight it's always down to one guy, and we have a plan to handle him and be quiet as we do it."

Susan said, "It still sounds dangerous. But I've no doubt we need to handle this now and Bailey you know what you're doing."

Charlie leaned back in his chair. "How're things lookin' here in Kansas City for Friday night?"

"I've put Briggs in charge of that part of our mission. The guys are ready. They've acquired explosives and studied the targets in detail. We know where to place the dynamite for maximum immediate destruction, and the balance of the structures will burn to the ground before the fire department can arrive and attempt to put out the fire. The team will meet at 2:00 am at a location kept secret from everyone except the team members. After they have placed their packages and watched the explosion, they'll return to a designated location and report their successes to Briggs. And I plan to call Briggs at our first fuel stop on our way home and get a report. Any questions about the Kansas City portion of the mission?"

Charlie looked at Susan and then back to Bailey. "No, I think the plan is straightforward. We need to get this done, so you can focus on gettin' the security company developed."

Bailey nodded and swallowed a sip of coffee. "I'll have what will be my original staff hired by the end of next month. Everyone hired already has been made aware our home office will be Tulsa. The balance of my hires will also be told, but I'm going to have people located all over the country at some point. We need to since we're creating security services for other companies. We'll develop and staff individual security plans for them."

Susan said, "We need to let you go, and I have a long list of honey-does for Charlie to complete before you two take off for Chicago."

***

The following evening Charlie was at his desk and was focused on a report from Boss when Susan walked in. He looked up at her and tilted his head. "Sweetheart, is something wrong? You look concerned."

"Can we talk? Let's go out to the conservatory so we can be alone."

After getting a bottle of Cabernet and two glasses, they went to their loungers where Charlie asked again. "What's wrong?"

Almost whimpering, "I don't want you to go with the guys to Chicago. It's too dangerous. Bailey and his highly trained staff can deliver our message. I know I've said to everyone I support the mission. And I do, but the more I think about it, I don't support it with you going with them."

Charlie rose, turned, and reached over and took her hand. "Susan, I've gotta go. Torrio would probably not go on somethin' like this and therefore wouldn't expect the leader of an adversary to do it either. It's the surprise element we need for this mission to be successful. I'm goin' into his home and deliverin' the message myself. Susan, I appreciate your concern, but even back at the 101 Ranch, there were some jobs only Boss would do. This is one of those jobs within Kramer I must do. Understand?"

"Yes, Sweetheart, I guess I do. But I don't have to like it. And I don't like it."

Chapter 48
Making an Impression
July 1920

CARRYING HIS BRIEFCASE, BAILEY walked into the Kelly kitchen Friday morning and found Charlie and Susan sitting at the breakfast table. Charlie was dressed and drinking coffee. "Are you ready to go?"

Charlie put down his coffee cup and said, "Yep, and your timin' is perfect. I just finished eating."

Susan placed her hand on Charlie's arm and said, "Please call me as soon as you can after you arrive in Chicago. I won't expect another call until about this time tomorrow morning. Promise me you'll get the job done and come home to me. Okay, big guy?"

They both stood, and Charlie pulled her to him and kissed her. He stepped back. "Sweetheart, you know my motto, if somethin' needs doin', Kelly Can. I'll be home tomorrow, I promise."

Susan pulled him to her and whispered. "I'm proud of you, even if I wish you'd stay home. But I guess if I'd wanted a man who didn't take charge, I'd have married Goodnight. I think I made the better choice."

"I do too."

***

Their train arrived in Chicago on time. After putting together the final details of the plan over dinner, Wyatt and Josh gave Charlie and Bailey a tour of Chicago's southside. While driving around the area, they pointed out warehouses, brothels, and clubs like the Four Deuces on Wabash Avenue where the Chicago Outfit did a lot of their business.

Wyatt said, "The Chicago Outfit has been into prostitution

for a long time and is becoming a powerful force in bootlegging. Torrio wanted to get into selling booze a long time ago. The Outfit's previous boss, "Big Jim" Colosimo, wasn't interested in booze. He was killed at his restaurant back in May. Everyone in Chicago is pretty sure that Torrio ordered the hit, but of course, there are no witnesses, and nobody going to risk their neck to come forward to say that."

Charlie had listened as Wyatt had talked. "Thanks for doin' a thorough job. It appears this Torrio fella is used to eliminating his problems and he doesn't care how it's done."

"That's the size of it," Josh said. "But he's also careful to not get himself directly involved. He's too worried about keeping up a respectable appearance for the citizens of Chicago."

"Well, good, maybe takin' this direct approach will scare him as we want it to."

Around 1:00 in the morning, they drove past the Torrio residence for the first time, which allowed them to evaluate the lighting around the house. As they drove past, Josh said, "We'll park here. As you can see, this is about a block away and around a corner. We'll approach the house from the alley. Torrio doesn't have dogs, and there are none close by in the neighborhood. The guard, if there is one, will be in the kitchen area. We haven't seen a guard since we arrived, but we know he uses one from time to time."

Bailey said, "I saw an all-night coffee shop about a half mile away. Let's go relax and run through our scenario one more time."

***

At 2:45 they left the coffee shop and arrived at their parking spot five minutes later. After they climbed out of the Buick, they opened the trunk and distributed their arsenal. Bailey said, "Wyatt and Josh, check your weapons." The three of them, including Bailey, carried .38 Smith and Wesson M&P revolvers, and all were wearing cartridge belts with forty bullets.

Charlie said, "I feel naked without a weapon. I can't believe I never brought the subject up. I expected we would all be armed."

Bailey reached into the trunk and pulled out a sawed-off 12-gauge shotgun. He turned to Charlie, smiled, and said, "You're a cowboy, bet you've used one of these."

Charlie laughed and reached for the gun. "Mine isn't sawed-off, but you better believe I know my way around a 12-gauge."

Bailey said, "We hope we don't need to use these, but we

don't intend to get shot either. Let's be very quiet and get to it."

They worked their way down the alley and into Torrio's backyard. Josh knew the house well and said, "I don't see a light on in the kitchen. It should mean there's no guard." He went straight to the back door and found it locked. In no time he picked the lock and opened the door. The team followed him inside. There was no guard there or on the first floor. Their eyes quickly adjusted to the dark and they crept to the bottom of the stairs without any light.

Josh motioned with his hand to indicate they would take the stairs up and then go to the right. Bailey nodded and took the lead, and the others followed. When he arrived at the top, he saw that the bedroom door was slightly ajar and opened into the room. Bailey turned and looked at each individual and held up his hand.

The others nodded. Bailey burst into the bedroom and found the bed located exactly where Josh said it would be.

Bailey shouted, "Don't move!"

Torrio gave a startled yelp. His wife screamed. As soon as he recovered Torrio growled. "What the fuck! Who the hell are you?" He started to get out of bed.

Bailey ignored the question, shoved him back onto the bed, and with his pistol aimed at the mobster went to the side table on Torrio's side of the bed and found a gun in the drawer. At the same time, Josh went to the wife's side table and found one there as well. They continued searching the room and closets for weapons as Charlie walked to the foot of the bed and held his shotgun cradled casually in his arms.

"Allow me to introduce myself. I'm Charles Kelly. I own The Kramer Group. Sixteen days ago, some of your assholes in Kansas City shot and killed my driver and put a bullet in my left shoulder. Lucky for you, they missed my wife. Otherwise, you'd be a dead son-of-a-bitch right now.

"You may think you're a powerful and tough guy. You may think that no one can get to you." Charlie leaned forward and grinned. "Well, buddy, I just did. And I can anytime I fuckin' want to. You may think you're rich. You may think your money will protect you. But you'd be wrong." He gave another grin. "There ain't more than maybe three people in the fuckin' world richer than me. And I am willin' to spend every last dime to make your life a livin' hell if you so much as sneeze in my direction again. As of tonight, you're done messin' with me, my family, and my businesses."

Charlie pulled the slide on the shotgun to chamber a round

and pointed it casually at Torrio's head. "Do you understand me, asshole?"

Torrio was wearing silk pajamas and had been full of bluster when they had first entered the room. But now the smell of urine filled the air. Charlie glanced with one eye and could see that his pajamas were soaking wet because he was lying in a pool of his piss. Torrio's wife had pulled at the covers attempting to cover her negligee and was whimpering next to him.

Despite the fear Torrio seemed to remember that he was a big man. "You won't get away with this. I have men too. You know I ain't afraid to kill. You and your wife—"

Torrio stopped as Charlie changed the angle on the shotgun to point at the mobster's groin. "Wrong answer, Johnny. You need to consider your next words carefully. Sure, you've ordered men to kill, but I've done it. The last man that harmed my wife is buried in an Oklahoma field. I think I can find a good spot for you too, but you won't have all your parts when I do it."

Now Torrio was shaking as he responded, "I... I... I underst... stand you."

Charlie grinned, "I'm lettin' you live Johnny because I know you won't let anythin' happen to me or any of mine ever again. If somethin' happens for the rest of my life, I'm gonna blame ya, and you're gonna wish I had killed ya quick. But, as long as things go along great. I'll let you alone. Run your fuckin' Chicago business however you want. I don't give a shit what you do. To make my point clear, tonight in Kansas City, my people are puttin' the DiGiovanni's out of business. What we're doin' there I could have done here in Chicago. Do you understand me, shithead?"

Torrio couldn't speak. After a while, he mumbled, "I... I get it. I messed with the wrong guy. I got your back from now on. You won't be bothered by me or any of my associates. There are too many ways for me to make money without touching your business ever again. Mr. Kelly, when I see you want a quarry or anything else, I'll not be bidding on it."

Charlie said, "Good." He turned and looked at Torrio's wife who was sobbing next to Johnny. "Ma'am, I'm sorry we had to disturb your sleep. I hope ya don't ever have to remind your man about tonight. If we ever need to come back here, you're gonna be a widow, and I really don't want that to happen."

Torrio said, "It won't, Mr. Kelly. I promise you. It won't. I'll always have your back, I promise you."

Charlie smiled and said, "Good. I'm a reasonable man. I was nice this time, just remember there better never be a next time."

Torrio said, "There won't be, Mr. Kelly, I promise you there won't be."

Bailey said, "I don't believe him. He'll come after you."

Wyatt said, "Maybe we should have blown up the Four Deuces earlier. Then it might have hit him closer to home."

Charlie said, "Nah, I think we've made our point. Mr. Torrio is a reasonable businessman. He knows what will happen if he breaks his word." Charlie finally lowered the shotgun. "Let's get outta here and let these folks get back to sleep."

The four men backed out of the room and hurried down the stairs. They were out the back door and to the Buick as fast as they could run. They were across Chicago and onto the road toward Bloomington and Springfield in less than thirty minutes.

When Charlie was sure they were safe and down the road, he looked at his watch and saw it was almost 4:00. He asked the group, "Well, do you think we were successful in puttin' enough fear into the asshole for him to do what he said he would?"

Bailey answered, "If you didn't, nothing or nobody ever will."

Josh said, "You literally scared the piss right out of him. Hell, I was impressed with you. I don't ever want to get you mad at me."

Wyatt said, "Charlie, you were fucking amazing. I can't imagine he will ever be a problem. If he's smart, he'll be the best friend you have against anyone in his world."

The ride back to Kansas City was quiet, even pleasant. They called Susan at their stop in Springfield. Bailey called the other team and learned that their side of the mission had gone off without a hitch as well. Back on the road, they would swap driving chores so each of them could get some sleep.

The Chicago mission crew pulled into the driveway at Westover Road that afternoon and parked the Buick around back by the garage. Susan came running out to meet them and jumped into Charlie's arms.

He laughed as he hugged her. "Boy, Sweetheart, that's the hardest my shoulder has been hit since the shot. But it felt good." He gave her a big kiss and continued his hug.

They all went inside, and Beverly had cold beers waiting for them. They sat in the living room and relaxed for a few minutes, and then Bailey, Wyatt, and Josh let out a loud "Hooyah!"

Charlie smiled big and said, "It's all I needed to hear. We'll celebrate a victory tonight."

About thirty minutes later the Kansas City team arrived. After everyone was there, they all wandered out to the patio where Susan, Beverly, and Kathryn had set up a table and chairs to celebrate. Platters of steaks, potatoes, corn, and biscuits were piled on the table, and several bottles of champagne had been opened and glasses filled.

Susan raised her voice enough to get everyone's attention and said, "Let's all sit down. I want to hear what happened in Chicago and here in Kansas City."

After everyone was seated, Bailey said, "Briggs, I know it was a success. Give us the low down"

Briggs stood, smiled, and said, "We had a perfect night. We kicked their butt. Every location is devastated. There is no way they can do anything at those locations without a complete re-build. We were able to rendezvous at our designated location earlier than we thought we could because things went so smoothly. We were eating breakfast at the American by 6:00 this morning. I drove around to every location this afternoon to con-firm what we accomplished. I'm happy to say we were successful."

Charlie burst with enthusiasm as he clapped his hands. "That's what I wanted to hear. Thanks, Briggs, and great work team."

Bailey looked at each team member around the table. He stopped his gaze and smiled at Susan. "Oh, how I wish every one of you could have been in Torrio's bedroom with us last night."

Richard shouted from the far end of the table. "So do we."

Bailey grinned at Richard and then continued. "Everything went like clockwork. Charlie was amazing in how forceful and clear he told Torrio how it would need to go if Torrio intended to stay alive. Susan, Beverly, and Kathryn, I apologize before I say this, but Charlie was so powerful that Torrio was lying in a pool of his urine when we left. Charlie's words scared him that much. I couldn't believe it. I would be shocked if we ever hear a peep out of the crime world again. But if something happens, Charlie warned Torrio what he's facing."

Susan raised her glass of champagne and everyone else fol-lowed. "To the Kramer Security Team!"

Author's Notes

Some of the events, people, and places described within these pages are based on fact, while most are pure fiction and hopefully make for a good story. I enjoy writing historical fiction. That's Fiction with a capital F. But I do try to be true to what was happening or could have happened back a hundred years ago. I sure hope you are enjoying the story and plan to stick around as there is a lot still to come.

Author Bio

E. Joe Brown pursues his passions as an author writing a series of historical fiction novels with Artemesia Publishing. He's a member of the Western Writers of America (WWA) and a board member of their Homestead Foundation. He is a member of the staff of the Roundup Magazine published by WWA. He is an active member of SouthWest Writers, a member of the Military Writers of America, and the New Mexico Westerners. He served as a New Mexico State Music Commissioner appointed by Governor Susana Martinez and on the International Western Music Association Board of Directors. In these roles, he influenced the culture of New Mexico and the American Southwest through literature, music, poetry, and education. He is a proud retiree of USAF.